Zach Forrester was back!

And the flicker of recognition in his eyes showed Dana that he remembered her. The grim set of his mouth told her that he wished he didn't.

"It's quite a surprise seeing you back in town," she managed. "Are you looking for a job here?"

"Nope." He met her eyes squarely. "Thought I'd get away from city life for a while."

"*I got to go potty.*"

The small voice from behind his knee startled Dana. Her gaze fell to a small hand gripping a fold of his faded jeans. *He's married?* Even as the thought twisted her heart, she shoved the past back where it belonged. "The bathroom's down the hall, first door on the left."

He bent and scooped up the little girl. She immediately dropped her head onto his shoulder, hiding her face.

The contrast of powerful, protective male and fragile child couldn't have been greater. And when he dropped a gentle kiss on Katie's forehead, nothing could have touched Dana's heart more.

He's back was all she could think.

Dear Reader,

Zach Forrester, son of a father he never met and a mother who drifted from town to town, hasn't spent much time thinking about white picket fences and settling down. His career as a special agent with the DEA has been his consuming passion, until one day his estranged sister drops her small, frightened child on his doorstep and begs him to keep her safe.

That moment launches him into a series of events that leaves him wounded and on the run to a tiny Colorado town with his newfound niece, where he encounters the one woman he truly loved, but had to leave behind long ago. And now, he must learn new lessons about parenthood, commitment and what matters most of all.

I hope you'll enjoy the story of Zach, Katie and a veterinarian in Colorado who is faced with choosing the life she knows, or daring to follow her heart.

I'd love to hear your comments, and hope you'll enjoy my next book, *Operation: Mistletoe*, which will be out in November of 2002!

Roxanne Rustand

e-mail: roxanne@roxannerustand.com
Web sites: http://www.roxannerustand.com
               http://www.superauthors.com
Or by mail: Box 2550, Cedar Rapids, Iowa 52406-2550

Books by Roxanne Rustand

HARLEQUIN SUPERROMANCE

Operation: Katie
Roxanne Rustand

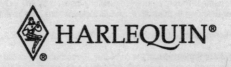

HARLEQUIN®

TORONTO • NEW YORK • LONDON
AMSTERDAM • PARIS • SYDNEY • HAMBURG
STOCKHOLM • ATHENS • TOKYO • MILAN • MADRID
PRAGUE • WARSAW • BUDAPEST • AUCKLAND

ISBN 0-373-71064-X

OPERATION: KATIE

DEDICATION

With love to Danielle. Welcome to the world, sweetheart!

ACKNOWLEDGMENT

Many thanks to Dr. Kathy Ross, DVM,
and Dr. Greg Winterowd, DVM, for your time,
patience and veterinary expertise.

Thanks also to weapons experts
Dave and Nancy Nicholson, who provided technical
firearms information, lessons on gun safety and hands-on
experience with the weapons used in this book.
Any mistakes are mine alone.

Thanks so much to Diane, Lyn, Monica and Muriel.
Your insights and encouragement are invaluable,
and I deeply treasure our friendships.

And finally, as always, love and thanks to Larry,
Andy, Brian and Emily—for your support
and understanding when deadlines loom.

PROLOGUE

"*WHERE'S MY MOMMY?*" The three-year-old stared up at him, her lower lip trembling, a faded cloth doll clutched against her thin chest.

Zach Forrester looked down into the bright blue eyes shimmering with tears and wished like hell he knew. "She went on a trip, honey. She'll be back soon."

For almost the entire day, the child had stood waiting just inside the front door of his condo, as if standing there might make that door open and her mother magically return.

He knelt down to the child's level and opened his arms, willing her to accept comfort, but she lifted her stubborn little chin and kept a wary distance.

Not that he blamed her.

Two days before, his sister Janet had appeared on his doorstep, thin as death, with darting eyes and a high, nervous laugh. He'd barely recognized her, but hope had rushed through him all the same.

It had been ten long years since she'd screamed invectives at him from across a courtroom. Five since she'd been released. He'd been there, wanting to take her home and help her, but she'd refused to even speak to him.

He'd pleaded with her anyway, until a surly guy with three nose rings and more tattoos than bare skin arrived to pick her up.

But maybe this time...

Those hopes had been dashed the moment she'd spoken. *"I gotta stash my kid someplace safe. Just for a while—so she can't be found. I'm in some trouble."*

So nothing had changed.

He'd looked down then, into the frightened face of the little girl, a niece he'd never known existed. And he'd fallen instantly and helplessly in love.

From her white-blond curls and blue eyes to the tips of her tiny, ragged sneakers, she was every child he'd ever tried to help, and the image of the sister he hadn't been able to save from herself. At least, not yet.

"Please, Janet, come in," he'd pleaded. "I can help you."

But she'd already shoved the bedraggled child and a backpack through the door, and he barely had time to slip a business card into her hand before she disappeared into the night with an eerie laugh. "Just keep Katie for me, but don't try interfering with my life again."

He'd scrawled his e-mail address and newest unlisted phone number on the first piece of paper he could grab from his pocket—a business card for his cover as a software sales rep—but she hadn't yet contacted him.

A smudged, notarized letter hidden in one of the pockets of the backpack asked him to keep the child until she returned. That she'd even thought to consider custody was a chilling postscript to her departure.

When she wasn't back by morning, he'd called the police. Notified some fellow DEA—Drug Enforcement Administration—buddies with skill at locating people. Called in an old favor from his friend, Jerry, a local P.I. After leaving Katie in the care of a trusted colleague and his wife for a few hours, he'd even cruised the back streets of Dallas, hoping to see some sign of his sister.

With all of his years as a special agent, he'd hoped finding her would be easy, but forty-eight hours later there hadn't been a word.

Now her child's eyes filled with fresh tears. "I want my *mommy*."

So do I. I want her safe, and here with you. But I don't think that's gonna happen anytime soon.

Zach managed a broad smile and prayed it looked convincing enough to reassure the little girl. "I'll bet she comes back real soon. She asked me to take care of you, and I promised I would. Would you like some pizza?"

"No."

"Peanut butter and jelly?"

That combination had been the only food that had worked so far, but now Katie's lower lip stuck out and a tear trickled down one cheek. Her blond curls bounced as she shook her head.

"Ice cream?"

Katie's head shook less vigorously at that.

Well…the child had to eat *something*. "Vanilla?"

Careful not to startle her, he rose slowly and headed for the kitchen. "With chocolate syrup?" he called over his shoulder.

Katie didn't move from her position at the front door, but her white-knuckled grip on the doll relaxed and she jerked her head in a single nod.

That's a good girl. We've got to get along here, or the County is going to give us trouble. Already, the Department of Social Services, alerted by the police, had left a message on his machine, questioning Janet's arrangements for her daughter.

Given the child's unkempt appearance when she'd been dropped off, they should have been on Janet's case a lot sooner.

His tug on the refrigerator door handle met unexpected resistance. Intent on finding the chocolate syrup, he tugged harder and the door opened.

His breath caught in his throat as he stared at the unfamiliar brown paper sack wedged between the left-over pizza and an outdated carton of eggs. A slender copper wire snaked through a hole in the bag toward the door.

A deafening explosion of light and noise and debris threw him across the narrow galley kitchen and slammed his head against the bottom cupboards.

He fought the darkness just long enough to look toward the front door of the condo. It was open. A bright green envelope had been tossed inside.

And Katie was gone.

CHAPTER ONE

"YOU AREN'T GOING to like what that note said." Paul Soderberg, a fellow Special Agent with the Dallas Field Division of the DEA, settled back in the hospital room chair and gave Zach a faint smile. "It's from that same guy. The one who calls himself 'El Cazador'—the Hunter—and he made the bombing sound real personal."

Zach concentrated on breathing slow. Steady. A throbbing headache threatened to detonate his skull. The hospital bed was hard as granite and with every movement, searing pain radiated down his spine. *At least I'm not dead.*

He could have been, he reminded himself grimly.

From what Paul said, his condo had been nearly destroyed, but there'd been only moderate damage to the other units in the building. No one had been killed, thank God. The heavy refrigerator door had flown forward, knocking him to the floor and shielding him from flying debris.

The entire day was a blank—he couldn't remember anything since putting Katie to bed the night before. "My...niece? Is she okay?"

"Scared. Won't talk to anyone—just keeps crying

for her mom. Pete and Alice will keep her until you're out of here.''

''If…that bastard…touched her…''

Zach closed his eyes and fought the mist spinning through his brain. Fought to stay awake, and alert. Had he been in the hospital a day? Two days? The passing hours had bled together, marked only by ghostly voices floating toward him on a sea of darkness and endless pain.

''There weren't any signs of physical abuse, Zach. She was frightened and dirty, but physically unharmed when she was recovered.''

Maybe she'd been physically unharmed, but God only knew what emotional trauma she'd endured. ''Tell me the details, dammit. I need to know.''

Paul shook his head slowly. ''She sure was lucky. Some customers at a truck stop outside of St. Cloud heard Katie crying in the back seat of an old LeMans. They said the driver seemed real agitated. When a woman approached the car and bent down to peer inside, Katie screamed.''

''Could any of them identify the guy?''

''Nope. He wore a dark, hooded sweatshirt and kept his back to the others who were fueling up nearby. After Katie screamed he didn't wait around—he dropped the gas nozzle, forced an elderly woman out of a nearby Ford Taurus, and peeled away in a cloud of burning rubber.''

The thought of Katie, terrified and helpless, sent fury pounding through Zach's veins. ''I'd like to find that bastard and tear him apart.''

"So would I, but at least he left her behind at the gas station."

"Any leads?"

"A clerk called 911 and the cops found the Taurus an hour later, abandoned at a freeway rest stop. The LeMans had been stolen, as well."

"Latent prints?"

"Nope."

"What about the note he left at my place?"

Paul sighed. "No prints, and the same message you got the other two times—'You don't have a prayer' hand-lettered in broad permanent marker. But this time he added something else. 'I know every move you make. And now I know about your girl.'"

Zach tried to sit forward, but the pain lancing through his shoulder and spine sent him back against the pillows in defeat. "He must..."

"Think Katie is your daughter?"

The threat made Zach's blood run cold. "I'm going to get this son of a bitch if it's the last thing I do. He could grab Katie the moment my back is turned."

"Or he could just off you both and be done with it. From the looks of things, he wanted to kill you this time, and left the note just in case."

"Yeah, but I think he'll go back to his cat-and-mouse game...waiting until I'm not on guard." Zach glared at the sling supporting the cast on his right forearm and wrist. "Which makes it a hell of a time to be out of commission with this."

"How long till you're back?"

"The wrist fracture is no big deal. The ribs will be

okay if I keep them taped. Supposedly the shoulder surgery means a long recovery, but I figure on just a couple weeks, tops.''

"Lie low until you can come back to work. Or take the girl and go to Tahiti. Head for Canada."

"I can't. What if Janet turns up? She'll want her daughter, and I need to be here to help her." *If she'll let me, this time. If she'll even sit down and talk.* "And I need to figure out who this El Cazador is before he strikes again."

"Hell, you've been involved in so many drug cases during the past five years, it won't be easy."

"Which means I can't stay away from my job a day longer than necessary."

Paul shifted uneasily in his chair. "Janet has your address and phone number at work, right? If she calls in, we'll contact you."

Unless she threw my business card in the gutter. It had been...what? Four days, now? Still not a clue—not an airline or bus ticket in her name, no records of charge card activity. No contact with any of her known friends.

If she was off having a fling with some low-life boyfriend, that was nearly unforgivable. Zach didn't want to think about the other, much darker possibilities.

"So what are you going to do about Katie?"

"Pete offered his wife's day care, but I don't want to put his family in danger. For right now, Katie's safer with me."

"How about foster care?"

"She's distraught over her mother's disappearance, but at least she knows Janet trusted me. I've got to keep her." *I've never been able to help Janet, but I can sure as hell help her little girl.*

Paul shook his head. "I hope you're doing the right thing." He glanced at his watch, then stood up. "The Dallas division is still researching past cases for new leads on this guy. I'll keep in touch."

"Thanks." With a sigh, Zach eased back against the pillow and tried to drift into the soft, welcoming darkness of sleep.

Instead, he lay awake long into the night, his mind racing through fractured images of explosions and blood and visions of his sister Janet screaming his name, begging for help.

But the images that tore at his heart were those of a frightened little girl who might never see her mother again.

THE NEXT FOUR WEEKS PASSED in a blur of pain and anxiety. Unwilling to risk Katie's safety by being drowsy, less alert, he didn't dare take his pain meds.

The days were long and the nights even longer.

They'd rarely spent more than two nights in one place, moving from Mesquite to Richardson, Fort Worth to a secluded cabin along Lake Texoma, and a dozen forgettable little motels in between.

But every time they moved to a new location, another threatening note appeared within twenty-four hours. Slipped under a motel room door. Or propped in the window of a small rental cabin in the back of beyond.

Always in a bright green envelope, with the same damn message—plus a chilling new addition. ''I owe you, pal. You and your kid are going to die.''

Katie mostly watched him silently, and clung to her doll, night and day. He had little experience with small children and she probably knew it, staring at him with those wary eyes, never cracking even the beginnings of a smile. That he could understand. The fact that she never cried, never showed any other emotion, was almost spooky.

He bought children's videos, books and small toys. But she just held on to the tattered doll and sat close to the door, or near a window where she watched in vain for her mother's return.

The fact they were being stalked surely made it all the harder for her.

She had to notice that Zach lingered at the windows, too, and had surely picked up on his watchfulness and tension. He figured she had, because she seemed to melt into herself a little more each day, as if she wanted to simply disappear.

Alone, Zach had always dealt with any threats with cool determination. With Katie to protect, the situation was much more difficult.

Every move to a new location was made in the dark of night, and he drove for hours to mask their trail. It didn't matter—the messages still arrived. And after he insisted on twenty-four hour surveillance, the envelopes started coming by mail, postmarked from post offices throughout the metropolitan area.

He'd always had good working relationships with the other Special Agents working out of the Dallas office, but he'd shared his personal life with just a few close friends and barely knew his neighbors at the condo complex. So how did El Cazador find him?

Someone very close to him was involved, maybe even someone at work, unless this guy was watching him night and day. Even now, in an isolated mom-and-pop motel outside Duncanville, he felt the hair at the back of his neck prickle.

Worse, he still couldn't remember a damn thing from the day of the bombing. If he could just recall *something*…an unfamiliar face, a car idling on the street nearby….

The sharp voice on the phone brought Zach back to the present.

"Rest that shoulder so it can heal," his boss said irritably, "or you'll be back to square one. You could even end up with medical retirement. Why take the chance?"

"My shoulder is fine." Zach gripped the receiver tighter. "So when the arm cast is off in two weeks, I'll be back."

"I've had rotator cuff surgery, myself, and I know you aren't going to pass medical clearance for duty anytime soon."

"But I'm perfectly—"

"Look, you haven't taken a vacation in years, and you've been involved in some damned rough undercover operations. You're burning out, and it's time you got out of here for a while. How the hell can you rest and heal when you're constantly on the move?''

''But—''

''You worry me, Zach. You've put yourself on the line far too many times over the past few years. Taken risks you shouldn't have.''

''That's my job,'' Zach snapped. His single-minded pursuit of the drug traffickers who'd caused such personal heartbreak for so many families was his only mission in life. And who else could do it better? He could afford the risks—he didn't have a wife and family at home.

''It's time you had some distance. As of today, you're on a three-month medical leave.''

''I've already been out for four weeks!''

''Yeah, but the medical report says your shoulder isn't healing very fast. My guess is that you'll be lucky if you regain full mobility.''

''I can't be gone that long.''

''Yes, you can, and now I've got the right excuse to make you do it. Show up sooner and you'll be at a desk job for the rest of the year. Got it?''

Zach cursed under his breath.

''Look, just drop completely out of sight for a while, so El Cazador can't find you,'' Martin continued in a softer voice. ''The other agents are as worried about his threats against you as I am, and they're working hard on this. As soon as we figure out who the guy is, we'll get him.''

''I need to find the bastard, not go off on some

damned vacation. This is a personal vendetta against me—so who would have better odds at getting him?"

"Then think about that little girl. Spend more time with her. I'll bet her mom's disappearance has been hell on her."

How well Zach knew.

Katie had simply retreated into silence, barely smiling, eating almost nothing. She'd finally allowed Zach to hold her, but last night the hopelessness in her eyes had torn his heart.

I need to keep working, and nail El Cazador.

But even as he fought the idea of leaving, Zach knew it was probably the right thing to do. He didn't know who to trust anymore, and he needed to take Katie to safety.

"If I've got to be on that damned leave, then I'm heading out of state for a few months."

"I wasn't thinking you should go that far," Martin protested. "Stay in this part of Texas so we can help you if need be."

"No. This guy has information he shouldn't have. I can't risk the chance that one of these days he'll make a successful hit, especially with Katie to worry about. It's safer to completely disappear."

"But—"

"No. I've done enough undercover ops in the last ten years to write a book on the subject. I'll be back in three months."

After hanging up the phone, Zach searched through his memories, revisiting the dozen or so towns he'd lived in as a kid. All but one—Fossil Hill, Colorado—

were places where he had relatives, where a smart man could track him down.

The one safe place was a town he'd never wanted to revisit, not even in his dreams.

Paul had said, "It's that same guy again. This time he made it real personal."

But Paul had been dead wrong. Zach had his reasons for choosing a career in the DEA, and *every* case was deeply personal.

Now El Cazador had taken it a step further, and in doing so had made a fatal mistake. Zach was going to bring him down if it was the last thing he ever did.

But the next three months of waiting were going to be hell.

"YOU'VE GOT TWO COLTS to geld out at the Michaelson place in Longford at nine. Back to Fossil Hill after that for spring tune-ups on two horses—vaccinations and worming—at Fallow Creek Stables, then twenty calves to vaccinate and dehorn at Bill Swanson's, eleven o'clock. *Then,*" Francie added with a smirk, "lunch at the Pink Petticoat Inn with your mother, one o'clock sharp."

Dana Hathaway groaned as she zipped up her heavy-duty coveralls. "After the calves?"

"You got it. But Bill says he'll have two guys running calves through the chutes, so you should be done there by twelve-thirty."

With all the spring rain they'd been having, Swanson's low-lying corrals and chutes would be a muddy mess. "Can you switch some appointments? I could do them after lunch."

"Nope. Bill is leaving for Denver with a load of cattle right afterward. He made the appointment weeks ago, and called this morning to confirm it. You know how testy he can be—he'll call the Lakeland Vet Clinic instead if you mess with his plans."

"I can't afford to lose his business. But my mother won't forgive me if I'm late."

Francie propped a mirror against the telephone at her desk and fluffed her glossy black hair. "That's *your* problem, not mine. What happened?"

"She…cornered me at the library."

"And you forgot which days she works there?"

"Alex and Molly both had overdues. I figured I could drop their books off and pay later, but I swear my mother has radar. She appeared from behind the stacks like an avenging angel—demanding to know where I'd been for the past few days. Wondering why I hadn't called. By the time she was through, I swear half the library patrons were rallied behind her, hanging on every word."

"She does have a…certain presence."

"And you have amazing tact. Maybe you could use it to call her and postpone our lunch?"

"Not on a bet." Francie swiveled her chair back to face the computer on the reception desk. "I've never understood people with a death wish."

"I thought you were hoping for a raise this year," Dana muttered as she snagged the truck keys from the counter and stepped over Gabe, her ancient Australian shepherd, then headed for the back door of the clinic.

Until last year, when his arthritis started slowing him down, Gabe had ridden along on all of her farm calls. Now he mostly snoozed his days away.

"When you can afford a raise, I'll be a lot nicer," Francie called out.

Dana chuckled as she stepped into the bright Colorado sunshine. No matter what struggles she'd faced, she could always count on Francie, a true friend since childhood. When Dana married Ken, a widower with two young children, Francie had been there with advice and encouragement. Just as she'd been when Ken died.

Losing him, making ends meet on the struggling horse ranch he'd left her, and running the clinic would have been overwhelming without Francie's unflagging support. The kids loved her like a favorite aunt.

Outside, Dana surveyed the Bowie vet box mounted on the back of her pickup, then checked through its refrigerated compartments, making sure she'd restocked the antibiotics and vaccines she would need. Then she locked each compartment door and headed to the cab.

A row of six registered quarter horse mares, ears pricked eagerly, hung their heads over the plank fence by her barn and whinnied. One of them pawed a cloud of dust into the air.

"Beggars," she called out as she slid behind the steering wheel. "You *had* your breakfast already."

They were the moms-in-waiting, mares who'd been bred later than the others last spring. The rest of the mares were grazing out on the grassy hills behind her house, watching patiently as their new babies played foal-tag with each other or slept flat as pancakes in the warm spring sunshine.

The sale of this newest foal crop could herald the bright future of Rocking H Ranch…or signal its downfall, Dana thought with a deep sigh. Time would tell. Every morning she stood at her kitchen windows, eating her toast, gazing down the hill toward the clinic and wondering what the future would bring.

Success, if hard work and determination made the difference. But there were so many other variables out of her control.

Her cell phone chirped as she started down the mile-long gravel driveway leading out to the highway.

Martha Benson's voice rang out loud and clear, and as always she got right to the point. "Remember that little blue house next to your place?"

Martha—who doubled as the postmistress and the town's only Realtor—had been trying to rent or sell the place for years.

"You found a buyer?" Dana pulled to a stop at her mailbox. To the east, the highway led out into ranch country. To the west, the driveway of Martha's vacant property was a mile down the road, and the town of Fossil Hill five miles beyond that.

Martha cleared her throat. "Not a buyer, unfortunately."

"You *rented* it?" The little one-story house offered just two tiny bedrooms, a living room, a single bathroom and a country kitchen, and had been empty for at least two years. Even the spacious old barn and fifty-acre pasture hadn't tempted anyone to make a decent offer on such a small house so far from town.

"Fairly short-term…just for the next four months."

Mystified, Dana drummed her fingernails on the steering wheel. "Do you need me to run over and check the place out before they move in?"

"I just thought you should have some warning. You know, so you'd be prepared."

"Prepared?"

"Well…now I'm wondering if this was a big mistake. But really, after all these years, how could it matter? I just hope—oh, dear me. They're already here. I'll call you later, okay?"

Martha hung up before Dana could say another word.

A big mistake? Dana threw the truck in gear and turned out onto the highway.

Martha was a sweet elderly lady, but she did love gossip, and nothing much exciting happened in a town like Fossil Hill. A visit by out-of-town relatives was almost headline news.

When Dana finished the Swansons' last calf at twelve-thirty, she was hot, dirty and darn curious. "You hear anything about some new people in town?" she asked Bill as she stood next to her truck and peeled off her muddy coveralls.

"Nope."

"The ones who rented Martha's place out on the highway?"

He gave her a blank look. "Nope."

She hadn't expected much of an answer. The reclusive old rancher probably wouldn't yell "Fire" if his boots were in flames, but he was a good neighbor who baled her hay on shares and he'd come over to work on her old tractor more times than she wanted to think about.

She was in her truck with the motor running before he spoke again. "Saw a stranger and his little girl in town, though. Guy looked sorta edgy."

"Thanks, Bill." Well, that sounded odd. Martha's new renter, maybe? But why did she think Dana would care?

Giving him a breezy wave, she headed back home, one eye on the speedometer and the other on the clock. Coveralls or not, she smelled like a cow barn and—she took at quick glance in the rearview mirror—her hair looked like something destined for the landfill.

Scraggly wisps of dishwater-blond hair hung in limp tendrils about her face. The light touch of makeup she usually wore was long gone, replaced by a smudge on her cheek and a streak of something unmentionable across her brow. Definitely not ready for the Pink Petticoat Inn.

Her small-animal clinic hours didn't start until two o'clock, so barring walk-in emergencies, there wouldn't be any clients waiting for her now. She could check in with Francie, then race the hundred yards up to her house for a quick shower—

Darn. An unfamiliar black Blazer was parked in front of the clinic.

Dana pulled into her usual spot behind the clinic and walked in the back door. "Francie? What's up?"

"You'll have to take care of this one, boss," Francie called out.

Dana walked up the hall, past the kennel room, the surgery and the two exam rooms, feeling a familiar sense of pride at the sparkling clean floors, the neatly arranged supplies.

Whatever dreams she'd once had, she was where she should be—close to her aging mother, in a safe, rural area where the kids could grow up with relatives nearby, surrounded by familiar memories of their late father. Despite the struggles ahead, she would make a success of the clinic, and the ranch, as well.

She stopped short at the doorway to the reception area.

"This guy just needs your key for Martha's place," Francie said, with an odd note of warning in her voice. "She gave him one but it doesn't work."

The words floated past Dana in an incomprehensible tumble of sounds as she stared at the tall, dark-haired man standing in her waiting room. The shock of recognition in his eyes matched her own stunned reaction.

She hadn't seen him in fifteen years. He was taller, broader, far more imposing than the reckless charmer she'd loved with all her heart during her senior year in high school. But he still had that indefinable edge hinting at danger.

After all these years she'd never expected to see him again. But Zach Forrester was back.

And she wanted to run.

CHAPTER TWO

THE RECOGNITION IN ZACH'S EYES showed that he remembered her. The grim set of his mouth told her that he wished he hadn't.

Well, fine. She'd recovered nicely, thank you. Married a kind, loving man with two beautiful kids. She hadn't given Zach a second thought in years.

Except for the occasional wish to meet him again someday, and let him know how cruel he'd been.

After that first, wrenching heartbreak had come anger, but after the anger faded she'd been left with a hollow ache that kept her watching for tall, dark-haired strangers long after she'd accepted the fact that he would never come back.

How many times had she relived that magical night of the senior prom, wondering what she'd said, or done, to make him disappear from Fossil Hill without a trace the next day? Her fragile teenager's heart, filled with the wonder and thrill of a first love, had been defenseless. A surgeon's scalpel couldn't have done a more thorough job of destroying it.

"It's quite a surprise seeing you back in town," she finally managed, eyeing the cast on his right arm. Had he been in an accident? A fight? "Are you looking for a job here?"

"Nope." He met her gaze squarely. "I'm…a sales rep for a software company, and I've got a few months' leave. Thought I'd just get away from city life for a while."

"I gotta go potty."

The shy voice from behind his knees startled Dana back into the present. Her gaze fell to a small hand gripping a fold of his faded jeans. He's *married?* But even as the thought twisted her heart, she knew her reaction was ridiculous. In fifteen years she'd finished college and married. Why wouldn't he have done the same?

She dusted her hands on the backside of her jeans and shoved the past back where it belonged, with childhood memories and things that didn't matter anymore. "The bathroom's down the hall, first door on the left."

The little girl edged farther behind Zach, a faded rag doll clutched against her chest.

"Can you go yourself, Katie?" he asked, his gentle voice achingly familiar, yet so different. It was now the deeper, testosterone-laden baritone of the man he'd become.

The rugged timbre of it danced up Dana's spine like a possessive caress, bringing back all the sensations of hunger and need she'd felt in his arms so many years ago.

He bent and scooped the little girl up with one arm, drew in a sharp breath—*of pain?*—as he lifted her, the fabric of his white polo shirt molding the bulk of his muscular shoulders, the color a sharp contrast to his dark tan.

The child hid her face against his shoulder as he strode down the hall. At the door he flipped on the light and whispered something to her, then awkwardly hunkered down and set her back on her feet.

She stood frozen—a frightened cherub with a nimbus of white-blond curls framing her delicate face—and then edged into the bathroom. Dana and Francie exchanged glances. The child's obvious fear went beyond a typical toddler's shyness. Why was she so afraid?

Zach stayed motionless until she finished, then stepped into the bathroom to help wash her hands. The moment her hands were dry she scrambled up into his arms again.

He shifted her into the curve of his left arm, and again she dropped her head to his shoulder, hiding her face.

The contrast of powerful, protective male and fragile child couldn't have been greater. And when he dropped a gentle kiss on Katie's forehead, nothing could have touched Dana's heart more.

"Do you have that key?" He met Dana's gaze, his eyes betraying turbulent emotions she never would have expected.

Perhaps there were marital problems or looming custody battles that accounted for the child's emotional state. "Of course."

Dana stepped past him and went down the hall to her office, then rummaged around in the top drawer for the extra set of house keys Martha had given her years ago.

When she stepped back into the hall, she found Zach idly scanning the framed diplomas and certificates that hung there.

"Impressive," he said, tipping his head toward the framed summa cum laude degree from Colorado State. "You've done well."

She dropped the keys into his hand. "I loved school. I was tempted to go on, and maybe teach veterinary medicine, but I wanted some years of practical experience first. And then, well...." *Shut up,* she told herself sharply. He'd barely acknowledged that he'd met her before. Why would he care to hear about what she'd done since?

"I'm hungry." The little girl's whisper, muffled against his shirt, was nearly inaudible.

Dana glanced toward the front windows. The Blazer parked outside had no luggage on top, no trailer behind. With a wife inside and all the paraphernalia of traveling with a child, there couldn't be enough space for the household items they'd be needing.

"You do know that Martha's house is furnished but has no linens, right? No housewares? I check on the place for her every few weeks. It's clean, but bare."

"We'll manage." His voice was tinged with exhaustion, and he gave her a faint smile. "I don't expect much. I agreed to work on the place as part of my rent."

"If you need anything, you could try Miller's on

the far side of town. It's a small store, but they carry most of the basics. Perhaps your wife—"

"It's Wednesday." Francie's voice floated down the hall.

"Wednesday?" Zach lifted a brow.

"Sorry." Dana gave a self-deprecating shrug. "This is still a very small town. Miller's closes at noon on Wednesdays, because Marge has her hair done, and Jim always plays poker with the old cowboys who hang out at Sonny's bar."

A flicker of amusement glinted in Zach's eyes, but then the child fidgeted, kicked her little pink tennis shoes against his hip. White lines of tension—or pain—deepened at the corners of his mouth as he shifted her weight.

"Hungry!" she repeated.

Dana waved a hand toward Fossil Hill. "There's a couple of places to eat in town—a roadhouse or two you wouldn't want to take her in, but the Cattleman is good. Or a new place...the Pink Petticoat."

She'd hesitated, knowing she and her mother would soon be there, but at the faint look of alarm in Zach's eyes she knew there'd be little possibility he would choose that one. No surprise, there. Cindy Walters's color scheme and froufrou decorating style scared off any guy who wasn't dragged in by an insistent wife.

"I'll stop at your house later on with some things so you can get by tonight," she added.

Zach pocketed the house keys. "Thanks."

He strode out of the clinic, nodding to Francie as he passed the front desk. The minute the door closed behind him, Francie launched out of her chair and rounded the corner of the receptionist area.

"Did you ever think you'd see Zach Forrester in this town again?" she demanded. "Of all the nerve!"

Well, *there* was one of the perils of hiring your best friend from childhood. Francie knew altogether too much about Dana's past. "It's a free country."

"That man ripped your heart out." Francie folded her arms across her chest. "Believe me, I remember. If he'd showed up again back then, I would have been happy to lasso that buzzard, hog-tie him and drag him behind my barrel horse into the next county."

Dana grinned. "I would have been visiting you in jail for the next ten years."

Francie gave her a searching look. "You aren't going to make any dumb mistakes with him this time, are you?"

"Don't worry. The guy is married and has a young child to boot."

"So where's his wife? While you were talking, I wandered outside to say hello, but there wasn't anyone in the Blazer."

"Francie!"

"I did have to go check the mailbox," she retorted. "Promise me you won't give Zach so much as the time of day."

"Believe me, I've had a lot of time to grow up. I know what matters. Honesty. Trust. Something deeper than just a handsome face."

"Anyway, the whole town figures you're practically engaged to Tom Baxter.'' Francie winked at her. ''Any good news, yet?''

''Hardly, and you know it.'' Tom was her neighboring rancher to the south and a lifelong friend, but this was a persistent local assumption she'd tried to tactfully dispel. Tom, on the other hand, didn't seem to mind it in the least.

''He's a good, solid guy. Maybe he's what you need.''

''Now you sound like my mother.''

Francie rolled her eyes. *''Puh-leaze!''*

A flash of panic shot through Dana. ''Oh, my God. She's waiting and I'm not even ready.''

She raced into the bathroom, reached for the bar of soap and began scrubbing up as best she could. There were a few basic cosmetics in the medicine cabinet, and she kept a clean shirt or two in the back room. That would have to do.

But as she rushed to get ready, knowing that an interminable lunch and her mother's caustic wit awaited her at the Pink Petticoat, only one thought pounded through her brain.

He's back.

ZACH HAD KNOWN all his life how stubborn women could be. He *hadn't* realized how young they started.

Surrounded by a dizzying melee of hearts on flocked wallpaper, ruffly tablecloths, lacy wall decorations, and a good two dozen women, he thought longingly of the barren park at the edge of town. He'd figured on going back out there with some take-out sandwiches from the Cattleman's Café.

But one glance at the lacy pink curtains and pink-bowed teddy bears in the windows of the Pink Petticoat Inn, and Katie had planted her little feet on the sidewalk and refused to budge. *"There!"* she'd said. "I wanna go there!"

Given the fact she'd never wanted anything so much in all the time she'd been with him, he couldn't have said no if she'd asked him to do cartwheels up to the door.

He'd scanned the tearoom when he and Katie entered, noting windows and exits, and the patrons seated inside. He'd requested a corner table as he always did, feeling comfort in having his back to the wall. The cautious habits lingered, even here.

A flurry of whispered conversation telegraphed that everyone present was well aware of the stranger's presence—a stranger all the more noticeable for being the only man in sight, save for an old rancher sitting with his plump wife near the front.

One woman had glanced his way, her eyes widening with sudden recognition. Then she scowled and pointedly turned her attention back to her menu. Something about her seemed so familiar…

In her early sixties, she wore a severe gray suit that did nothing to complement her angular body. Since glancing his way, she'd checked her watch twice, her rising agitation apparent in the stiffness of her spine and the rapid tapping of her fingertips on the tablecloth.

She had to be Dana's mother.

A pretty, middle-aged redhead came to a stop at his table, a pencil poised above an order pad. "Hi, I'm Cindy. Are you ready to order?"

Zach ordered the usual glass of milk and a peanut butter and jelly sandwich for Katie—all she'd ever eat except for ice cream—and a steak sandwich and salad for himself.

Cindy jotted down the order. "What a beautiful little daughter you have there." She reached out to stroke Katie's bright curls, but the child jerked away in alarm. Cindy's cheeks turned pink. "Oh, I'm so sorry. I didn't mean to scare her!"

Some women at the next table gave him a suspicious glance, and he knew they were thinking the same thing he did: someone had been physically abusive to Katie. But they were figuring it might be *him.*

The thought of anyone laying a hand on this child in anger made his stomach clench. It also made him wary.

To cover his tracks, he'd used only cash on the way to Fossil Hill. En route, he and Katie had stayed one night at a crumbling, mom-and-pop motel unaffiliated with any nation-wide chains, on the edge of a small town.

El Cazador's identity was still unknown, but it didn't take much guesswork to assume he'd been nailed during one of Zach's undercover operations and now wanted revenge. Somehow he'd already tracked down Zach's real name—but did he know Zach was DEA instead of a low-level drug dealer?

If not, finding out the truth could blow the covers of agents still on related cases.

So now Zach faced three months of healing until he could go back on duty. Three months of trying to attract as little attention as possible, so no one could show up in the dead of night and catch him unaware.

If Katie's fearful reactions triggered any sort of investigation of her situation, inquiries could possibly lead the guy to Fossil Hill…and put her at risk.

"We were in an accident recently," he said smoothly, just loudly enough for nearby patrons to hear. "Doctors, nurses—anyone in a uniform still frightens her."

He'd used that excuse several times, letting people assume he referred to a car wreck on the drive north from Dallas. He'd prayed that Katie's shyness would preclude any hint of denial in front of others. Each time, she'd dropped her gaze and sort of closed in on herself, just as she had when he'd said she could call him "Daddy" until her mother returned.

She'd never once used the word.

"I'm so sorry," the young woman gushed. She glanced at the cast on his arm and seemed to take his words at face value. "Were either of you badly hurt?"

Shaking his head, Zach shifted his gaze to the newspaper he'd picked up at the drugstore, hoping she wouldn't pry.

"Would you like to color, sweetie?" At Katie's brief nod, she withdrew some crayons and a coloring book from a deep pocket in her apron and set them on the table, then turned and headed for the kitchen.

The decor wasn't intended for male customers, but the service was fast and Zach's steak sandwich was perfect. Apparently enthralled with the feminine atmosphere, Katie even relinquished her death grip on her doll and placed it on the empty seat next to her.

"How's your food?"

"Okay." She looked shyly up at him from beneath her eyelashes. "It's like a dollhouse in here."

Dollhouse? Guilt lanced through him at all she'd lost in the past weeks. What little she had now. She was safe, but all she had was that bedraggled doll, the faded clothes he'd found in her backpack, and the few books and small toys he'd bought her. What did a three-year-old play with? What did she need?

A search of Janet's shabby apartment had turned up only basic housewares, scattered clothing, a mattress on the floor and a few battered toys. So few possessions—had she been on the run even before dropping off Katie?

She'd disappeared over five weeks ago and they still had no leads. It didn't take much imagination to guess that she might be dead.

He'd mentally prepared himself over the years. After not seeing her since they were kids, he'd gone out East to find her, but he'd been too late to make a difference in the life she'd chosen. Into marijuana and wild friends as a young teenager, she'd moved on to methamphetamines and worse by the time he'd caught up with her. He'd known her addictions and refusal to accept treatment would probably lead to her death. But logic and forethought didn't lessen his gnawing anxiety now. *Another chance. Just give me another chance.*

Lost in thought, he didn't look up when the entrance chimes trilled at the arrival of yet another customer. Awareness slid through him.

It was Dana. He knew without looking up. And once again, he knew it had been a mistake coming back to Fossil Hill, because the moment he'd seen her at her vet clinic, the past exploded into his thoughts in a dizzying rush. Her sweet, shy smile. The wit and intelligence that had charmed him from the moment they'd met. The ravenous hunger he'd felt when they'd first made out behind the school.

She'd been so innocent and awkward at first, and then suddenly she'd caught on fire with need that drove his own beyond reason, beyond his ability to turn back. He'd never loved anyone as much as he'd loved her.

He'd reasoned that she would have gone off to school, won some guy with a great future in medicine or law, and would now be living in a fine house on either coast. "I'm going to make something of myself," she'd said long ago. "I'm not staying here."

He should have checked. Done a little research on the Internet, looked up her name. Asked a few questions and found out for sure. He'd carelessly left that little detail up to chance, and now he'd signed a four-month lease on a house right next to hers. "Serves you right," he said under his breath.

Her short cap of blond hair gleamed in the subdued lighting and her soft, creamy complexion glowed.

She'd changed into a silky peach top and tan slacks, but nothing about her hair or clothes or makeup spoke of pretension. She seemed completely unaware of how she looked. And yet, in this sea of femininity, he would have picked her out in a split second.

She sauntered over to the woman sitting alone, her stride confident, but another emotion flashed through her expression as she sat down. Weary acceptance, maybe. As if she wished she were someplace else.

He watched her profile as she spoke to her mother. He'd only met Vivian Denton twice, and that had been before middle age had added lines to her face and even greater bitterness to her eyes.

Katie fidgeted in her chair. She'd nipped tiny half-moons from the center of each sandwich now lying forgotten on her plate. He must have missed her first request, because her voice rose to whine. "*Potty. Now.*"

Again?

Some of the older women at the neighboring table glanced over at him with reproving expressions. Apparently he wasn't passing their private daddy-test with flying colors.

Rising gingerly to protect his ribs, which were starting to ache again, he dropped three fives on the table—a fifty-percent tip, but not worth the time to ask for change. Had he remembered his ibuprofen at eleven? Probably not. "Come on, honey."

He offered his hand but she drew back, an overtired glaze in her eyes and her mouth forming a mutinous pout. "Carry," she whimpered, her doll held tight against her chest.

Taking a steadying breath, he carefully leaned over and picked her up, steeling himself against the searing pain radiating through his damaged shoulder joint.

His expression must have betrayed him, because Katie instantly burst into tears. She stiffened and kicked back, knocking over a glass that sent ice water across another customer's back.

The woman gave a startled yelp. Customers around the room stared as she jerked her head around toward Zach, but the thin line of her mouth softened when she saw Katie staring at her with frightened, tear-filled eyes.

"I'm sorry, ma'am," Zach began. "She suddenly decided she had to—"

"I heard." She raised her voice to be heard over Katie's wails. "Don't worry, I'm not wearing anything that won't dry."

"Thanks," he murmured. He started sidestepping through the crowded room, corralling Katie's legs with one arm. Not for the first time, he wished that kids came with a guidebook or online instructions.

He'd reached the restroom door when he felt a warm hand on his arm. It was just a light touch, but he felt it even before she made contact. He didn't need to turn around to know who it was.

"Want me to take her?" Dana's voice was filled with quiet amusement. "This is probably enemy territory to you."

Gratitude flooded through him, followed by other, deeper emotions he didn't want to acknowledge.

It had been far too long since he'd had a close relationship with any woman. He'd been undercover so much, sometimes it was even hard to remember who he was. Relationships based on honesty and commitment were something he couldn't give.

Not even here, over eight hundred miles from Dallas...because one slip might make it easier for El Cazador to follow him.

"Thanks." He eased Katie into Dana's arms.

He'd expected Katie to cry even louder, twist in her arms and reach for him, but Dana matter-of-factly set her on the floor, bent down and took her hand. "Only *girls* can go in this special bathroom. It's way too pretty for the boys."

A final, giant sob racked Katie's thin frame. She gulped, then nodded shyly and allowed herself to be led inside. Through the door, Zach could hear the singsong of Dana's silly chatter, then the sounds of splashing in a sink and the rustle of paper towels.

He imagined her married to someone else. Caring for her own toddlers, making a perfect life for herself in this town...and felt an aching hollowness in his heart for all he'd missed over the years by not finding the right woman and settling down.

In a few minutes they reappeared. Katie's tears were washed away and she wore a tentative smile.

"We girls," Dana announced, "think that bathroom is pretty. Right?"

Katie nodded slowly, her outburst apparently forgotten.

"Thanks for the help," he said quietly.

"Anytime." Dana gave Katie a wink, but when she looked up at Zach her expression was blank. "I'll…send Francie over with some household things to help you out tonight."

Before he could answer, she'd moved between the crowded tables and sat down to her lunch.

"Let's go, honey." He took Katie's hand and stepped out into the bright sunshine, resolutely shutting away his memories. What mattered now was keeping this child safe.

Prior to leaving Dallas, he'd made some calls. With luck, the phone and electricity would be hooked up, and he'd have everything unloaded and in the house by supper.

The fact that he'd lived in Fossil Hill during his senior year of high school should satisfy any local curiosity about his decision to return. He and Katie could settle in for a few months while he recuperated, unless Janet turned up to claim her.

He looked down at the child's blond curls, at the trusting way her little hand fit inside his own, and felt his heart expand until it barely fit in his chest.

At first he'd been overwhelmed by the unfamiliar task of caring for his niece. But now, if Janet showed up and didn't have a logical excuse for disappearing—and at this point, only amnesia would be close to acceptable—it was going to be damned hard to give Katie back.

SUPPRESSING THE INSTINCT to spin around and check behind him, El Cazador stopped at the Holy Mother of God Church on West Fifth and made his way down the hushed, darkened aisle to light candles for the dead.

He smiled when an elderly priest shuffled past, feeling suddenly powerful. Invincible. No one knew his secret. No one could stop him.

Lingering odors of incense and furniture polish and musty old parishioners filled his nostrils, bringing back a thousand memories of childhood.

The ill-fitting suits his grandmother had made him wear every Sunday. The endless homilies, during which he tried to count the sections in the ornate stained glass windows that rose three stories to the cavernous ceilings above. The sharp toe of her lace-up shoes connecting with his tender ankle bone if she caught him daydreaming. She was dead and buried, now, God rest her soul. At least she hadn't lived to see the disgrace of the family name.

He crossed himself, then stepped into a pew, pulled down the kneeler and dropped his head in silent prayer. *Help me bring back our honor....*

Because of a traitor in the family organization, it had been ten years, four months and twenty-three days since he'd had the freedom to walk these streets, and he'd spent every minute of that sentence planning his revenge.

With his computer skills, he'd been a valued part of the family business, but he'd lacked his older brother Eduardo's courage and threatening presence.

That failing had never weighed heavier than on the day he'd stood helplessly by, his trembling hands in the air, while Eduardo and their father fought back and were killed in a DEA raid on their warehouse at Fiftieth and Balster.

They'd been murdered in cold blood—shot like animals before his eyes, and he'd only been able to watch in horror.

The reproach in Eduardo's eyes as he lay dying had been a constant nightmare these past years; retribution for the slaughter an obsession that stole sleep and dominated every waking hour. The silent vow he'd given Eduardo became his constant litany. *I'll avenge you both—and see justice done.*

Unfortunately, he'd made a slight miscalculation on his first attempt.

Foolish mistake, staying in a stairwell of Forrester's building…but he'd wanted to make sure the bombing was a success. When that little girl appeared in the hallway, crying and confused, she'd *seen* him.

Could a kid that young testify in court? God only knew, but he'd panicked, grabbed her and ran before anyone else arrived at the scene. And now there'd be kidnapping charges—and the possibility of life in prison—if she ever identified him in a lineup.

Unless he got to her first.

It was all part of his plan now. Forrester's family would be eliminated, then Forrester himself would be dealt with.

The first of them had already been located. And though Janet had managed to slip away, it wouldn't

take long to find her. A woman with her...appetites...
would soon surface.

When she did, she would provide useful information whether she wanted to or not.

And then she would die.

CHAPTER THREE

ALEX THREW another bale of alfalfa onto the conveyor, then shielded his eyes against the late afternoon sun as he looked up at the open door of the hayloft.

"You aren't going over to welcome those new people?" His fourteen-year-old sensibilities were clearly affronted by Dana's lack of common hospitality. "Not even to take over those boxes on our porch?"

"Francie is dropping them off on her way home, right after she finishes riding her horse." Dana grabbed the bale as it tottered at the top of the conveyor, tested the twine with her curled fingers, then flung it high onto the stack behind her. "She ought to be back in a half hour or so."

"I think we should go, Mom," Molly called from her perch on the stack. At the age of eleven she had the easier job of settling the bales into even rows. "You said he had a little girl, and was alone and everything. Shouldn't we bring them supper, or something?"

Guilt born of lifelong duty to such rituals of country life had settled around Dana's heart since seeing Zach trying to manage his little girl at the Pink Petticoat, warring with her equally strong need for self-preservation.

Fortunately, she knew that several other women present had already volunteered. "After he left the Petticoat, Kim Nelson and Lila Frasier said they were going to take him supper tonight and tomorrow. By the time word spreads, he won't have to worry about fixing dinner for the next month."

"But we're the closest neighbors." Alex lifted another bale from the hay wagon, but tossed it to the ground instead of sending it up the conveyor. "This one's real heavy, Mom."

Meaning it was damp inside, and would mold if stored for winter. Dana sighed. "Another one we'll have to break open to dry out. That bottomland hay wasn't quite dry enough when Bob baled."

She'd figured out the number of massive round bales she needed for cattle and range horses, and the number of small bales for the horses kept up by the barns. This first cutting had been lighter than she'd hoped, and if much of it was poorly cured...

"Maybe Molly and I could go visit."

Exasperated, Dana blew her bangs out of her eyes. "He doesn't need crowds of people disturbing him. We'll go over one of these days."

"What's he like?" Molly called out. "Francie says he lived in town when he was a kid. He doesn't have relatives here, though. Why did he come back?"

Why, indeed. Maybe he was drifting, like he had in high school. Maybe he hadn't been able to hold his last job and needed a cheap place to rent until that arm healed. "It's his business, you guys. I hope you know better than to ask him *anything* personal."

"But—"

"Okay. You win. We'll take those boxes over and say hello." The kids had inherited their father's stubborn streak along with his strawberry-blond hair and freckles, and she knew there'd be no peace until they made it over to meet Zach and Katie. "But we have to get this load of hay in the barn."

The bales hit the conveyor belt faster after that, until Dana and the kids were hot, sweaty and covered with prickly hay chaff. In twenty minutes Alex heaved the last one onto the belt with a grunt. "Done. Let's go."

Molly, her grimy face streaked with rivulets of sweat, scampered down from the bales. "I'm ready!"

"Oh, no you're not. Showers first, young lady, and you too, Alex. You don't want to scare that little girl, do you?"

"Like a three-year-old kid would notice."

"No arguments. Now scoot, Molly. Maybe you can beat your brother to the hot water."

Dana peeled off her leather gloves and leaned against a support post, inhaling the sweet, comforting smell of new alfalfa, thankful for what was already in the barn.

Another two cuttings and they'd have enough for the next winter. *If* rain fell when they needed it, and the skies stayed clear when they didn't. Last year had bordered on drought, and she'd had to buy an extra fifty round bales—money she hadn't had to spare—to make it through spring.

She straightened and tucked her gloves into her

back pocket, then started for the rickety wooden stairs leading to the main floor of the barn.

Since Ken's death everything had been harder—the night calls and long hours at the clinic, the ranching, trying to raise the kids on her own. But despite her own mother's doubts, she was doing okay. She hadn't lost the ranch or her practice yet.

And no matter what Mom thought, she definitely didn't need marriage to a neighboring rancher or anyone else to survive.

THE PHONE AND ELECTRICITY were both hooked up when Zach and Katie arrived, just as he'd hoped. The little blue house wasn't fancy, but it was a good five miles from Fossil Hill and another half mile off the highway, down a curving lane and well out of sight.

Not that much traffic passed by on a road leading to nowhere—the next town was fifty-three miles to the east and boasted a population of eighty-six. Beyond that, there wasn't a town of over a thousand people for another three hundred miles.

He'd arranged the lease by phone, after finding a local Realtor through an Internet business directory. The lease offered an additional bonus: a fifty-percent reduction of the rent for working on maintenance projects around the place.

Just as well. He'd brought his laptop and planned to spend a lot of his time researching case files from the past five years, looking for any clues related to El Cazador, but without something physical to do, he'd go stir-crazy in less than a day.

People took care of their own in these parts. The evidence stood before him in the four cakes on the kitchen counter, and a refrigerator brimming with a collection of casseroles and salads. Eating at that ladies' den of frippery had apparently set the informal news network afire, because an hour after he and Katie arrived at the house, pickup trucks and dusty Suburbans had started pulling in.

Which fulfilled his immediate goals of being known around town and having something edible to feed Katie. Fortunately, with her overtired whining in the background, none of the ladies had stayed long.

When yet another set of tires crunched along the lane, his first impulse was to stay inside and feign sleep. Dredging up another smile, another few moments of introductory chitchat, was almost more than he could handle. But at the sound of slamming doors and the eager voices of several kids, he knew he couldn't ignore them.

"Hey, Katie, we have more company," he said brightly, offering her a smile. "Want to come see?"

With her dolly clasped tightly against her chest, she braced herself in the corner of the faded green couch and jerked her head in a decisive no.

She'd needed a nap since lunch but had been too wound up to fall asleep. He'd walked with her, tried lying down with her, even took her for a long ride in the car, but she'd alternated between fitful crying and all-out wails for the past hour.

"Okay, honey. I'll just be at the back door, okay?"

Her lower lip trembled. Fresh tears welled in her

eyes. The slight nod of her head was a whole lot less decisive than the no had been.

Oh, sweetheart. This hasn't been easy for you. Without asking her a second time, he dropped a kiss on her cheek and lifted her up against his good shoulder, then started for the back door. She instantly wrapped her little arms around his neck.

What was it like, losing your only loved one when you were just three? He'd never known his dad, and his mom had never been a shining example of parenthood, but at least she'd never pulled a stunt like Janet's.

He'd assumed Katie's custody without hesitation, determined to keep her safe, his strong, instinctive need to protect a driving force that had served him well throughout his career. But she was a different sort of operation than he'd ever taken on before—mystifying, challenging and emotional, though no less dangerous. Because this time, he could so easily lose his heart.

He opened the door to find Dana and two kids, each barely visible behind the cardboard boxes and piles of bedding they carried.

"Sorry we didn't get here sooner, but I knew you had supper covered," Dana said as she sidestepped past him into the kitchen.

"You knew?"

"The only problem after you left the Pink Petticoat Inn was how those women were going to figure out who would come out first." She dropped her load of boxes on the kitchen table, then turned to take the top box and pillow from the girl who followed her in. "These are my kids. Molly, eleven. Alex, fourteen. They've been badgering me all afternoon about coming up to meet our new neighbors."

And without that, you probably wouldn't have come, he realized. Which was no more than he deserved.

"Nice to meet you." He offered a hand to Alex after the boy set his load of boxes on the floor.

"Hello." The boy's voice was still at that rusty precipice of manhood, but he was already a good five foot eight and met Zach's gaze with a measuring look. His handshake was that of a kid who knew responsibility and wanted respect for it.

Molly made no pretensions of maturity. She danced from one foot to the other, with a broad smile on her face. "She's sooo cute!" Reaching forward, she danced her fingers up Katie's leg, then landed on her tummy with a brief, butterfly-light tickle.

Zach steeled himself for a howl of outrage, but instead Katie relaxed against him and a faint chuckle vibrated through her.

"You've got your work cut out for you." Dana walked through the kitchen, opening and shutting drawers and doors. "I've kept things clean, but there's still a lot to do."

"I'll manage. Thanks for all the loans."

She bent over one of the boxes on the floor. "We'll help, and then it will be done. Alex, you make the beds." She nudged a box with her foot. "Molly, you put the food away."

Without waiting for an answer, Dana began stowing basic utensils, a mismatched set of china, and some cookware. Zach took over another box and stored an assortment of glasses and mugs in the cupboard by the sink.

"We brought over just a few basics—bread, milk, eggs, some canned goods. Enough to see you through until you can get to the store."

"If you need something, you can always call us. We're the closest ranch," Molly chimed in as she wedged the gallon of milk between the casseroles in the refrigerator.

"These household things are from our foreman's cabin," Dana said. "We don't have a foreman anymore, so you might as well hang on to all of this until you move away. No sense buying anything new."

She emptied the last box, then tossed it on top of the others at the back door. "See? Took just a minute." Then, apparently checking through a mental list, she braced her hands on her slender hips and frowned. "Let's see…if you want the local paper, you can pick one up in town and get the address."

"We used to get it, but we can't anymore," Molly interjected.

"There's trash service out here, but it's expensive. You might want to use the burning barrel out back for all you can." Dana tugged a business card from the back pocket of her jeans. "Here's our number, in case of emergency. Do you have a phone yet?"

Zach grabbed a pen from the counter and jotted his new number on a scrap of paper. He wanted to ask her why their foreman was gone. Why they couldn't afford the newspaper anymore. Where her husband was, maybe. But Dana was already at the door, mission accomplished and keys jingling in her hand.

And there really wasn't much point. His cover was already in place—his software career, his supposed status as Katie's dad. There was no future for him here.

As soon as Alex reappeared in the kitchen after making the beds, Dana lifted her keys. "We should go, kids. I'm sure these two have had a long day."

Though he knew he shouldn't ask, and knew what she would say, he found himself asking anyway. "I've got a ton of food in the fridge. Would you three like to join us for supper?"

"We still have kennel chores, horse chores...Molly has a calf to feed..." She spared him a brief smile that didn't reach her eyes. "You should wrap those extras in foil and put them in the freezer."

He shifted his attention to Molly, who looked crestfallen, and Alex, who was studying his mother as if she'd just morphed into an alien.

"I can't freeze the salads," he pointed out. "They look mighty good, but they won't all keep with just Katie and me here."

"Please, Mom? I could play with Katie, or set the table. I'll help with dishes." Molly folded her hands in front of her as if in prayer. "Pleeease?"

"Yeah, Mom. We'll do chores when we get home. It doesn't take that long. We didn't even have a chance to talk to Mr. Forrester."

There was a hint of longing in the boy's voice that spoke of a need for male companionship, and suddenly Zach knew there wasn't a Mr. Hathaway in the picture any longer. So she's doing it all on her own, he realized. No wonder she looks so harried. "It was just a thought. No big deal. Your mom needs to get home."

Dana wavered, clearly torn between social graces and the personal desire to leave. Her gaze settled on his cast. "How are you managing bath times?" she said finally, her voice laden with resignation.

He knew she referred only to Katie's care, but an image of her helping *him* sent a warm rush of sensation to body parts that had no business being interested. Not now, not during the next three months. "We do okay," he said slowly. "She does pretty well with supervision."

Dana shoved the keys back into her pocket. "Molly, go find some towels. You can start running bathwater for Katie right after we eat, and help her with her bath. Alex, take the empty boxes out to our truck, then come in and set the table. I'll take care of the food. Everything ought to be ready—we'll just have to heat something up. Deal?"

Gone was the timid little girl who'd hung on Zach's arm and stared up into his eyes with awestruck wonder after he had kissed her at the prom. Now, he'd lay bets that she could manage an army platoon or a herd of cattle with equal calm.

"Thanks for staying," he murmured. Setting Katie

down on the floor, he gave her nose a little tap. "Want to go see what Molly is doing?"

After just a heartbeat of indecision, Katie tucked her doll under her arm and made a beeline for the living room.

"So tell me," Dana said as she peered into the refrigerator and began peeking beneath coverings of foil and plastic wrap. "How did you get hurt, and how bad were you?"

The lie now came easy as sin. "A fender-bender accident on the freeway. Broke a few ribs, tore the rotator cuff. Broke my wrist."

"No seat belt, right?"

Her tone of derision rankled. "Uh…yeah. Actually, it was more of a side hit. Totaled the car."

"So the airbags didn't deploy?"

He suppressed a surge of defensiveness, then had a sudden flash of insight. "No, they didn't. Did you lose your husband in a car accident?"

She straightened, bearing an oblong glass dish in one hand and a large bowl in the other, and nudged the refrigerator door shut with her hip. "There's not much contest between a semi and a pickup. We lost him three years ago."

"I'm sorry."

"The kids are doing okay, now. It was hard. Still is, on all those special holidays and anniversaries." She lifted the containers in her hands. "Lasagna and fresh fruit salad? I didn't see any lettuce salads in there."

"Look, I—"

"I'd better get this going. The lasagna is still warm, but it's going to need fifteen or twenty minutes in the oven." She put the fruit on the counter, then slipped the pan of lasagna into the oven and turned the temp to 350 degrees. "I've got to run out to check my cell phone—it's charging in my truck, so I couldn't bring it in."

In a flurry of efficiency she was out the door, leaving him bemused and staring after her.

When he realized she still lived in the area, he'd hoped she hadn't been nursing a serious grudge for the past fifteen years that would make his stay in Fossil Hill difficult. Or worse, that she'd built up some sort of romantic fantasy over time, and would be impossible to avoid.

He gave a short laugh as he headed into the living room to check on Katie. Living this close to Dana Hathaway wasn't going to be the problem he'd expected. The more he saw of her, the more his old memories and longings flooded back. He'd never been able to forget her.

But she clearly had no feelings for him at all.

BACK HOME, after an awkward evening at Zach's place, the usual round of chores and a colic call out to the Gregorsons' ranch, Dana slipped out onto the wide porch with a glass of lemonade and headed for her favorite spot.

The big old porch swing could seat four, and with the new cushions she'd bought last year and a pile of puffy pillows at either end, it was the perfect place to unwind after a long day.

Gabe thought so too. He was already curled up against the pillows at one end with his paws hanging over the edge, taking up over half the space. Now and then his legs twitched and respirations speeded up as if he was dreaming of the fast rabbits and long summer days of his youth.

Careful not to rock the swing, Dana eased down at the other end and held the cool condensation of the glass against her cheek before taking a long sip. Tart and lemony, with just a hint of sweetness, it tasted like heaven after a long, hot day.

Fireflies flickered like a host of dancing stars in the yard. A mellow breeze ruffled the pots of petunias flanking the steps. The warm, familiar scents of cattle, horses and high country pine washed over her like a soothing balm.

Two minutes later, Alex appeared.

He stepped forward to brace his hands on the railing of the deck and leaned over it, peering into the darkness toward Zach's place.

It was two miles away by car, but just over a mile as the crows flew. Breeze-tossed branches blocked the view of his house, save for an occasional twinkle of light that might have been the security lamp set high above the barnyard.

"Who was that guy, Mom? I saw him looking at you sorta funny."

"Just an old friend from long ago." That didn't really encompass the long-term effect Zach had had on her life, the weeks and months and years when she'd done her best to forget him, but none of that mattered now. "He didn't live here very long, though. Just during his senior year. Why aren't you in bed?"

"I couldn't sleep."

"Too much cola?"

The moonlight silvered his red hair as he gave his head an impatient shake.

"Busy day," she murmured.

"Yeah."

"We got a good load of hay in. Thanks for all your help."

He lifted a shoulder. "Gotta be done."

"How are the babies coming along?" Alex worked with the foals every day. In return, she paid him twenty-five dollars a head when they were finally halter broke and gentle.

"Four of the older ones were real good today. Banner's filly and those two paint colts are still real spooky, but they're better. Rowdy still goes berserk when I turn on a pair of clippers."

"You've got your dad's touch, though. I swear, he could have gentled a tornado."

Alex stiffened. Fell silent.

"Come sit with me," she urged, patting the cushions next to her, but he stood at the railing with his back to her, resolute as ever. "We can move Gabe over a bit more. Please?"

"Guess I oughta get back to bed."

"What have you been thinking about?" she asked gently.

He stared up at the stars, then sighed heavily. "Nothing that makes any difference."

She wanted to pull him into her lap as she had when he was a young child, dusty and bruised from his latest fall off a calf or his latest escapade on his old mare. She wanted to smooth back his hair and kiss his forehead, and tell him his heart would heal, in time.

But beyond shouldering a man's load on the ranch—more than she would have ever asked of him—he remained as remote as he had the day state troopers came to their door.

Molly had cried over her father's death. She'd been angry and hurt, and for a few months, she'd had nightmares about terrifying car accidents. But she'd also talked about her feelings night after night, tearfully railing against the unfairness of it all, and in a year's time she had moved past the worst of her grief.

Alex had barely said a word.

Knowing that he was suffering and unable to get through to him, the weight of the past few years settled like an anvil in Dana's chest. *If his own mother hadn't died years ago, would she have been able to reach him?*

"Talk to me, sweetheart," Dana whispered gently. "It's time to get this out in the open and find a way to heal."

Turning away without a word, he went back into the house. Minutes later she heard his slow, measured footsteps ascend the stairs.

Though he no longer talked about his dreams of

becoming a lawyer someday, he'd finally showed more interest in activities around him during the past year. His grades had climbed back up to solid B's.

But Dana couldn't remember when she'd last heard him laugh.

CHAPTER FOUR

"IT'S BEEN OVER SIX WEEKS. You haven't found *anything?*" Ignoring the dull ache in his shoulder, Zach paced the kitchen of the rental house, a cell phone at his ear. "What about Janet's friends? Past landlords? Neighbors?"

"I don't know where she is right now," Jerry retorted. "But I do know where she's lived, where she worked, and who she saw for the past four years."

Leaning against the doorway to the living room, Zach shoved a hand through his hair. "And?"

"She quit or was fired from six different jobs in three towns during that time. Arrested once in Chicago for drunk driving, once for possession of marijuana—a party situation where a dozen people were hauled in. Other than that, she's stayed out of trouble with the law."

So either her drug habits were gradually coming under control, or she'd managed to steer clear of the dealers who'd been her downfall. They'd hooked her on meth, then used her to deliver. After being caught with fifty grams, she'd ended up serving five years.

The sound of shuffled papers came across the line. "Katie's birth certificate doesn't list a father."

No surprise, there. Zach closed his eyes. "My sister isn't exactly a model citizen."

"But there's nothing to show that anyone is after her. Her roommate back in Madison said Janet never talked about Katie's father, never asked for or got any child support. No one ever showed up claiming the child was his."

"Her employers?"

"The co-workers I talked to said she showed up late a lot. Always seemed tired. Didn't work hard. She'd get fired, or quit just before it was likely to happen, but there don't seem to be any rumors about embezzlement or other problems."

"Her supervisors?"

Jerry gave a short laugh. "These days, management is afraid to say anything for fear of a lawsuit. No matter how bad the employee."

"What about Janet's father?" Not that much help was likely from that quarter.

With no other siblings, Zach had never thought of Janet as just a half-sister, but his mother had been divorced for years when she'd had an affair and become pregnant. Initially, the man had sent sporadic child support, but later he'd sued for full custody of their eighteen-month-old daughter and won.

Soon after his victory his company transferred him back East, and Zach hadn't seen his sister again for almost seventeen years.

"He still lives out in New York. Got a little defensive when I called. He immediately announced he wasn't responsible for any of Janet's debts."

"Even after you told him she was missing?"

"Yeah. He said this was nothing new. Interesting lack of concern, given the grandchild involved. I'll check in again tomorrow and let you know if I've found anything else."

"If Janet doesn't show up, we'll need to look into custody issues for Katie. I sure hope he doesn't decide to fight for her."

After the call ended, Zach put down the phone, then braced one hand high on the door frame.

With her arm curled tightly around her doll, Katie had fallen asleep on the couch an hour ago. Her tousled blond curls and long lashes made her look like an exhausted cherub. What kind of future did the poor thing have? A mom with drug addiction. An intolerant, uninvolved grandfather. Zach's mother lived in a cozy retirement village out in California and could hardly take on a child.

As a kid Zach hadn't had much stability, with a mom who was forever moving to somewhere else. There was always another town, another school, and early on he'd learned to stand up for himself, but that didn't make him good parent material. This little girl deserved better.

Zach searched his memory. Perhaps there were other, more distant relatives. Nice people, who would give her a loving and stable home. But during all his years growing up, he'd met a lot of his relations, and right now he couldn't think of a single one worthy of becoming Katie's guardian.

What would happen to her if Janet turned up dead?

Lord knows *he* wasn't much of a choice as a substitute father. What he knew about kids could be summarized on the back of a credit card.

Katie whimpered and clutched her doll tighter. Then she raised her head and looked around with sleep-glazed eyes. Were those rosy cheeks a sign of fever? Zach moved quietly over to the couch and touched her forehead—cool, thank God—then leaned down to rub her back. Soon she drifted back into fitful sleep.

He hoped her dreams were happy ones, of sunshine and laughter and a loving mom who sang soft lullabies at night.

And wondered if those dreams would ever come true.

"YOUR BOYFRIEND IS PULLING UP out in the parking lot," Francie called out. "Should I send him back to your office?"

Dana sighed. Tom was a good man, an honest man. So why didn't her heart beat a little faster whenever he came by? Maybe, she decided, that reaction belonged only to those in the early years of hormones and naïve passion.

"Tell him to wait. I'll be out in a minute."

Clipping the last suture along Muffy Anderson's belly, she gave the young calico cat a quick rub behind an ear and slipped her into one of the stainless steel cages along the wall.

"You've healed well," Dana murmured. "And

now you'll keep your girlish figure for good. No worries about corralling kittens, either.''

The cat flew to the back of the cage and glared at her through slitted eyes.

A light knock sounded on the door of the room. ''She doesn't appreciate your efforts, apparently.''

''Hi, Tom.'' Dana turned and smiled at the man she'd known since grade school. Pudgy and awkward as a child, he'd grown to nearly six feet, and now his stocky build was hardened by years of ranching. ''Get those cattle shipped?''

''Jim left an hour ago. I needed to run into town for milk replacer for a couple of calves, so I figured I'd stop by and see about Saturday night.''

He looked at her expectantly, but she could only give him a weak smile. ''Saturday?''

Annoyance flickered in his eyes, though his easy smile didn't waver. ''The Cattlemen's Association dinner. We went last year, and the year before that.''

Had he asked her, or just assumed she would be available? ''Um...right.''

''I'll be by to get you at six-thirty. Wear something nice...that red dress with the silver buttons.'' At her raised eyebrow, he added, ''It'll be a real special night.''

She stared after him as he walked out the door. With his blond, Nordic good looks, he was the kind of guy women looked at twice when he passed by. His hint at a special evening should have made her heart sing.

Instead, she could only imagine how tired she'd be

by then, after another day of taking emergency calls and hauling hay. But though she could get along fine on her own, there were the kids to consider. They both were still young, needed a good, strong father figure to help them through the treacherous waters of their teen years. Didn't they?

"You look," Francie announced, "as if your favorite dog died. What happened, did ol' Tom finally throw in the towel?"

"We're just friends, and you know it."

"Tell that to him. He left looking sorta upset."

"I forgot about the Cattlemen's dinner Saturday night, and I guess he just assumed I'd be going with him. Honestly, I'd rather not."

Sagging against the wall, Francie lifted her wrist to her forehead. "You poor thing. A dinner date with a handsome guy, a great meal—that's far worse than your dog biting the dust."

"Thanks."

Francie straightened and gave her a sympathetic smile. "Why don't you cancel?"

"I shouldn't let him down."

"Has your mom been talking to you again?"

"She still thinks he's the perfect guy for me." Dana sighed. "I guess it's a logical, reasonable relationship, all things considered. Maybe I just need to try harder."

"That's the logic you'd use for picking out a used car." Francie shook her head slowly. "You need to find someone you can love with all your heart, and who'll love you just as much."

"You've been reading again, Fran. Those magazine articles on romance and passion are probably written by people who are delusional in their spare time."

"They're *experts*. Social workers. Counselors. Psychologists...."

"Who've set hopes and expectations way too high for an entire generation of women."

Francie laughed. "One of these days you're going to find out just how wrong you are, and I sure hope I'm around to see it."

"It won't be in this lifetime." Dana glanced at the wall clock, then turned to the back door. "I've got those five farm calls, but hope to be back by four-thirty. When the kids stop in after school, tell them to fill the water tanks in the corrals by the barn."

"Will do. But think about what I said, okay? You used to talk about how you wanted to teach at some vet school, maybe get your advanced degree. Will you be sorry someday, if you give up those dreams for someone you didn't love, heart and soul?"

"I haven't given those dreams a thought in years," Dana said firmly. "This is my life now."

But heading out onto the highway in her vet truck, Francie's words played through her thoughts again.

She'd never planned to remarry after Ken's death, and Tom certainly hadn't ever asked her. But lately he *had* been hinting at an unspoken element of inevitability.

Probably because in a remote town the size of Fossil Hill, there weren't a lot of choices, and all too often people chose practicality and compromise rather than being alone. Which was not the way one should address matters of the heart.

Feeling as though a weight had lifted from her soul, she pulled to the side of the road, reached for her cell phone and made the call she should have made long ago.

The phone rang six times before switching to his voice mail, but this wasn't something to leave as a recording. She'd try again tomorrow.

Before this went any further, she and Tom needed to talk.

ALEX SLOWED HIS GELDING to a walk as he neared Martha Benson's old place. A mile as the crow flew, it had been an easy ride through the Rocking H north pasture.

Francie had given him homemade bread and a plastic container of chocolate chip cookies for the new neighbors. He knew he could just set them inside the back door of the house and leave.

But maybe the guy and his daughter were around. It would be sort of cool to see them again. Nothing much happened in Fossil Hill, much less this close to home.

He pulled up at the gate marking the Hathaway and Benson property line, leaned down and unfastened the chain, then sidestepped his horse neatly through it. The pasture behind Martha's outbuildings and house was fenced, but there'd been no livestock at her place for years.

As he rode his horse closer, he saw the new guy's

car parked in the driveway and a shiny new pink trike by the back door. From inside the house came the sound of a soft lullaby playing on a tape recorder.

He dismounted and tied Blaze to the hitching rail at the side of the barn, then lifted the bread and cookies out of his roomy saddlebags and headed for the house.

The windows were all open, and gauzy white curtains fluttered against the screens. Through a window at the back—a bedroom, he knew—he saw Zach's shadowy form bend over some small, dark objects on the bed.

The man's movements were swift and sure. Knowing he shouldn't, yet too curious to stop himself, Alex stepped a little closer to the window. A breeze lifted the curtain higher.

He stared in shock.

The quiet city guy, the one who'd told Mom he was some sort of computer salesman, swiftly loaded cartridges into a clip, then slid it into the butt of a semiautomatic. Then he reached inside a box on the bed and took out another gun.

Alex had been around rifles and shotguns all his life. He'd started target shooting when he was seven. But only at the movies had he ever seen anything close to these.

City cops carried semiautomatics like Zach's.

And bad guys on TV.

Apparently sensing someone outside, Zach stilled for a split second, then spun toward the window with one of the guns in his right hand and an expression of cold determination.

He stared at Alex, then slowly lowered the weapon.

Alex jerked back. Stumbled. What kind of guy kept guns like those—and kept them *loaded?*

Just keep walking, like you didn't see a thing, an inner voice whispered.

Frozen with indecision, jackrabbits dancing in his stomach, Alex hadn't taken a single step when Zach opened the back door and stepped out onto the wrap-around porch.

His air of tension and controlled power, coupled with a black T-shirt that molded to his muscular chest and major-league biceps, reminded Alex of some dude in an action movie. His hands—thank God—were empty. But the coiled tension in the man's stance said he wouldn't need a weapon to take on anyone who crossed his path. He scanned the property, then settled his intent gaze on Alex.

"You should be more careful, son," Zach said quietly. "I thought you were a prowler. Are you here alone?"

Mom's every word of caution about strangers came back to him. "Uh…yeah."

Zach raised a brow. "You hiked?"

"R-rode. My horse Blaze is tied to a rail behind the barn."

"I didn't hear you come down the lane."

"Uh…I came over through the pasture gate between our property and this place." Alex lifted the sacks in his hands. "Francie wanted me to bring these over."

"I see." Accepting the proffered gifts, Zach visibly relaxed. "I'd be neighborly and ask you in, but Katie's asleep." He gestured toward two chairs on the porch. "Want a Coke?"

Alex wavered. "Well..."

"Sit. I'll be right back."

A moment later he returned, two cans cradled in one hand and a bag of chips in the other, and eased the back door shut without a sound. He tossed one can to Alex and settled into a chair, then ripped open the bag of chips and laid it on the small table between them.

"Nice day to go riding." Zach lifted a brow.

"Yeah, I guess."

"I suppose you have your own horse?"

"Course. Dad gave him to me the day he was foaled, and helped me start him as a two-year-old under saddle." It was hard to keep the note of pride out of his voice. "Blaze was the first horse I finished on my own."

Zach smiled a little at that. "You still in school?"

"Yeah." Alex slid a thumb along the condensation on the can. "Two more days."

Cracking open his own can of soda, Zach took a long swallow. "Late this year, isn't it?"

Alex gave a self-conscious shrug. "We had like seven snow days, so we had to make up the time."

Zach laughed. "I used to hope for blizzards when I was a kid. Never much liked having to go longer in the spring, though. Warm weather...baseball...fishing... would have been better just to never miss days during winter.''

"Yeah." Alex thought about the guns he'd seen through the window. He wanted to ask, but didn't dare. "Do you hunt?"

"Not much." Studying Alex over the rim of the can as he took another swallow, Zach eased deeper into his chair and stretched out his long legs, crossing them at the ankle. Just an average guy relaxing on a warm day, Alex thought, except for the intensity of his gaze. "Does this town still have a high school baseball team? Football?"

"Uh...yeah. Not very good, though."

"So the Fossil Hill Giants haven't exactly taken the world by a storm?"

Alex snorted. "Hardly."

"How about you? You must be what—a sophomore?" Zach gave him an approving glance from head to toe. "You look like you could be a pretty mean quarterback."

A flicker of pride warmed Alex's heart. "I'll be a freshman this fall."

"Going to try out?"

The warmth faded. "Nah."

"Why not?"

Because my dad is dead, and there are horses to feed, and stalls to clean, and I have a sister to look after...and if I don't keep my grades up I'll never earn scholarships to get away from here. "Just not interested."

"You should go for it." Zach finished the last of his cola. "I never got to play in sports. Moved around too much, so that made it tough to get involved. Always wished I'd played football."

"Why?"

"Why did I want to play?"

"Why did you move so much?"

"I guess we just liked the open road," he said lightly. "New places, new people to meet."

Exactly what I want. "Cool."

"There's a lot to be said for a stable home, kid. Being around people who know and love you. I'll bet you and your mom get along really well."

Alex jerked upright. Looked at his watch. "Holy cow—I've got to get back."

Only after he was on his horse and halfway home did he remember what he had seen.

Zach Forrester had come off as a friendly guy. He'd talked like they were equals—old friends shooting the breeze on a summer afternoon. But he'd said almost nothing about himself, and he had major weapons stowed away in Martha Benson's house.

Who was this guy—and what was he really doing in Fossil Hill?

THE BITCH HAD SURFACED, just as he knew she would. Putting the word out on the street in Dallas had snared her within days. Finding a card in her pocket bearing Zach Forrester's e-mail address had been a nice bonus.

He'd thought Janet was Zach's ex-wife, and that

the child was his daughter. The truth had been... disappointing. Still, they'd both be useful. Since they were family, they would die.

He opened the door to the room and studied the jittery woman clutching a bundle of blankets around herself on the floor.

One hand never ceased, just constantly picked at the flesh of her other arm, as if she were removing an endless legion of ants crawling across her flesh. Now and then she cried out, answering voices only she could hear.

He'd used an old family friend to help him keep tabs on Forrester's every move, but they'd lost him, dammit, and Janet had refused to talk. It wouldn't take long. The craving would build and build and build until she would give him the location of her own daughter and brother for just one more hit. She had to know where they'd hide.

He smiled to himself as he locked the door. He'd always abhorred the carnage created by guns. But messy, disagreeable weapons weren't necessary when a user was involved.

Once the woman gave him all the information he needed, she would be given the biggest—and most deadly—high of all.

CHAPTER FIVE

"IT'S LATE, but we need to talk." Dana stood on the other side of his screen door, her arms folded over her full breasts. The determined tilt to her chin told Zach that she wasn't leaving anytime soon.

"Sure." Zach unlatched the hook he'd installed high on the door, to make sure Katie didn't wander away, and ushered her in. Outside, the sounds of crickets and bullfrogs echoed through the damp night air. An eerie, faraway whinny to the west invoked the distant, answering calls of other horses unseen in the darkness.

"Hey, when did you get rid of your cast?"

Zach shrugged. "A local doc took it off this morning. He said everything looked fine."

"Is Katie awake?"

"Nope. She's asleep in the back bedroom, already. I've come to believe that naps and early bedtimes are a gift from above."

He smiled, but Dana ignored his subtle bid for friendship. She swept past him, the lemony scent of her shampoo trailing behind her, and he found himself wanting to run his fingers through that silky blond cap to see if it felt as soft as it looked.

He had a pretty good idea of why she'd come, though, and it wasn't to start where they'd left off fifteen years ago. There was little doubt that her son had seen too much. "Anything wrong?"

She halted in the middle of the kitchen and turned to face him, her expression troubled. "Alex was over here this afternoon."

"Your friend Francie sent him over." He gestured toward the sack still lying on the counter. "Want some coffee and a taste of her chocolate chip cookies?"

Eyeing him closely, she shook her head. "Why are you back in Fossil Hill?"

"A few months of vacation. Some time to heal," he said easily. "I figured it would be nice to step back in time for a while."

"But you don't have relatives here—probably not even any close friends, since you were here for less than a year as a kid, right?"

Now there was an understatement. By the time he and his mother had landed in Fossil Hill, they'd lived so many places that he no longer bothered to make friends, and he'd had a chip on his shoulder the size of Texas. Dana, with her ready smile and big blue eyes, had been his salvation. "We were here as long as anywhere else."

"Are you in trouble?"

He feigned ignorance. "We've settled in just fine."

She stepped closer, until they were practically toe-to-toe. "My son came home worried about something. He didn't want to tell me, but..." She colored slightly.

"He finally told me that you have weapons here. Is that true?"

"It's hardly unusual. A Colorado pickup without a gun rack across the back window is rare as an albino Angus."

"The average cowboy carries a rifle."

"True."

"They don't carry automatics—much less several. My children live right next door, Forrester. Believe me when I say that I won't allow anyone, or anything, to place them at risk."

He lowered his voice. "You must not remember me very well."

Unfolding her arms, she impatiently waved away his comment with one hand. "I don't think you'd hurt them. But if you're in some kind of trouble, that could bring danger to my back door. Are you on the run?"

"I'm not wanted by the law, no."

"*That* I wouldn't be worried about. If you were, I'd turn you in myself."

He had to smile at that. She'd probably enjoy doing it, too. "And no, I don't have any drug-dealing cohorts who are after my money or my nonexistent stash. Whatever you think of me, I've never been arrested, never spent a day on the wrong side of the law."

"But Alex said—"

"Alex caught a glimpse of my guns, true. But I'm a collector, not a criminal." Zach chose his words carefully, regretting the fabrication he had to use.

"They came from a gun shop during our trip up here."

"You just *collect* them?"

Just as he'd feared, the boy must have seen him loading clips. "I also do quite a bit of target practice, so you might hear the noise now and then. But believe me, my guns are safely stored in a locked case, with the clips and cartridges stored separately. There are too many tragedies each year involving children and guns to ever be careless."

She studied his expression, not giving an inch, and he had the uneasy feeling that she was far too perceptive. "You do understand my concern?" she asked finally.

"Of course."

"My son has had a hard time dealing with his father's death." She extended her hands, palm up. "His grandpas are gone, his uncles are too preoccupied to give him the time of day. I worry about the wrong kind of influence."

That hurt. "Like me?"

"I didn't say that. I only want to keep him safe, and to raise him right. These days…"

"He's a good kid, Dana. You're doing a great job."

"I'm trying. I want him to understand that his word means everything. That he needs to learn to face up to problems and deal with them head-on, instead of running." She met Zach's gaze, silently challenging him to deny ever failing to do just that.

"For the record, I agree completely." Though she'd never find out how much, because he could never tell her about his last night in Fossil Hill so many years ago.

"Really. Then…" Her voice faded away as she stared at him, and he wondered if she felt the same mesmerizing connection he did—if she felt the old longing and desire wrapping around her heart, too, despite the way their relationship had ended.

She was only inches away. He could have reached up and smoothed back her hair, or rested a reassuring hand on her shoulder. Perhaps even settled a kiss on those full lips to see if the magic had survived.

Which was far too foolish to contemplate. Not now, when he'd be here only long enough to recuperate. When he had a career back in Dallas, a major-league case to solve. When—if his luck didn't hold—the very man he was after could turn up in town and threaten the lives of anyone close to him.

He stepped back and motioned toward the kitchen table. "Coffee? I just made some."

"No, I really need to—"

"Please?"

She wavered, glanced at the clock above the stove. Then she lifted the cell phone hooked to her belt and hit a single speed-dial digit. After a brief conversation with Molly, she laid the phone on the counter. "Ten minutes, then I have to get home. I don't like to leave the kids at night if I don't have to."

Zach poured two mugs of coffee and set them on the table with a plate of Francie's cookies. "They're alone?"

"Ben is our only full-time ranch hand. He lives up

the hill in a cabin, just a couple hundred feet from our house.'' She took a sip of coffee, then reached for a cookie. "He's sort of a reclusive old guy—won't even eat with us very often. But he loves the kids, and without him close by, I couldn't leave on night vet calls.''

A vet practice. A ranch. Kids to raise. A full plate, even if her husband were still alive. Was there another man in the picture by now? "Your schedule must be nonstop.''

"It had better be. If I don't—'' She caught herself abruptly. "You must really rate if Francie is baking for you already. She's not exactly the most domestic type, but her oatmeal raisins are the best ever.''

Zach didn't want to talk about cookies and the woman at the clinic. He wanted to know what Dana had done over the past fifteen years, day by day. And he wanted to know what would happen if she didn't keep busy. Was she on the verge of losing the ranch? Her practice?

"It's good to see you again, Dana,'' he said finally, opting for safer ground. "And it's good for Katie to be with other people, too. I hope we'll be good neighbors.''

From outside came the sound of a diesel pickup, the crunch of gravel under its wheels. A door squealed open, then slammed shut. Zach stilled. Judged the distance to his bedroom, where he'd left his guns in locked, portable gun safes on a high shelf in the closet. "You know anyone who'd stop this late?''

Dana raised a brow. "You look as if you expect trouble."

"It's a reflex after years of traveling to unfamiliar cities."

"From the sound of that truck, it's Tom Baxter." She smiled, but there was resignation in her voice. "He must have called my place and heard I was here."

"Is he...a good friend of yours?"

"Since grade school."

The guy was near her age? Zach stalked to the window and stared out into the darkness. "He still follows you around?"

"He checks up on me, yes. If I go out on night calls and he happens to see my truck, he'll stop to see how things are going."

"Was he in our class? I can't place him at all."

"He's a few years older, and would have been in the service then."

Older—so with luck, the guy was short, fat and bald.

Heavy footsteps crunched across the gravel, then climbed the back steps. A fist banged against the door. "Dana—you in there? Everything all right?"

Before he could knock again, Zach reached the door and jerked it open. "It will be unless you just woke up my little girl." He tried for a welcoming smile. "I'm Zach Forrester. Want to come in?"

"Tom Baxter." Tall, blond, with the kind of face some women might find attractive, the man didn't hesitate for a second. He took off his hat and stepped inside, surveyed the room and then headed to Dana. "I was out to your place, but they said you were over here." His brow furrowed. "Are you here on a vet call?"

Annoyance flashed through Dana's eyes. "No."

"I figured you might need some help."

"Thanks, but everything is fine. I'm just visiting."

Tom spared Zach a dismissive glance, then riveted his attention back on Dana. "If you're done here, I can follow you home."

"Thanks, but I don't think so. I'll be here a while longer."

"I want to make sure you get home safely. It's late."

"I don't think the lady wants to do that just now," Zach said mildly. He sauntered back into the kitchen and leaned against the counter by the sink, folding his arms across his chest.

"This isn't your damned business."

"You've made it mine by coming here," Zach said softly.

Tom glared at him, hands flexing at his sides. He was heavily muscled but overweight, and had probably downed a few beers before showing up here. It might take more than a few moves to take him down. Given the positioning of the table, chairs and countertops, it would also take a measure of luck to avoid hurting him in the process.

"No one wants any trouble," Zach said.

"I'll bet you don't."

"Tom, for heaven's sake! I—" Dana seemed to

catch herself, then her voice softened. "Look, we need to talk. I tried calling you this morning and didn't get through. Can we can meet tomorrow sometime?"

"But—"

She gave Zach a swift, apologetic glance, then turned back to Tom. "Go home. Have some coffee. I think I have some free time around ten o'clock in the morning. Can you stop by then? If not, call and we'll work out something else."

Tom stared at her, a dull red flush rising up his neck as he self-consciously ran his fingers over the brim of his hat. After a long moment, he finally nodded and left.

Long after he was gone, Dana stared at the back door.

"Are you going to be all right?" Zach asked finally. "Is he going to come after you?"

"Tom? Of course not."

"I'll follow you home to make sure he isn't waiting for you there."

"That isn't necessary."

"Yes, it is." Zach smiled. "For my peace of mind, if not yours. I need a good night's sleep."

"What about Katie?"

In answer, he went back to the child's bedroom, wrapped her up in a blanket, grabbed her pillow and carried her out to his car. In moments he had her snuggled up on the back seat with her dolly and extra blankets. "She won't even know she left home," he whispered. "If she does wake up, I'll just read a few dozen books until we both fall asleep."

Dana started for her truck, then turned back. Moonlight glimmered through her hair and turned her eyes dark and mysterious. He wondered if she'd ever realized just how pretty she was. "Thanks, Zach."

"No problem."

But it was. As he followed her down the mile of highway and additional mile of private lane leading up to her house, he tried to quiet the memories that kept coming back. Dana befriending him, the new kid in school. Teasing him, drawing him into her circle of friends. Kissing him in the moonlight.

He'd never forgotten her. Never should have returned. Because once again he would have to leave, and it would take forever for his heart to heal a second time.

TOM SHOWED UP at the clinic at ten-thirty in the morning, his eyes bloodshot and his walking-on-eggshells gait that of a man who'd had too much to drink the night before. Dana had never seen him with a hangover, and it saddened her.

"I'm sorry about all of this, Tom. I really am."

"Things were going real well until Zach showed up."

"No—you and I are just friends like we've always been, and always will be, I hope. He didn't change anything."

"Didn't he? At least give me some credit. I'm not blind."

"Look, I'm not dating him, either. I've got too much to handle right now, to even think of a steady relationship with anyone."

"So what happens when he leaves?"

"Life will go on as it did before."

"But—"

"No, Tom. Be honest—can you say you truly love me? That you're filled with incredible passion when you see me walk into a room? Does your heart race?"

"*Jeez*, Dana." Dull red rose up his neck. "I do care about you."

"But not like when you fell in love with Anna. Remember?"

"And that didn't last. I never should've married her."

At the bitterness in his voice and the bleak look in his eyes, Dana's heart twisted. "You need someone who'll love you with all her heart, Tom," she said quietly. "That person isn't me."

"But we get along," he protested. "You aren't the romantic, flighty type, and neither am I. Hell, just think what we could do with the Rocking H and my spread combined. We'd be one heckuva team."

"The next time you court someone, you might want to leave that approach at home," she teased gently. "Telling a woman she isn't the appealing, romantic type and offering her a business deal won't win you many points. That's just a suggestion."

"I didn't mean—"

"I do understand. You deserve the best, and I'll

always be hoping you find it. No hard feelings, okay?''

Long after he was gone, Dana sat at her desk and stared out the window toward the hills, wishing she could have given him a different answer. But someday he'd find the right woman to win his heart.

DURING THE NEXT FOUR DAYS, Zach unpacked everything. Went to town to buy ruffled pink curtains and a bedspread covered with pink balloons. Found toys and a new doll and, with the help of a grandmotherly clerk, bought Katie new outfits and underwear and a light jacket. *She'll need it all later,* he reasoned. *When her mother shows up.*

Through it all, Katie silently clung to his leg like a burr, that faded doll as much a part of her as her baby-soft hair and sad blue eyes. It was as if she already knew that her mother wasn't coming back.

Now, while he stood out in the midafternoon sunshine, giving the exterior of the little house a fresh coat of paint, she played with her doll on the porch swing, where he knew she kept a close eye on his every move. *She's afraid I'll disappear, too.*

At the distant sound of hoofbeats, he stilled, looked across the rolling pastureland toward the Hathaway place and saw two riders approaching at a dead run. Dana's kids, he realized after a moment. Riding bareback and racing to an impromptu finish line. A few hundred yards away, they slowed to a walk and Molly leaned over to give her horse a hug.

Katie stared at them in awe. "Horsie!" Her doll

forgotten, she slid off the swing and stood at the porch railing.

Zach tapped the lid back on the paint can and dropped the brush into a jar filled with thinner, then put the jar up high where she couldn't reach. "Would you like to pet the horses?"

Her vigorous nod made him smile as he scooped her up into his arms and headed for the gate at the far side of the barn.

He'd come up with a long list of chores, well beyond what his lease agreement required, and it felt good to keep busy. He'd already replaced several window screens and scraped blistered paint from the weathered house. Now that his cast was off, he'd be able to make faster progress.

They stood along the split-rail fence as the Hathaways pulled to a stop on the other side.

"Hi, Katie!" Molly waved exuberantly.

Alex, his efforts at masculine reserve painfully obvious, nodded once and touched the brim of his hat. "Francie and Mom are grilling steaks tonight to celebrate the end of school. They…uh…wanted us to invite you over."

"Can you come? Please?"

"What do you think, honey? Want to go visiting?"

"We've got puppies in our barn," Molly cajoled. "And Mom has baby birds in the clinic." Her voice rose dramatically. "I could even catch old Penelope, and see if she'll give you a ride. She was Alex's first pony, and mine, too. Supper is at seven, but can you come sooner?"

"We were supposed to ask you hours ago," Alex said, giving Molly a long-suffering look. "But *some-*

one left the south pasture gate open. We had to round up over a hundred cows and calves heading down the highway.''

"It wasn't me," Molly retorted. "I didn't even go through that gate this week. Honest.''

"Right. Like you didn't leave the clinic's back door unlocked after feeding the dogs yesterday—'' Alex gave Zach an apologetic grin. "Sorry. You won't want to come over if you have to listen to us.''

Zach glanced at his paint-spattered watch. "We'll be there as soon as we can. Katie needs a quick bath, and I could use a shower first.''

"Perfect!" Molly beamed at him.

Katie watched with rapt attention as the two Hathaways turned their horses toward home. *"Ponies,"* she breathed.

Her bath done in record time, her eyes sparkling with anticipation, she was waiting at the door long before Zach had finished his shower and dressed.

"Just a second, sugar," he said, pausing at the laptop he'd set up on the small desk in the living room.

Before leaving Dallas, he'd bought an 800-number telephone calling card at a discount store. He could use the card and no calls could be traced to his own name.

Still cautious, he now varied between using his cell phone and the prepaid calling card. Knowing that special software could trace e-mails, he only rarely went online, via a major Internet provider, to check whether Jerry had any news about Janet. He never sent any in return.

Definitely not a perfect system, but the best he could do under the circumstances.

Maybe today there'll finally be some information about Janet.

After powering up his laptop, he hit a series of keys, then waited impatiently for his messages to appear. Not that he expected many. He'd set up this very private, personal address in April, and only a handful of people even knew what it was.

One message from Jerry, succinct as ever: *Nothing yet. Still trying.*

He scrolled to the next message. Icy fingers crept down his spine at reading the sender's name. *El Cazador.*

Damn. How had the guy tracked down this personal e-mail address, and what else did he know? Zach's breath caught in his throat at the first paragraph...and the danger it represented to an innocent little girl.

I'm far closer than you think. Maybe I'll take the kid first. Or maybe I'll just arrange a nice, final party for you both. Wouldn't that be fun?

The last paragraph made his threat crystal clear.

Bring in the law, and I'll end this even sooner. You can bet more people will die—and that girl might just be the first.

CHAPTER SIX

AFTER READING the threatening e-mail, Zach's first thought was to contact the closest DEA office and request assistance. His second thought was that it might be a major mistake.

Out here, in an isolated, rural area, it would be nearly impossible for a team of Special Agents to move in unnoticed. Their visibility would elevate the risk.

If spooked, the guy could turn violent. Or he might disappear for days...weeks...months. Then suddenly reappear and take Katie in the blink of an eye. And so far, Zach didn't even have a physical description to help identify him in a crowd.

But while the arrival of Special Agents would be obvious, so would the arrival of anyone else from far away. A stranger hanging around town would be hot news at the café in minutes.

That gossip could prove more helpful to Zach than what little the field office back in Dallas had been able to find. They'd turned up nothing conclusive. Zach hadn't had much more luck, though he'd spent hours each day, poring over old records on his computer, searching through old case files.

Now he grabbed his binoculars from the kitchen counter, then stepped outside and scanned the rolling hills surrounding the house—barren except for the trees filling ravines, and a scattering of distant cattle.

By daylight a stealthy approach to the house would be almost impossible, given the long driveway and lack of trees for cover. At night...

He thought about Martha Benson's place, just north of town, and smiled. Several times, when driving past, he'd pulled over and parked for a few minutes, because the woman's flocks of poultry enthralled Katie. Especially the peacocks and bossy geese.

He and Katie would pay Martha a quick visit before going to Dana's ranch, and then he'd stop at home to install an instant alarm system no city guy would ever expect.

"IT'S GRANDMA ON THE PHONE," Molly shouted down the steps. "She wants to talk to Mom!"

Ben tucked his paycheck into the front pocket of his heavy flannel shirt and edged toward the back door of the kitchen. "Guess I'll be goin', then."

"I still don't see why you won't eat with us." Dana looked up from the lettuce she'd started chopping for salad and waved the knife blade in his direction. "You could meet the new neighbor and his girl, and we're having good steaks on the grill."

Ben harrumphed. "Cain't chew them steaks, anyway. My new teeth don't work."

"I could grill you a nice juicy hamburger."

Ben shuddered. "No, ma'am."

"Cottage cheese, then? A grilled cheese sandwich?"

"You know I like eating by myself in front of *Wheel of Fortune* and turnin' in early. But thanks for the invite."

At the sound of Molly's feet thundering down the stairs, he settled his stained Resistol low over his brow and started out the door. "Tomorrow I'll be headin' up into the north pasture, ma'am. Fencin'. Since the boy's out of school now, he's welcome to come along."

The door closed behind him as Molly slid into the kitchen on her stockinged feet. "Did you hear me? It's Grandma. She's kinda in a hurry, so you better get on the phone."

"One of these days we're going to get that man to join us for regular meals," Dana muttered as she stepped over Gabe and reached for the phone on the counter. "I swear he's more of a recluse with every passing year."

"Recluse?" Vivian's sharp voice was audible even though the receiver was still a foot away from Dana's ear. "Are you talking about me?"

Grinning, Molly leaned both elbows on the counter and propped her chin on her hands to listen.

Dana shooed her away. "Go back upstairs to hang up that receiver, then come back and set the table. *Now.*" Then she took a deep breath. "Hi, Mom."

"I haven't seen you in a week. What have you been doing?"

"Office calls. Vet calls. Chores around the ranch...nothing new."

"And how is Tom?" The thinly veiled accusation in Vivian's voice suggested that she already knew. "You're so lucky, Dana Marie. He's a fine man. Did you enjoy the Cattlemen's dinner Saturday night?"

"Actually, no." Taking the phone with her, Dana stepped over Gabe again and went back to her cutting board and the lettuce.

A long silence fell. "You didn't enjoy your evening?"

"He and I didn't actually have one. We had a talk, Mom. We both agreed that there wasn't much future for us."

"You need a father for those children. Tom is a good man, with a good heart," Vivian said firmly. "You couldn't do better."

"I don't love him, Mom. If I ever get married again, I want shooting stars, and fireworks. I want to feel as if the earth has stopped in its tracks, just for me."

"Foolish dreams. It's not too late to change your mind. I can call him—"

"*Mother!*"

"I only want what's best for you, dear, and for the children. You need to be thinking about *them.*"

"I do. All the time."

"There are a lot of men around who'd be a bad choice. Old mistakes are best not repeated, don't you think?"

"I don't plan to, Mom." Dana lifted her gaze to the window and watched Ben hobbling back to his cabin, then gave Molly a thoughtful look. *Someone* had been talking about Zach. Ben? One of the kids? Maybe even Francie.

"Then keep your distance from Forrester. A few years difference doesn't make him a better man. I remember like yesterday how you felt when he dumped you flat and disappeared. You think he wouldn't do that again?"

Gritting her teeth, Dana silently counted to ten. *She means well, she really does.*

"Dana, are you there?"

"I'm a thirty-three-year-old professional woman, Mom. It's thoughtful of you to give me advice, but I can't guarantee I'll take it. Um…thanks for calling, but I need to go now, okay? I'm in the middle of making supper."

Long after she hung up, Dana rested her palms on the counter and stared at the lettuce she'd decimated during the phone call.

However abrasive or calculating her mother could be, she did have a point.

It would be all too easy to be lured by Zach Forrester's potent charm and devilish grin. She'd have to take care. He had a career in Dallas; she had total commitment to her kids, the ranch and her practice. There truly was no way to compromise.

Going beyond being just friends and neighbors would be a painful mistake.

"YOU BOUGHT *WHAT?*" Dana looked at Zach across her dining room table in frank amazement. "Because *why?*"

He grinned back at her. "I think geese are fascinating. And peacocks—amazing creatures, don't you think?"

"That's cool!" Molly announced, a spoonful of strawberry shortcake halfway to her mouth.

They'd grilled massive steaks and had polished off baked potatoes and several dozen ears of early sweet corn. Zach couldn't remember when he'd enjoyed a meal more.

"Do you have any idea how noisy they are?" Dana set aside her half-finished dessert. "How territorial?"

Yes, indeed. "I just figured they'd be interesting to watch."

"Will they even let Katie play outside?"

"The entire yard is fenced, but there's also a fence dividing the front and back. I can herd the peacock and geese to the backyard and lock the gate."

"Good plan, because they sure can be aggressive. We've had geese that would chase horses away from the feeders. One old gander even intimidated our younger bulls."

"Until one of them finally got fed up and hooked him over the fence," Alex pointed out with relish. "Broke that—"

"Alex!" Dana interrupted sharply. "We don't need the details right now."

Francie, seated to Zach's left, rolled her eyes. "Some peacocks can scream like a dying woman, and you can hear 'em a half mile away. Maybe Martha will give you a refund if you bring those birds back."

Katie, who'd climbed onto his lap a few minutes ago, twisted around to look up at him, her eyes filled with silent worry.

He gave her a reassuring smile. "Martha said she'd take them back when we leave the area, but I think we'll keep them until then. Okay?"

She nodded, then snuggled closer to whisper in his ear. "Can I see the pony? And the puppies?"

Molly jumped out of her chair. "I'll take her."

"Not just yet, young lady," Dana said. "Who's on dishes tonight?"

"But Mo-om," she pleaded, drawing the name out into several agonized syllables. "Katie wants to go, and I did catch the pony for her. Can't I take her now? Please?"

Francie stood up and gathered the plates and utensils within reach. "I'll wash, Molly dries, and Alex can put things away. Deal?"

Alex moaned. Molly scowled. But they both dutifully began clearing the table.

Zach swallowed the last of his coffee and took in the warm, welcoming atmosphere of Dana's kitchen—the soft yellow walls, the airy curtains. The refrigerator plastered with old school notices and pictures and lists of things to do.

A project of Molly's, involving clay and poster paints and a rainbow of construction paper, dominated the dining room, so they'd eaten at the kitchen table instead.

The comfortable setting and constant family banter were as foreign to Zach as upscale Dallas restaurants would have been to Molly and Alex, but he had no doubt as to who had the better deal.

This was what Katie deserved. The warmth of a family. Stability. The love and support of a mom who would always be there for her, who would give her firm guidelines and help her grow up into a strong and independent young woman.

He doubted Janet had handled parenthood very well but knew without a doubt that he was even less qualified than she. This one evening meal had just brought it home to him with absolute clarity.

Katie scrambled off Zach's lap and grabbed for his hand, then reached for Dana's. "Let's go!"

Over the child's head, Zach gave Dana a rueful smile. "Guess she's impatient."

"Of course she is—puppies and ponies are a little girl's dream." Dana turned to Francie. "You really don't need to help with the dishes. The kids can handle it."

"I eat here more often than I eat at home. So what's the problem? Go make that child's day." Francie flapped her hands at them, shooing them out the door.

Gabe rose from his favorite spot by the kitchen sink and followed them all outside. Once they left the porch, Katie let go of their hands and danced ahead with Gabe loping along beside her.

Zach fell into step with Dana. "Are things always this busy here?"

"I think you mean noisy. And that answer is yes."

Almost of its own accord, his hand found hers as they walked side by side toward the barn. She drew in a sharp breath and pulled away.

"Sorry. Just instinct, I guess."

"I...well, I just don't want you to get the wrong idea."

Zach chuckled. "Must be tough, fighting men off at every turn. You need to carry pepper spray." He waited a beat, then added, "Maybe on a necklace."

She laughed at that. "Believe me, I would rarely need it."

"Heard any more from your old friend?"

She walked a few yards in silence. "Tom? I think we've got things straightened out."

"Meaning?"

"Tom's wife has been gone for a long time. He's been lonely, and started seeing possibilities that just aren't there. And I...well, I just let things go on too long."

"How about you—do you get lonely sometimes?"

Her laughter, soft and sweet, charmed him completely. "Take one look around here, and tell me when I'd have time."

When they reached the cool depths of the barn, Katie looked up at the dusty swaths of spiderwebs hanging from the old timbers and hesitated to step inside.

"Come on, sweetie, the puppies are over here. And," she added with a wicked grin, "there might just be one with your name on it."

"Named *Katie?*" Her voice filled with awe, the child followed close on Dana's heels.

Dana laughed. "So to speak."

A month ago, Zach's life had been on an even keel. Work, sleep, work. Barring midnight call-outs on a case, he'd been able to predict what might happen from day to day. Now a mental image of puppies, geese and peacocks threatened to overwhelm him. "I really don't think we can take on a dog."

But then he looked down. The puppies, a fluffy, tumbling mass of gray, white and black spots, scrambled at the walls of the pen, yelping and barking and fighting to lick Katie's proffered hands. She squealed with delight and gave him such a look of joy that his heart skipped a beat. Whatever they cost, Katie would have a new puppy if she just said the word.

"There you have it, their total devotion to me has gone straight out the window," Dana said. "They definitely like you best, Katie."

"How come they have different color eyes? Can they see?"

"Gabe is the daddy. Did you see how he has one brown eye and one blue? Australian shepherds are often like that. And yes, they can see perfectly well."

"Where's their mommy?"

"Susie probably disappeared the minute she heard us coming." Dana glanced both ways down the aisle. "A family mistreated her before she came here, and she's really afraid of children and strangers. Mostly she keeps to herself."

Katie's eyes filled with worry. "What about the puppies?"

"Don't worry, honey. They're weaned already. Some of them have already gone to new homes. Susie will, too. All the commotion here makes her nervous, and a widowed client of mine wants her for a companion."

"Can I play with the puppies?"

"Sure, if it's okay with your dad. But they'll probably knock you over."

Dad. Since leaving Dallas, he'd presented himself as the child's father, figuring the fewer questions, the better, especially if anyone was trying to track him. A twinge of regret hit him as he lifted Katie into the pen.

He'd allowed Dana to make that assumption, too. Remembering her sense of honor and abhorrence of lies when still a teenager, he wondered what she'd say when he told her the truth.

Katie's excited giggles filled the air as the puppies crowded around her, begging to be petted. "They're funny!" she squealed, trying to hug two at once.

Standing next to Dana, watching Katie become a carefree child for the first time since he'd met her, Zach's heart suddenly seemed too large for his chest. Not trusting his voice, he reached over and caught Dana by the waist. Snuggled her next to his hip.

This time, she didn't resist. "I can almost imagine Molly and Alex in there at that age. They were already five and eight when I married their dad, and I missed so much." She sighed, closing her eyes.

"Kids and puppies. Don't you wish they'd always stay small?"

"There are a lot of things I wish for," he said slowly. He looked down at her gleaming hair, the smoky crescents of her lashes lying against her cheeks. She seemed smaller, more fragile than she had a moment ago, and he couldn't stop himself from running a finger lightly along her high cheekbone, the firm line of her jaw.

Her eyes fluttered open and widened as he stared down into the darkening blue depths.

"I—"

He didn't give her the chance to finish. When he dropped a feather-light kiss on her forehead, she stilled. When he brushed a kiss against the curve of her cheek, she swayed into him and reached out to steady herself with a hand against his chest.

The sounds of childish laughter and exuberant puppies faded when he lowered his mouth to the sweet warmth of hers. His sudden, explosive desire caught him unaware, a heady mix of tension and hunger and sensations he could barely name.

She opened beneath him, her hands sliding up his chest and curving around his neck, pulling him closer. Silently welcoming him. It felt like coming home—

"Which one is Katie?"

Dana stumbled back and blinked, clearly disoriented.

"You said one puppy is named Katie," the child repeated, her eyes shining. "Which one?"

"I—uh—don't remember. See if you can pick one

out." Dana's hand flew to her swollen lips as Katie turned back to the mass of eager puppies at her feet. "We shouldn't have done that," she whispered. "I swore I wasn't going to, and I did anyway."

So she'd been thinking about him, then. A sense of male satisfaction filled his chest. "What happened?"

From outside came the sound of approaching footsteps. "Look," she said, "we both know this can't go anywhere."

"Maybe there's something more."

"It doesn't matter, because I won't take that risk." She reached out, laid a hand on his arm. "You and Katie are welcome here anytime. We're neighbors, and perhaps we can be friends. Let's leave it at that."

"Have dinner with me this weekend?"

"I don't think—"

"Please." He gave her a rueful smile. "Just dinner, some grown-up conversation."

"I'll...think about it." She took a deep breath. "But you're wasting your time if you're hoping for anything more. You broke my heart once before. I'll never let it happen again."

"I NEVER, EVER SHOULD HAVE said yes," Dana muttered as she finished laying out the surgical instruments. Stretched out before her, in a state of blissful unconsciousness, lay the Hendersons' beagle, its shaved belly illuminated by the bright surgical lamps overhead and the endotracheal tube already in place. "I stood there and told him I wouldn't...yet before he and Katie left, I'd agreed to dinner."

"Maybe you buckled because he was so nice about letting her have that puppy."

"That must have been it." That, and the total adoration in Katie's eyes when she'd looked up at him, as if she couldn't even comprehend so wonderful a gift.

"I'm still mad at him for hurting you in high school, but watching how sweet he is with that little girl has restored my faith in men. Maybe there *are* a few guys around who are capable of commitment and fatherhood." From the other side of the stainless steel table, Francie wiggled an eyebrow as she swabbed the beagle's belly with a povidone-iodine solution. "Who knows? Zach might have changed enough over the years that he could be a good prospect."

"Francie!"

"Just a thought. But hey, tell him you can't go. Then tell him your beautiful, sensuous and *very* intelligent friend happens to be available instead."

"I can't." Her Bard-Parker Number 15 scalpel poised, Dana measured off two finger-widths distal to the dog's navel, then started the first, careful midline incision through the skin, then through the subcutaneous tissue. "Molly is excited about her and Alex getting to baby-sit Katie, and now it's too late to cancel." She glanced up at the clock and sighed. "It's already five o'clock."

Francie laughed. "You make this sound like a dreaded dental appointment."

"He insisted he owed me a dinner for helping him

out, and said he just wanted to be a good neighbor. What could I say?"

"No?"

"He looked so…so earnest."

But that hadn't been it at all. An electric fence couldn't have given her a greater jolt than she'd felt the moment she first saw him again. The mesmerizing appeal he'd had as a teenager was nothing compared to what he possessed now.

"Earnest, huh?" Francie gave her a knowing grin.

"He said he hoped there were no hard feelings between us. Refusing would have made it seem like I'd held some sort of torch for him all these years—or like I'd been so pathetically in love that I never forgave him."

Which had been the case, for more years than she'd ever admit. It scared her even now. Long after the heartbreak and initial anger, he'd dominated her dreams and filled her thoughts, until she might have given everything she owned just to see him one more time.

With a history like that, she needed to keep her distance, not play with fire.

"To tell you the truth, I couldn't take your place tonight, anyway."

"Do you have a date with Jack? Kip?" Dana laughed, thankful for a switch of topics. "I swear, I can't keep up with you and your guys."

"Jack is history—said he's going back to his ex-wife. Kip's cast came off and he's back on the rodeo circuit, so he probably won't be back for months. One of these days I'm going to find a keeper, and that cowboy isn't going to get away.''

''Who's your best prospect now?''

''I don't have one.'' Francie checked the pulse oximeter monitor, then pressed a finger against the dog's gingiva to check capillary refill time. ''She's at 85 percent oxygenation. You want me to decrease the anesthesia a little?''

''Let's go with one percent for now, and increase the oxygen flow.''

Francie adjusted the dials. ''Got it.'' Her breezy tone softened. ''Gil Tabor asked me to go out dancing tonight. Remember him? We dated a few years ago and it just didn't work out, so here's to second chances.''

Dana carefully isolated one of the dog's ovaries. After clamping off the blood supply, she removed the ovary and then began ligating blood vessels. ''If I remember right, he was an awfully nice guy.''

The phone starting ringing in the front office. ''Are you okay in here?''

Dana nodded without looking up. ''Go ahead.''

Stripping off her gloves, Francie went up front to answer the phone. In a few minutes she returned to the door of the surgery. ''Walterses' place. One of their cows went through a fence, and has several full-thickness lacerations on the chest and forelegs. She needs sutures.''

''Did she nick any significant arteries?''

''They've got the bleeding under control, but Pete

wants you out there as soon as possible. He says this is one of his best cows."

"That's what he always says. Tell them I'll be out as soon as I finish here. Twenty minutes, tops." Dana completed the procedure, then checked for any intra-abdominal bleeding before suturing the layers of tissue back in place. "I may have to cancel my evening plans after all."

"As if you'd be sorry." Francie helped move the dog into a clean pen. "Honestly, barring any further emergency calls, you should be done in plenty of time."

But for once, I think I'll be hoping for the telephone to ring.

GLANCING BEHIND HIM to make sure Katie was still safely up on the porch, Zach reloaded and switched the Sig Sauer semiautomatic 9mm to his left hand, then emptied another fourteen rounds into the target he'd set up next to the barn.

Backed by a half-dozen moldy bales of hay he'd found in the loft and a high swell of earth another fifty yards beyond, the setup wasn't bad. But he'd started the session with his Smith & Wesson .38, switching to use both hands, and the weight of the revolver plus the individual trigger pulls for each round had wreaked havoc with both his right wrist and damaged left shoulder.

He glared at the cardboard target he'd set up. Barely seventy percent had hit the kill zone on the male silhouette he'd drawn with a marker. His accuracy had decreased with every reload.

Hardly good enough to qualify for duty.

Not high enough to feel confident of his aim. Most agents shot above ninety percent when they qualified twice a year, and he'd usually topped ninety-five.

And now his shoulder hurt like hell.

With a soft curse of frustration, he holstered the weapons and strode back to the house, remembering only at the last minute to fix a smile on his face for Katie.

His lessened accuracy and endurance was bad enough. The fact that he still couldn't remember the day of the bombing at his condo made it all the worse. The entire day was still a blurred haze marked only by the images from the hospital hours afterward.

If he could remember the make of a suspicious car, or the face of anyone hanging around the area, it might help him figure out El Cazador's identity. His ongoing search through old cases hadn't yielded anything yet, either, and that failure placed both Katie and him in danger. He still had no idea of whom to watch for.

She sat on the porch swing, her sleepy new puppy cuddled in her lap. Her eyes were big and round at his approach.

"That was noisy, wasn't it," he said, pausing to stroke the pup's mottled gray and black fur. "But now I'm going to put my guns away and we're going over to Dana's house. Won't that be fun?"

She held the puppy tighter. ''Can Buffy come, too?''

''Do you think she'd like to visit her brothers and sisters?''

Katie nodded. ''She'd be scared here without me.''

''Then you hold on to her, and I'll be ready in a few minutes.''

Zach stowed the guns back in the gun safes and set them back on the high closet shelf, well out of reach of curious fingers, then he quickly showered and dressed. When he stepped out onto the porch a short time later, the puppy had wriggled out of Katie's arms and was romping the length of the porch, wrestling with one of his loafers.

The black spot encircling her one blue eye like a pirate's patch and her fierce puppy growl might have been amusing if not for the gnawed edges of his shoe—one that until today had been in perfect shape. ''Uh, Katie? We need to watch out for what she chews on. No shoes, got it?'' He looked around for the other one.

He found it at the far end of the porch, the insole chewed to shreds.

''She didn't mean to be bad,'' Katie whispered. ''She doesn't have to go away, does she? Like my mommy?''

He pivoted, intending to reassure her. Her pale face and trembling lower lip made his heart turn over. Katie had said so little to him these past weeks. What went on in the mind of a three-year-old who'd faced such loss?

He opened his arms and swept her into a bear hug, then kissed the top of her head. "Honey, there's nothing your puppy could do that would make me take her away. Ever. I promise."

"W-will my mommy come back?"

"I don't know, sweetheart. We'll keep her in our prayers, okay?"

Katie hadn't asked since they'd left Dallas, and he'd wondered if she was afraid to even give voice to her fears. He just wished he could give her the answer she wanted.

Because after all this time, a feeling in his gut told him that she would never see her mother again.

THE STUPID WOMAN had been tougher than he'd expected. He'd thought Janet would grovel at his feet and sell her soul for the hit she so desperately craved.

Instead, she'd refused to say one word about her brother, or his friends, or where he might have taken her daughter.

Even after Marco worked her over, the bitch had just stared back with crazed, dilated eyes, her limbs trembling. Then she'd fought back with strength she never should have possessed. If they'd still had her kid, she would have talked plenty, dammit.

Enraged at her rebellion, Marco had gotten too rough…but it didn't matter. She was a dead woman anyway. Then they'd slipped her some angel dust so she'd be seen as just one more overdosed addict.

A scrap of paper in her purse had already yielded enough information. When confronted with it, she'd finally caved in. She'd admitted that she'd tracked down her mother's phone number through directory assistance, then begged her for the names of towns where Zach had lived as a child. Places he might think to hide if he was on the run.

The e-mail address had already been very useful. With a high-tech, black-market software program, it had been easy enough to track down Zach's current phone area code by tracing his own message. Given the vast area covered by that area code, it might have been impossible to locate Forrester. But the name of the town scrawled on that scrap of paper—Fossil Hill, Colorado—was within that same 719 area code.

El Cazador smiled. He'd chosen his own nickname—the Hunter—very well.

Now he'd arrived in Fossil Hill, and soon the vow made at the graves of Eduardo and Reuben Alvarez would be accomplished.

All he had to do was kidnap the girl, and then he'd have all the leverage needed to make it happen.

CHAPTER SEVEN

ZACH HAD EXPECTED Dana to answer her front door in something simple—maybe slacks and a silky blouse, or a nice little dress that clung to her curves and accented her slender form. His more hopeful expectations had involved something scarlet, with a neckline that ended somewhere in the vicintiy of her naval, and black stiletto heels.

But when she greeted Katie and him at the door wearing stained coveralls, battered hiking boots and a ball cap, with a cell phone at her ear, her businesslike handshake startled him more than her attire.

Come on in, she mouthed silently.

She listened to someone on the other end of the line, and then glanced at the clock on the wall. "I'm on my way."

After hanging up, she gave him an apologetic smile, though he'd have bet it was born of relief and not regret. "I'm afraid I'll need a rain check for tonight. I had another late call before this, and now the Meyerses' stud is colicking."

"No problem. I understand." He knelt down at Katie's side and rested a hand on her shoulder. "Dana has to go take care of a sick horse, so I'm going with her, okay? You can still stay here and play."

She been subdued on the way over, even more somber as they parked outside. Now her lower lip trembled. "Can I go with you?" The puppy in her arms twisted vigorously, trying to reach the floor.

"I think Buffy wants to stay here, don't you?"

"You don't have to come along, Zach," Dana said. "Really. This call could take quite a while."

With Gabe at her side, Molly loped into the living room in stockinged feet, smiling from ear to ear. "Hi, Katie! You brought Buffy to see us? Cool!" She skidded to a halt against the sofa. "Want to go out in the backyard?"

Katie looked uncertainly from Zach to Molly.

He dropped to one knee, and gave Katie and her armful of wiggling puppy a quick hug. "You'll have lots of fun, honey. Go ahead. That pup needs to use up some of her energy."

"W-will you come back?"

Her fear tore at his heart. "Don't ever doubt that. If you're asleep, I'll carry you out to the car and you'll wake up tomorrow in your own bed. You'll see me first thing when you wake up, I promise."

Tears welled up in Katie's eyes. "I want to go with *you*." She let Buffy scramble to the floor, then she launched forward and wrapped her little arms in a death grip around his neck. *"Please."*

She held on as if he were her last hope for survival in a frigid North Atlantic sea. As if she thought he would disappear any moment and never return. The warm dampness of her tears against his neck and the surprising strength of her embrace erased all desire to leave for an evening. How could he enjoy even a minute away if Katie was left behind, heartbroken?

He rose to his feet, holding her close, and gave Dana a helpless look. "Maybe you're right. I could let her play awhile, then we'll go home."

"All little kids do that," Molly said breezily, bending to ruffle the ears of the puppy wrestling with one of her shoelaces. Gabe moved closer, sniffed at its ears and back, then playfully bunted the puppy with his nose. "They cry and hope you'll stay, but then they have a good time when you leave. Hey, Katie— look! Buffy wants to go play with her old family." Sliding into a tempting singsong tone, she made a goofy face when Katie pulled away to peek at her. "Remember all the cute little *puppies?* Next time you come, they might all be gone! Don't you want to play with them one last time?"

Katie studied her, her expression wary, then she gave a tentative, watery nod.

When she and Molly finally headed out the door hand-in-hand, Zach didn't know whether he felt relieved or bereft. "Well, I guess we're on."

"Unless *you* want to stay and play with the puppies." A glimmer of a smile lifted the corners of her mouth as Dana snagged a set of keys from her back pocket. "She'll be fine. Alex is out with the pups right now. The two kids will watch her like a hawk, and Ben is close by. Gabe barks at strangers. If the kids need anything, I have my cell phone in my pocket."

"You're right, I guess." He gave her a rueful smile. "A short time ago I was on my own. Now I've got Katie, a puppy, geese, a house to fix up and a cranky peacock. It's been an adjustment.''

A few minutes later, as they sped down the empty highway, Dana spoke without taking her gaze from the road. ''How long have you had her?''

''Only a month.'' He hesitated for just a beat, feeling regret at allowing Dana's false assumptions to stand, and hoping that when this was all over, she would understand and forgive. ''Her mother is…away right now. I'm not sure when she'll be able to take Katie back.''

At a gravel intersection, Dana slowed and took a left. ''How's it going so far?''

''Harder than I thought, yet much better than I thought. Now that she's been with me this long, I can't imagine life without her.'' Until he said the words aloud, he hadn't realized how true they were.

Dana gave him a sympathetic glance. ''I know what you mean. Already the thought of my kids going off to college makes me sad—and Alex is only fourteen.''

Resting an arm along the backrest of the seat, he leaned into the corner of the cab so he could study her.

''Ever thought about a second career as a Formula One race driver?'' he teased as the truck jounced over a series of potholes and rattled over a stretch of washboard gravel.

''I'm only going forty-five!'' She eyed the speedometer on the dashboard. ''It always seems faster when you aren't the one behind the wheel, and in control.''

The truck fishtailed as she took the next turn and headed up a steep hill.

He drew in a sharp breath. "So…if I have control issues, and want to drive, will you let me?"

She laughed. "Not on your life. I've got control issues too, and being a passenger drives *me* crazy."

At the top of the hill, a sweeping panorama of gently rolling grassland spread out before them. Countless cattle. Herefords, their rich russet coats gleaming in the sun. Black baldies, their white faces and ebony bodies a sharp visual contrast to the grasses rippling like waves in the early evening breeze.

"We're almost there," Dana murmured. "This fence line marks the start of the Meyerses' place."

"Looks like a big cattle operation."

"Twenty thousand acres. Only God and Bill Meyers know how many cattle, but this is one of the more successful cow-calf operations in this part of the state."

"He raises horses also?"

"He's stood a few quarter horse stallions for as long as I can remember, and still has a successful production sale each year. It's not unusual for his proven brood mares to go for over twenty grand. Last year a yearling halter prospect sold for fifty, but they've gone higher than that."

Zach whistled under his breath. "A lot of money for something that could colic and die."

"That's why people keep up their insurance. My husband," she added with a hint of resignation, "dreamed of building up a good herd using Bill's bloodlines."

"Is this where your mares came from?"

"Entirely too many."

"You don't care for horses?"

"I've been a horse lover all my life. But sheer common sense tells me that one shouldn't risk everything they own to have them. Not when there are vet school loan payments and a big mortgage hanging over your head."

She drove another mile or so in silence, then turned into a long driveway marked by massive stone pillars at either side. Ahead, the lane forked. To the left was a massive home set on a hill, and to the right, a cluster of large barns.

"I might as well tell you, because you'll hear it anyway," she said as she pulled to a stop next to the largest barn. "Small towns being what they are. My husband Ken was a sweet man, but he didn't have a lot of business sense. Just before he died, he invested most of our savings and took out a second mortgage on our ranch to buy six good mares at one of Meyerses' sales."

"That would have been a hell of a lot of money."

"It was. He was sure that the colt crops each year would bring in a huge return on the investment. But, well…" She shrugged. "Two years in a row, a couple mares aborted in the fall, which is too late to rebreed. Some of the foals have been downright disappointing."

"Could you sell the mares?"

"We'd be in the classic buy-high-sell-low situation. With their recent reproduction records, they're worth less, not to mention that the entire market is down right now. Maybe this year's foals will be the answer, but those sales might come too late."

Zach thought about the pretty ranch house and buildings back at the Rocking H. Nestled in a grove of massive old oaks, the place radiated a sense of tradition and of the strong family ties still missing in his own life.

"The sales would be too late for what?" he asked, though he already knew.

"The bank wasn't eager to write up the loan, but Ken pushed until they finally agreed—at a high interest rate and terms that will be hard to meet. If I don't come up with the money by August thirty-first, our ranch and everything we own will belong to the Fossil Hill Community Bank."

"LET'S GO UP TO THE HOUSE," Alex muttered. He'd promised to keep an eye on Molly and Katie, but watching them was *really* boring. "If you'll come up to the house, I'll make you guys some popcorn and let you play video games on my PlayStation."

Molly shook her head. "Maybe later."

With a sigh, Alex slumped against the front of the stall. If not for Katie and Molly, he could have been riding Blaze out in the hills to watch the sunset and hear the coyotes teaching their pups how to howl. As much as a true rancher hated the coyotes, it was still sorta fun listening to those off-key yips and warbles.

Molly, sitting in the puppy stall with her back against the wall and legs outstretched, burst into renewed laughter as one of the more aggressive pups tried to wrestle her sock off. Two others scrambled onto her lap and vied for the chance to lick her face.

Zach's little girl had been quiet all evening. Weird. What kid didn't have fun with a box stall full of puppies? She'd sat in the corner of the stall petting the pups that ventured over to her lap, and had watched Molly with interest, but now and then she'd stare at the door and whimper as if hoping her dad would show up and take her home.

At least she wasn't crying anymore. The first half hour had seemed like eternity.

"Five more minutes," he warned. "Then we're going to the house."

"And who made you the boss?" Molly glared at him from across the stall. "I was the one who wanted to play with Katie."

"But I'm supposed to keep everyone in line," he retorted. "Remember? Mom said."

"Like I need you to do that!"

Ignoring her, Alex leaned down and scooped up the pup he'd named Terminator, a salt-and-pepper gray with a perfect black spot around its left hip. Exhausted from play, it snuggled up against his chest, so he held it there, stroking its velvet-soft fur and breathing in its milky scent.

This one was quiet, more of a loner. With luck, maybe no one would want to buy him and he could stay at the ranch, even though Mom said they had way too many animals already. *What happens if we have to move someday?* she'd said. *How could we take a dozen dogs and cats somewhere else?*

Guilt slithered down Alex's throat and landed in his stomach, where it wrapped cold tentacles around his insides. The future of the Rocking H—the only home he'd ever known—was uncertain, and that was partly his fault. He also knew there wasn't a thing he could do about it.

Lost in thought, he didn't hear anything beyond the sounds of the puppies and Molly until a sharp rap sounded at the door of the barn.

"Hello, anyone here?" a male voice called out.

In the corner of the stall, Katie's eyes grew wide. Her face paled. She cringed against the wood planks as if trying to disappear—no surprise, since she seemed to be afraid of just about everything on the planet.

Alex opened the stall door a crack, blocking the puppies' escape route with his leg, and looked out. Silhouetted against the setting sun, a man stood in the open doorway of the barn and peered down the long row of box stalls. He didn't seem familiar.

Odd, given that everyone knew everyone else in practically the entire county…and with the ranches so far apart out here, chance visitors were rare.

Suddenly wishing he hadn't left Gabe up at the house, Alex lifted a forefinger to his lips, signaling the girls to be quiet, then he stepped out of the stall and closed the door behind him. "Can I help you?"

The stranger silently watched him approach. Silhouetted against the brighter light outside, his face was shadowed, but he looked like any old tourist— new jeans, a navy T-shirt, a Nike ball cap pulled low over his eyes. Despite the relative gloom of the barn aisle—the lights weren't turned on—he still had his sunglasses on.

"I'm looking for the Kowalskis' place," he said. "I'm passing through on my way to California and wanted to say hello."

"Who?"

"Frank Kowalski." The guy gave a little shrug. "He and his family are new out here, so maybe you haven't met them yet. They moved to Fossil Hill during the past month or so."

"I've never heard of them." There was something weird about the guy. Not the clothes, exactly, or the words he said, but a watchfulness that made the hairs rise at the back of Alex's neck.

"You sure?"

Given that strong, ethnic name, Alex had absolutely no doubt. "Maybe you could ask at the post office."

"It's closed. Someone in town said some new people moved out this way. What about that place a couple miles from here?"

"Martha Benson's old place? That's—" A warning bell sounded in Alex's head before he could get the words out, followed by a series of images from crime shows on late-night TV. Who knew what this guy might be up to? And he was looking for a Kowalski, not Zach Forrester. "Uh…those people have been there a long time. Years, even."

The stranger studied him for a long moment. "Thanks, kid," he murmured. "You've been a big help. Maybe I can repay you sometime."

Those weren't the words of someone just passing through, Alex thought uneasily as he watched the guy saunter up the driveway.

His car was parked up at the edge of the front lawn, a good hundred feet away. The angle made it impossible to see the license plate, and in the long shadows of sunset its color was dark, indistinct. But it sure wasn't the cool car of some major-league criminal.

Alex watched the man get in it and drive away. Then he turned back down the aisle. Just some guy who was lost, he realized. No big deal.

All the imagination in the world wasn't going to bring any *real* excitement to Fossil Hill.

"WELL, MY DATE WAS sure memorable," Francie said dryly. "How about yours?"

Dana lifted another tortoiseshell kitten from the tan plastic carrier on the exam table, then peered into its ears with an otoscope. "Ear mites."

"He had *ear mites?* My, you certainly were intimate on a first date!" Francie flashed a wicked grin. "I didn't even get to first base."

"The kitten, as you well know, is the one with ear mites." Dana nodded toward the clipboard at the end of the table. "Write it down and don't get cute. Her temperature...is normal at 101.5. Eyes clear...skin and hair-coat are healthy."

Adjusting her stethoscope, she listened for normal

cardiac and pulmonary sounds. "This one has a good ticker, too. Hand me some Accarex, would you?"

Francie shook one of the small foil packets, tore it open and lifted out an ampule of medication. After snapping off the cap, she handed it to Dana. "This ought to make her feel better."

Dana squeezed the contents of the ampule into the kitten's right ear canal and massaged the base of her ear for a few seconds, then repeated the process on the left side. After vaccinating her with Feline Combo vaccine, she stroked the kitten and cuddled her for a moment, then moved her into a box on the floor with her littermates.

"What I'd really like is for Sadie to bring in the mom for a nice, quick spay."

"Which she won't, because every time one of her cats has a litter, she tells us how sweet and precious the kittens are, and how she loves each and every one."

Dana sighed. "If the County health department ever visits that house, they'll condemn it and put Sadie in a nursing home."

"Giving up her animals would break Sadie's heart. But is that woman even safe, living alone? From what I've heard, she belongs in the Pack Rat Hall of Fame. Not," Francie added, "that I would ever win any housekeeping awards myself."

Dana finished the rest of the kittens, then bent down to survey the inhabitants of the cardboard box on the floor. Seven bright-eyed faces peered back up at her, while one of the kittens sulked in a corner by itself.

"Do you want to drop them off at her house, or should I?"

"I have to go through town anyway, so I will." Francie rested a slim hip and one crimson-tipped hand against the counter. "But first you have to tell me about your Saturday night."

Dana reached for a spray bottle of sanitizer and cleaned off the table. "Okay, I had a colic call at the Meyerses'. We arrived around eight, and the horse was showing the usual signs. They'd turned him out in the corral adjoining his stall, and he was pawing, biting at his flanks. Went down and rolled a couple of times. His bowel sounds were almost absent, his pulse at over seventy beats a minutes. I gave him some Banamine IV and—"

"I know the routine. I want to know about Zach. Did he sweep you off your feet? Take you on a major trip down memory lane? Is he still the hottest kisser you ever met?"

"Francie! I never, ever said that."

"I'll admit that you're one of the more *repressed* people I've ever met. But I also remember the stars in your eyes back when we were high school seniors. When you and he dated back then—" Francie tipped her head back and fanned herself with one hand. *"Oh, baby!"*

"I think," Dana retorted as she started transferring kittens back into the carrier, "that you must be confusing my life with yours."

"Not likely. *I* never went out with the James Dean of Fossil Hill High."

"Okay, here it is. He went along on the vet call. He assisted me, made polite conversation and didn't make a single inappropriate move the entire night. We didn't get back until eleven or so, and when we walked in the door Katie was awake and crying for him. So he took her home. That's it."

Left unmentioned was the brief, soul-searing kiss he'd given her on the porch of her house after they returned.

If they'd been anywhere but there, listening to the sounds coming through the door of Katie crying and Molly's efforts to placate her, Dana would have threaded her hands through his hair and pulled him down into a deeper, longer, unending kiss. Just the memory still sent flickers of heat racing through her.

"Inappropriate?" Francie pursed her lips. "Exactly what would an 'inappropriate' move be with a thirty-three-year-old ex-girlfriend who hasn't had a date with someone exciting—and Tom doesn't count, because you say he doesn't make your heart race—in three years of widowhood?"

"Weren't you recently warning me against becoming involved with Zach again?"

"I don't know...he seems different, now. More mature. Maybe it wouldn't be such a bad thing."

"But he's not staying in town, and I'm not a one-night-stand kind of gal."

Dana turned to look at herself in the mirror over the hand sink in the corner. Her dishwater-blond hair was a tumble of wisps going in every direction. The light makeup she'd applied in the morning was long gone. "I am truly pathetic, aren't I? It's crazy to think any guy would look at me twice."

"You could let your Aunt Francie help you out a little." Francie fluffed her newly platinum hair and ran her palms down her size-five hips. "It's fun to experiment with hair color and makeup, and we're *almost* the same size."

"Yeah, right." Clad in that tight red T-shirt and those epidermal Levi's, Francie could stop a speeding train with a single sultry glance. Which probably wasn't the image a small town vet and mother of two ought to impart. "There are miracles...and then there are hopeless cases. But thanks anyway." Dana lifted the carrier and handed it to her. "I think I'd better just concentrate on keeping the financial wolves at bay."

CHAPTER EIGHT

BY WEDNESDAY Zach had finished painting the eaves of the house and the spindles on the porch railing white, a crisp contrast to its freshly painted pale blue siding.

He'd also emptied over four hundred .45 caliber rounds into the target out by the barn, stopping only when the ache in his shoulder and the pain in his right wrist grew unbearable. The 9mm Sig would have created less repetitive stress with its lighter kick, but he'd been determined to push himself.

The house looked better. The paper target and thin plywood frame behind it were reduced to shreds. And still he couldn't stop thinking about the time he'd spent with Dana on Saturday night.

If Katie hadn't been so upset when they'd arrived back at the Rocking H, he had no doubt that he and Dana would have taken that kiss to the next step, and well beyond.

Which would have been a major mistake.

She had a life here, with roots as deep as those of the old oaks shading her home. The minute he could obtain medical clearance Zach would be back in Dallas, using every resource at his disposal to track and capture the bastard who'd threatened Katie's safety.

Even after this guy was caught, there would always be other cases. Other situations to take him away from home for weeks and or even months at a time. It was no life for a family man…and not a life that could be pursued from Colorado's back of beyond, either.

Zach rubbed a weary hand over his face and sank into one of the wicker chairs on the porch. Out in the yard, the peacock and geese poked through parched grass in search of food. Katie's puppy lay on its back in the late afternoon sun, all four feet in the air.

At the sound of small bare feet and the screech of the screen door behind him, he turned. "Hi, honey. Did you have a good nap?"

One arm wrapped tightly around her doll, she rubbed her eyes and silently shuffled forward into his open arms. He settled her on one thigh and she sank against him, her soft, warm body limp and trusting.

She hadn't slept well for four nights. The first night, she'd whimpered, tossed and turned, crying out for her mother, barely settling down before the cycle started once again.

The last three nights, she'd awakened screaming, her eyes wide-open and staring into the night, yet she hadn't seemed to be aware of him, and hadn't responded to any of his efforts to comfort her.

These were night terrors, according to the paperback parenting book he'd bought at the drugstore in Fossil Hill, and the episodes were leading to utter exhaustion for both of them.

At first he'd figured it was all a delayed reaction to her mother's disappearance and Katie's brief abduction after the bombing of his condo. Now he wasn't so sure.

"Do you know what we should do?" he asked, giving her an extra hug. When she didn't look up, he continued anyway. "We should go over to Alex and Molly's place for a visit."

He felt her stiffen.

"Wouldn't that be fun? We could stop at the clinic and ask Dana where the kids are. Maybe you could ride the pony again, and see the puppies."

The sharp shake of her head couldn't have been more adamant.

"Why don't you want to go over there?"

She burrowed closer to his chest.

"Were you afraid of the animals?"

Silence.

"Did...the kids play too rough?" At her lack of response he searched for what else it could be. "Was it that I left you there? I promise—we can go together, and I won't leave you, okay?"

When she gave an almost imperceptible nod, he dropped a kiss on her forehead and scooted her off his lap. "Let's see, young lady. Are you still clean enough to go visiting? Hmm...you look as pretty as a petunia."

She didn't respond to his gentle teasing. Instead, she just looked up at him from under her eyelashes, the faded doll still wedged in the crook of her arm, and he wondered what it would take to ever reach the child behind that renewed wall of reserve.

Just to see this dejected little cherub laugh and sing

and play like a normal three-year-old would be worth almost any price.

"Hey, I've got a good idea. After you visit Molly, would you like to go into town? I think you need some more outfits, and I think I saw some awfully pretty dolls in the front window of the Pink Petticoat. Do you suppose they might be for sale?"

One small shoulder lifted in a halfhearted shrug, but if nothing else, he *knew* she loved going into the lace-and-ruffle infested place.

In less than twenty minutes they pulled into the parking area in front of the vet clinic next to a gleaming white Lincoln Town Car and a battered '67 Chevy pickup.

A lanky rancher, his arms folded on the countertop and hat resting on the counter beside him, looked over his shoulder and gave a brief nod as Zach and Katie walked in.

From behind her desk, Francie leaned to one side to peer past him. "Howdy, strangers. Dana's with a client right now, but she should be out in a few minutes."

"Are the kids around?"

"Molly was in back a minute ago. Alex…he's supposed to be here cleaning kennels, but he might have slipped out to ride his horse." A faint blush crept up her cheeks. "Zach Forrester, this is Gil Tabor. He has a ranch ten miles west of here, and raises Herefords and rodeo stock."

The rancher gave him a lazy smile and extended a

callused hand. "I've heard tell about you. Martha Benson's place, right?"

He had a good handshake, honest and true, and the steady gaze of someone to count on. From the gleam in Francie's eyes, he was more than just a clinic customer.

"Don't let us interrupt anything," Zach said. "We just had a couple of questions for Dana."

A moment later one of the exam room doors opened and a slender, tan woman in her fifties strolled out with dog that resembled a furry Polish sausage.

"Just remember, the geriatric formula dog food. *Nothing else,* okay?" Dana followed her, then handed a slip of paper to Francie. "We've got some samples here if you'd like to try what we carry." Her gaze shifted to Gil, and she gave him a warm smile. "Hey, there. How's old Buckshot? Is he doing better since you started him on those pellets?"

"Yep. If he keeps doing good, we might start riding him again. This last winter was sorta tough on him." He canted his head toward Zach. "You've got a visitor."

She stepped forward, and Zach saw her expression freeze. "Hi, Dana. I know you're working. I just need a minute of your time."

She focused on Katie. "Hi, sweetie. I'm sure glad to see you. I see you have your dolly with you again. Hmm…I can't remember her name. Is it… Mable?"

Katie melted against Zach's side and shook her head.

"Oh, now I remember. She's Lulu!" Dana gave her a wink. "Or...is it Polly?"

"She's *Bonny*."

"Oh!" Dana hit her forehead with the heel of one hand. "Of course. Now I remember."

Katie wiggled in her seat, and Zach looked down in time to see her mouth curve into a fleeting grin.

"Well, what brings you and Miss Bonny to see me?"

"Actually," Zach said, "I just needed a couple of minutes. Alone, probably." He stood and laid a hand on Katie's shoulder. "Francie is right here, honey. I'll be back in a flash, and then we'll go to town, okay?"

Back at her office, Dana stepped over Gabe, who was snoring peacefully in the doorway, then rounded her desk, clearly putting it between them.

Her obvious wariness made him feel all the more guilt at not calling her since their time together on Saturday night.

"Have a chair. Or should we just make this fast and easy?" Bracing her palms on the desk, she met his gaze steadily. "I do understand that any further involvement would be a major mistake. I totally agree."

"You do?" He'd been busy convincing himself of that fact for the past three days, but hearing her say it made it seem...wrong.

"We're temporary neighbors. We're adults. A little... fling...in the past shouldn't affect how we deal with each other now, right?"

A fling? He still remembered those weeks of his

senior year in vivid detail. Still regretted his midnight departure from town and the fact that he hadn't had the chance to say goodbye. But explaining now would only hurt her more. "Uh…right. Neighbors."

A memory of Saturday night's kiss slid through him. There was something between them still—a connection, a level of need, that hadn't dimmed in all the years they'd been apart—and he had a feeling that his reaction to her was never, ever going to change.

"Since that's settled, was there anything else?" Her breezy tone suggested that she was on the verge of heading back to the front of the clinic.

"Actually, yes." He settled in one of the chairs and crossed one ankle over the opposite knee. This wasn't going to be as simple as he'd thought. "I have something to ask you, and then I'd like to talk to your kids about the night Katie was here. With you present, of course."

"The kids?" Dana's eyes widened in alarm. "Whatever for? I'm sure they took good care of her."

"I'm sure they did. It's just that Katie was so upset when we got back after that vet call. At first, I figured she was crying because I left her for a few hours."

"She must have been overtired. All the excitement of the animals, getting to play with other children—"

"It's more than that." Zach drew in a deep breath as he decided how much to say. "You've seen how shy she is. Fearful, even. This past week or so she seemed to be doing much better, especially once she got the puppy. But now, she's more withdrawn than ever. She repeatedly wakes up at night, crying inconsolably.''

"You think my kids did something to hurt her?" Dana's voice cooled. "Molly adores young children. Alex is more responsible than a lot of adults."

"No, I'd never think that they were cruel. I'm just trying to figure out what could have changed for her. Maybe they said something. Maybe she saw something frightening on TV...or one of the animals scared her. Hell, I don't know. Finding out what happened might help me get her through this."

Dana drummed her fingers on the desk, considering. Then she settled into the chair behind the desk and hit a button on the intercom box. "Francie, could you track down the kids and send them back to my office?"

"They're out here with Katie right now, playing with those stray kittens the Jenkins brought in yesterday." Francie's voice sounded tinny over the speaker. "Katie, too?"

"Not yet. If she gets bored with the kittens, maybe you could show her the Millers' cockatoo?" Dana turned off the intercom. "Not that I've ever seen a young child tire of a basket full of kittens." She gave him a searching look. "Have you heard from Katie's mother lately?"

"Not a word." Zach rubbed at the back of his neck. "It's been almost two months, already."

Dana's eyes widened. "How could a mother do that? Unless she's hurt...or..." She sank back into her chair. "You must be so worried. Whatever happened between you two, she'll always be your daughter's mother."

Suddenly he needed to tell Dana the truth. "Well—"

Molly and Alex appeared at the door, clad in faded T-shirts and dusty jeans. "I got most of the cages clean," Alex began. "There's just three more and then I have to feed the boarders. Then can I go to the game in town? Please?"

"Me, too. All my friends are going to be there. We're supposed to meet on the bleachers. You promised, if I got my chores done." Molly held up her hands and started ticking off what she'd accomplished. "I filled the three water tanks, and fed the mares, and cleaned my room and—"

"Whoa!" Dana beckoned them both into the room. "Shut the door, will you? We just need to ask some questions."

At the extra commotion, Gabe lumbered to his feet and wandered down the hall toward the front desk. The children stepped farther into the room, warily glancing between Dana to Zach.

"Zach says his little girl has been especially upset since she was here Saturday night. He's wondering if maybe there was something that scared her while she was here. A television show, any of the animals, or games you might have played…"

"She liked the pups," Molly offered. "We mostly played with them. And when it got dark, we came in and had ice cream, and built a fort out of blankets in the living room."

Alex rolled his eyes. "She cried a lot when you left. And later, after we'd been out in the barn a long time, she started again. I don't think she was very happy about being here."

"But I tried really hard, honest!" Molly's voice quavered. "I don't know why she cried so much. She did like the puppies. At least at first."

"I'm sure she did," Dana soothed. "I don't doubt for a minute that you did your best. But was there anything that could have given her nightmares? Anything on TV? Or did any of the animals frighten her?"

Alex shrugged. "She cried for her dad a lot, but she never screamed, or anything."

"Thanks," Zach murmured, offering them all a smile. "I expect she's just going through a phase. You all have a good afternoon."

He'd reached the door of the office when Molly spoke up. "It was sort of weird, though. She sure is scared of strangers."

"What?"

Molly shrugged. "She was doing okay with the puppies, but then some guy stopped to ask directions. She never saw him, or anything. He was way up in front of the barn talking to Alex. But that's when she *really* started to cry."

ALL THE WAY TO TOWN, Zach weighed the possibilities. Neither Molly nor Katie had seen the guy, and when Zach asked Katie if she'd ever heard the voice before, she just vehemently shook her head. Alex only remembered he'd worn sunglasses and a Nike ball cap, and "looked like any other dumb, lost tourist."

Probably. But what if he wasn't?

Zach's first inclination was to stay out of sight. His second was to cruise through Fossil Hill, check for out-of-state license plates and then keep his promise to Katie.

"Here we are, honey." Zach glanced at his watch, then pulled into a parking space in front of the library, between two dusty pickups. Five o'clock—which gave them two hours until the entire five-block business district rolled up its sidewalks and turned off its lights. So far, he hadn't seen a single suspicious car. "What do you want to do first, go to Miller's and find some new clothes, or eat at the Pink Petticoat?"

When she didn't answer, he tousled her white-blond curls and released her seat belt. "*This* time around, I'll remember that your little knit play clothes don't do well in a hot dryer full of jeans. I promise."

For the past ten years he'd taken extensive, ongoing training; worked countless high profile cases; traveled throughout much of the country, using his knowledge, determination and tenacity to track and capture guys who made headline news.

Nothing in that life had prepared him for Operation: Katie.

There were a lot of things he'd learned in the past few weeks. The art of detangling baby-fine, curly hair without making a little girl cry.

The fact that there was only one way a peanut butter sandwich could be prepared—light *grape* jam, *no* butter, sliced diagonally, with the crust removed.

The mysteries of laundry loads requiring "delicate" settings. Hell, he'd sent out all of his own laundry for years, but he'd finally mastered the cantankerous old washer and dryer sitting in one corner of his kitchen at the rental house. *Life Skills 101.*

At Miller's General Store he led Katie by the hand past the housewares, saddle display and hardware section to the clothing department in the back. Fortunately, he found the same white-haired woman who'd helped him once before.

"Well, if it isn't little Miss Sunshine," she exclaimed, her broad, wrinkled features lighting up with pleasure. "Are you here for some pretty new outfits, again?"

Katie nodded shyly, her hand still gripping Zach's.

"We need three or four sets of play clothes. I... uh...had a little problem with the laundry."

"Let me guess." The woman leaned down and looked at Katie's pink knit coveralls over her half glasses. The pants legs were now well above Katie's ankles, and a blue tinge marred the area over her chest. She waggled an arthritic forefinger at Zach, though a merry gleam danced in her eyes. "Going to try cold wash, cool dry?"

"From now on."

"Sorting darks and lights?"

Zach laughed. "Scout's honor."

"Okay, then, we're in business." She held out a

hand. "Come with me, young lady. Let's check out the big girl racks over here."

Bemused, Zach leaned against a pillar and watched the friendly clerk waddle away with Katie in tow. She stopped at one rack, then the next, selecting one outfit after another for Katie's inspection.

In fifteen minutes they were both back and the clerk held an armload of clothing, all in varying shades of pink. "I checked the size label inside her collar so these should be about right. There are six or seven outfits here, and the only thing our little customer knows for sure is her color preference. We need Daddy's opinion."

Daddy. He'd reminded Katie often enough that she could call him that, but when Janet showed up, Katie would be gone, probably without ever saying the word. Just once...

A small hand tugged on his. "Please?"

Shaking off his thoughts, he looked down into her hopeful face. "Yeah. We'll take them all."

"The bow socks, too?" Her voice filled with wonder. "An' ruffle panties?"

"Those, too."

"You don't want to have her try these on?" The clerk nodded toward the dressing rooms in back. "I think they're the right sizes, but brand names do vary."

Being cooped up in a tiny dressing room, trying to manage hangers and buttons and what-went-with-what sounded worse than a stakeout parked on Dallas asphalt in July.

"I'll just keep the receipt and the tags, and exchange anything that doesn't work out, okay?"

"No, problem, sir." The clerk trundled to the front of the store. "I imagine your friend is tired of waiting, anyway."

A chill raised the hairs at the back of Zach's neck. "Friend? I didn't come in with anyone but Katie."

"Oh." Confusion flashed through the woman's eyes, then she shrugged and began ringing up his purchases. "There was a guy who came in after you, and he seemed to be waiting over by the housewares." She motioned toward several crowded displays where a man could have lurked unseen. "He left after a few minutes, though, so I must have been mistaken."

"Must have been." Zach dropped a hundred and two twenties on the counter, then waited as she counted back four ones plus change.

He'd made no long-term friends during his brief stay in town as a teen. There wasn't anyone in this entire town who would hang around wanting to talk. Which left...the guy who just might have tracked him to Fossil Hill.

"What did he look like?"

"Not very tall. Sunglasses. A hat—but it's always hard to see someone's features when they have on those dark glasses, don't you think? You two have a good day now, okay?"

Probably ninety percent of the people outside wore sunglasses and a hat of some kind. The description wasn't unique. *But it matched what Alex remembered.*

Out on the sidewalk, he held Katie's hand tightly as he scanned the street in both directions. No out-of-state license plates. No one who looked out of place in a town dominated by cowboy boots and jeans.

At the end of the block, a dusty black Mustang backed from behind a pickup with a camper top.

Slowly…cautiously…as if a ninety-year-old woman was at the wheel. Zach stared at its smoky windows. Leaned forward, trying to catch the license plate.

But a ranch wife with an armload of groceries and three kids in tow blocked his line of vision at the critical moment.

Zach scooped up Katie and her packages into his arms and strode into the street, trying for a better view. He caught just a glimpse of the plates before a red Ford dual pickup pulled in behind the Mustang. *Texas?*

An image from the past exploded in his brain—of an old black 5.0 Mustang hovering near his Dallas condo.

On the day his condo was bombed, he and Katie had passed that car as they walked across the street. He'd given it a second glance, because at the end of the block there'd been trees and shady parking spots. Who sat in an idling car for any length of time, under the fierce Texas sun, if there was shade close by?

If Katie hadn't been with him, he might have circled back and kept an eye on that car for a while, just to see if any deals were going down. With an elementary school a half block from his condo and a park just beyond that, he damned sure always investigated any suspicious activities in the area.

Now Katie tugged at the collar of his T-shirt. "Let's go!"

Shaking off his memories, he smiled at her, then scanned the street again. The car was probably local. Who would drive a battered Mustang clear up here from Dallas?

Yet recently a stranger had asked directions out at the Rocking H, and now someone had just lingered close by.

A coincidence, or something more?

At his Blazer, he'd just hit the unlock button on his key ring when a thin, all too familiar woman stepped out of the library entrance and headed straight for him.

"You're still here," she hissed.

Startled, Katie pulled back.

"It's okay, honey," Zach said. "This lady is Dana's mother." He opened the back door and lifted Katie into her car seat, then fastened her in and closed the door. "Hello, Vivian."

Dana's blond, fresh beauty sure didn't come from her mother. From those pinched, thin lips to the hard look in her eyes, Vivian hadn't mellowed over the past fifteen years...at least toward him.

"Stay away from my daughter," she said through gritted teeth. "She has a good life here. A future with a good man who would be a wonderful husband and father."

He'd once wondered what he would say to this woman if he ever had the chance. Now he could only feel pity for her. "Is that what she wants? Your daughter is able to make her own choices, Vivian."

"I'm warning you—"

"And I'll just offer a piece of advice. Let your daughter live her own life."

The woman's eyes narrowed, but not before he caught a flash of fear. "How *dare* you."

"I just want Dana to be happy." He opened his door and slid behind the wheel. When she stepped forward to rap on the glass, he rolled down his window.

"You were never good enough for my daughter," she snapped.

As he turned the key in the ignition, the engine roared to life. "The funny thing is, that's one point we agree on. I never thought I was."

CHAPTER NINE

"HOW'VE YOU BEEN DOING, Tom?" Dana set aside the Fluffy Henderson chart and gave him the best smile she could muster. "Your kids have been over to see mine, but I haven't seen you in a while."

He shifted his muscular bulk in the chair on the other side of her desk, then leaned forward to fold his hands on the edge.

"All these years...I've cared about you, Dana," he said slowly. "Way before you even married Ken. But I want you to know there are no hard feelings." His mouth quirked into a lopsided smile. "I still think we could make a go of it, if you ever change your mind. But I'm not going to be chasing after you, or anything. I want us to stay friends like we've always been."

He really was such a good, kind man. Dana resisted the urge to reach over to lay her hand on his. "I'm glad, Tom. Somewhere out there is a woman who's going to knock you off your feet."

"Probably not. I don't think I believe in all that anymore. But thanks."

Francie appeared at the door. "Grace is waiting in the second exam room with her black lab. He seems to...uh...have quite a problem with diarrhea, so you

might want to come right away. Are you free?'' Her
brow furrowed as her gaze settled on Tom. ''Hey, do
you have a minute to listen to a weird sound when I
start my truck? I don't know if it's the starter or the
transmission....''

By the time Dana finished with the black lab, Tom
had left and Francie was back on the computer at her
desk. As soon as Grace and her dog went out the door,
Dana gave Francie's shoulders a quick hug. ''*Diarrhea*? That dog didn't have any such thing.''

Francie swiveled around in her chair. ''I wasn't
sure how things were going with Tom—if he was giving you trouble over what you told him. Honestly, I
feel so sorry for that man.''

''He came to tell me there were no hard feelings.''
Dana gave her friend a sad smile. ''I just wish I could
have been the right woman for him, but I couldn't,
and I guess I just made things harder for him.''

Francie's gaze slid away. ''I...um...hope you don't
mind, but while he was looking at my carburetor,
I...sorta asked him over to my place for dinner next
weekend.''

''Meaning...''

''Well...he turned me down, but he was real nice
about it. Maybe he'll think about asking me out someday.'' Francie bit her lower lip. ''I never would have
made a move if I thought you wanted him, honest.''

''What about all the other guys you see?''

''Gil is a charmer, but he's never going to settle
down. The others—'' Francie waved her hand dis-
missively. ''Well, they're either in love with rodeo,

the show circuit, or with themselves a tad too much. I've come to realize that all the flash and excitement doesn't hold much water when it comes to real commitment.''

Dana hesitated, searching for the right words. ''Tom took his divorce really hard. I don't want to see him hurt again.''

''And I had to be absolutely sure you weren't going to change your mind about him, but maybe now it looks like the field is clear.'' Francie's smile lit up her entire face. ''That man reminds me of a big ol' teddy bear—capable of a lot of love, and just needing the right gal to come along. I'm hoping that gal is me.''

''For your sake and his, I hope it is.'' Dana gave her another hug. Feeling oddly melancholy, she went back to the lab to collect supplies for the day's farm calls.

Out at Ed Bailey's place, twelve of his newborn calves were scouring…all of them out of replacement heifers he hadn't vaccinated for rota-corona-E. coli, as Dana had recommended last spring. At Mildred Kastner's place, there were fifty calves to dehorn, castrate and immunize. Afterward, she had a lameness recheck over in Grenville and an equine prepurchase exam in Rock Springs.

A busy day ahead, for which she was thankful, because every good day meant a better chance at meeting the looming financial bombshell awaiting her on August thirty-first, when the balloon payment on the mortgage came due.

She'd do everything in her power to give the kids a stable and loving home, even if she had to sell out and move somewhere else. One way or another, she would succeed.

But still, there was a small, empty corner in her soul.

Back in high school, Zach—the boy she'd loved with all her heart—had ditched her without a backward glance. Her marriage had been...comfortable. Even Tom had wanted just more of the same—a relationship based on mutual friendship.

He'd even implied that she simply wasn't the kind of woman who inspired romance, and he was right.

What would it be like to have a relationship filled with hunger and passion and the kind of love that lasted for all eternity and beyond? She'd probably never know, because after seeing Zach again, she knew she'd never again settle for less.

Grabbing the last of the supplies, she headed out the back door of the clinic and into the bright Colorado sunshine. Several mares whinnied at her from their pasture next to the barn. From somewhere back in the rolling hills of the Rocking H came the sound of a cow bawling, and the answering call of her calf. Carried on a soft breeze from the southeast came the scent of newly mowed hay.

The sounds and scents of the ranch surrounded her, filled her with a sense of peace. Letting her kids grow up with memories of this place was what mattered most.

ALEX HOSED out the last dog run behind the clinic, then sent a fine mist into the air and watched a shimmering rainbow form within the spray. Some of the droplets drifted back on the breeze and settled like cool dew on his face.

He glanced at his watch, then irritably snapped off the spray nozzle and coiled the hose back up on its rack at the rear door of the clinic. Mondays were so boring.

Sammy and Trish from the neighboring ranch should have been here by now. The girls were younger and more timid, but he and Sammy often swam their horses in the creek, and then stopped in belly-deep water to jump off their horses' broad backs.

Maybe Sammy and Trish had ended up with a big list of chores and weren't even going to show up. Molly and he could ride to the creek on their own, but swimming wouldn't be near as much fun without the other two.

Not that he'd wanted them to all end up as one big happy family. The thought of their dad Tom and his mom together made him shudder. What did Mom need someone like him for?

Luckily Molly said she'd heard Mom talking to Tom last week, and it sounded like *that* threat was over.

A good thing, too.

Lost in his thoughts, feeling out of sorts and aimless and wanting nothing more than to head for the creek, he didn't realize Mom was talking to him until she waved a set of keys in front of his face.

"Hey, there!" Smiling, she still held the back door open with one hand. "Want to come to town with me?"

"To do what?" For a decent-size store you had to go down to Bixby, and even that town didn't have a fast-food place or a theater.

Her brow furrowed. "A little testy, aren't you? I thought you might like to stop in at the Cattleman for lunch, and then check Miller's sale with me. You've been needing some new jeans and I'm guessing you might need a different size."

"No."

"Just…no?"

"I don't want to go. Sammy and Trish are coming over and we're going to the creek to swim and fish."

"Are you sure? Francie ran into their dad at the post office this morning, and he said something about going to a livestock sale."

The rest of the day opened up like a yawning chasm. Hot. Boring. Aimless. While untold adventures awaited his friends.

Anger and frustration exploded in his chest. "And we're stuck here, right? Work all the time, nothing fun to do—this is such a lousy summer! I wish I had a d—"

He caught himself just in time. Choked back the words as he wheeled around and ran for the barn.

Inside the dark, cool depths, he scrambled up the worn wood slats against the far wall and found his usual refuge in the hayloft—the open loft door facing out onto the empty, rolling, endless grassland to the east.

Where nothing—absolutely nothing—broke the utter boredom clear to Nebraska, for all he knew.

Before he'd even plopped down on the soft loose hay on the floor, a trio of kittens appeared and began rubbing against his ankles. "Go away," he muttered.

A light sound on the ladder rungs told him he'd soon have more company than just the cats. He looked longingly outside, wishing he could simply spread his arms wide and fly away. Which was nearly as useless as the dream where he saddled Blaze and headed for Denver, then kept on going until he'd been everywhere, seen everything there was to see in the whole United States.

"Hey," Mom said as she dropped down next to him.

There just wasn't anything to say in return.

More patient than Job, she sat quietly next to him for a good ten minutes. "Nice place to just come and dream, isn't it?" She said at last. "Of faraway places, and adventures? When I was a kid, I loved sitting up in the hayloft on rainy days with my books. I'd spread a blanket out and pretend I was camping." Leaning into him, she gave him a playful nudge with her elbow. "How about you—what do you dream about when you come up here?"

"What does *that* matter?" he snorted. "Look how you ended up." The words were out of his mouth before he could catch them, and hung like razor-sharp arrows in the air between them. "S-sorry."

A heavy silence lengthened, and he almost wished she'd just yell at him and get it over with. When he was a kid, she'd had a low tolerance for back talk and he'd probably accumulated a year of time-outs on a kitchen chair before his twelfth birthday. Instant punishment was better than guilt and regret.

"How do you think I ended up, Alex?"

There was no anger in her voice, just quiet curiosity, but he still waited, expecting a lecture on respect. When it didn't come he finally said, "I didn't mean anything."

"No—tell me."

The fact that he was responsible for so much of the hardship turned his words bitter. "You're on-call twenty-four hours a day at the clinic. Have us kids to feed. A ranch to run on your own. Except for old Ben and me, and the two of us probably don't add up to one good man."

She smiled at that. "I could never do this without you guys."

"But you have to say that, 'cause you're a mom." He took a deep breath. "You can't ever go out for parties and fun stuff without ending up on an emergency call in some feedlot. You never travel because you're stuck in the middle of nowhere with all of this. Doesn't it make you angry sometimes?"

"What if I told you that I loved being a mom? That I loved being a vet, and seeing that I could really help my patients? Or that I think these wide-open spaces are the most beautiful place on the planet?''

''You never wanted anything else? Ever?''

A shadow crossed her expression. ''I suppose. Would we even be human if we didn't dream?'' She reached out and laid a hand on his knee. ''What do you want, Alex?''

Too many things, and most of them are impossible. To turn back the clock, and take back everything I said to Dad before he died. To change what I did that day, so he'd still be with us. To get away from here and never look back, and hope that I could leave all those memories behind.

''Well? There must be something.''

The gentle tone in her voice made him feel worse. ''Nothing. Absolutely nothing.'' Jumping to his feet, he slapped the loose hay from his jeans as he headed for the ladder. ''I need to go work with the foals, because I missed yesterday.''

''Alex—''

He didn't slow down.

EVERY DAY, for a week after he'd seen the black Mustang, Zach had found reasons to head for town. There'd been no further sign of the car, but Katie had certainly enjoyed her series of lunches at the Pink Petticoat.

Today he'd taken her back to Miller's after lunch, just for a change of pace, and had purchased another new outfit and a pair of pink shoes. Surveillance in Fossil Hill was proving to be an expensive affair.

All the way home from town, Katie held that sack as if she'd been given the greatest treasure on earth. Zach concentrated on the road ahead and tried to picture the car he'd seen last Wednesday. A dead ringer, he was sure, for one he'd seen in his neighborhood the day of the bombing.

If he could remember that much, maybe his brain was finally starting to clear. Perhaps he'd remember a stranger loitering near the building, waiting to view the results of his handiwork. Or someone on the other side of the street...

Or perhaps he hadn't really seen the Mustang the day of the bombing, and he was confusing memories from other days. Other totally ordinary days.

At home, he stopped at the mailbox to collect the mail, which included just an electricity bill, then cruised slowly up the narrow lane to the house. Everything looked the same, with the windows and doors closed securely.

The geese—stupid birds that they were—came rushing at the yard fence in a great, flapping display, honking to high heaven at the intruder in their territory. The peacock, far less demonstrative, gave one ear-piercing shriek.

"Quite an alarm system, right?"

Katie nodded. "I don't like those birds anymore."

No wonder. The geese had chased her once, and after that Zach had confined them permanently to the backyard, where they still raised a ruckus at the sight of anything new. "They can't get at you, honey."

"They hurt my ears!"

"That's because they've got a job to do. Did you ever have a doorbell?''

Katie thought for a moment, then shrugged.

"Doorbells are little buttons by an outside door, and when you push them a sound rings inside the house, and the people come out to see you.''

She was talking more, becoming a shade less withdrawn with each passing week, but he'd checked into an Internet site on language development and found that she seemed to be below the baseline for three-year-olds. Not surprising, if her mom had been inattentive or had left her in poor child-care situations.

So now he chattered to her. Named objects and asked questions and told her silly stories and jokes, read nursery rhymes and fairy tales and even magazines aloud. And as she responded—picked up new words, began initiating more conversations, he couldn't have been more proud of her if she'd just won the Nobel Prize.

God, it would be so hard to give her back. What had he done with his time before she came into his life?

After bringing the pup out into the front yard to play with Katie, he locked the front gate and then went inside. Keeping one eye on them through the living room window, he set up his laptop on an end table, plugged into the nearby phone jack, and logged onto the Internet, then connected to his e-mail server.

Amidst a collection of irritating spam mail—all an automatic delete—he found one message from Jerry.

I know you don't like to call much, but we need to talk ASAP. Call me night or day.

He logged off, then stepped back and sank into the upholstered chair nearby. *Please, don't let it be true.*

After a long moment he reached for the cell phone in his pocket. Hit Jerry's one digit auto-dial number. His heart picked up a faster beat. Cold sweat trickled down his back as he waited. The phone rang in slow-motion three…four…five times.

He nearly hung up when the answering machine clicked on, but Jerry answered a split second later.

"Tell me," Zach growled. "Now."

Jerry sighed heavily. "I'm really sorry, man. They found her this morning."

Oh, God. "Are they sure it's her?"

"The cops who discovered the body didn't know her. She was ID'd through photographs and finger-prints already in the system."

Grief settled like a cold weight in Zach's stomach. "Where'd they find her?"

"An abandoned house a few blocks from Sylvan and Singleton in West Dallas."

"How…how did she die?"

"The cops said it looked like an OD. There was a substance at the scene—looked like angel dust." Jerry hesitated. "From some of her injuries, it also looks like she could have gone ballistic—you know, how they go violent and paranoid sometimes? And…jeez, I'm sorry, man. She'd been there awhile. Maybe six or seven days."

Zach leaned back and closed his eyes. A thousand

images sped through his mind—colliding and fusing into a disjointed collage of regret and failure. He'd tried, but he hadn't tried enough. What if he'd returned, again and again, and forced her back into rehab? Stayed with her, night and day?

They hadn't grown up together, but he'd always hoped that they could develop a strong bond, in time. That someday they would become a get-together-at-Christmas kind of family. But now she'd died tragically at the age of thirty, and she'd been alone.

His own voice seemed to come from a million miles away. "Has…her father been notified?"

"Yeah. They took the body down to the Parkland Hospital complex. The Dallas County Medical Examiner's Office contacted him, and he said he'd let your mom know."

What a call to receive—announcing the death of a daughter she hadn't seen in decades.

"Katie and I will fly back as soon as I can arrange tickets."

"Uh…how well do you know Janet's dad?"

"Not at all. Never saw him again after he took her away to New York. The next time I saw my sister she was nineteen or twenty."

"Well, there may not be much reason to come back."

"Of course there is. Funeral arrangements, the services…"

"Her father told the Examiner's Office he wanted her cremated as soon as the autopsy was complete. It might already be done. And he told me he didn't plan on any sort of services. Real nice guy.''

Grief welled up in Zach's throat. A young woman with all the promise in the world had been brought to early death by addictions she couldn't control. And now the man who'd set it all in motion didn't care enough to give her final respect.

''I want her ashes sent here, Jerry, so I can arrange something for her. Organize it for me and let me know if there's a problem. She was born in Colorado and never should have been taken away. Maybe her whole life would have been different. It's the last thing I can do.''

After hanging up, Zach dropped the phone on the end table, then buried his face in his hands to mourn the sister he'd lost, and the loss of innocence for the little girl who played outside.

Every night, Katie said the simple prayer he remembered from his own childhood. *Now I lay me down to sleep…*

After a few days, she'd learned it by heart, and then had started adding a brief litany of blessings—*God bless Buffy and my dolly Bonnie. And God bless my mommy, an' please bring her back.*

How did one tell a small child that her hopes and prayers for her mother's return would never be answered?

CHAPTER TEN

"Of course I'll come. Right away." Dana handed the front desk receiver phone back to Francie. "That poor man."

"Is Zach's daughter okay?"

"She's fine…so far. He's heard news of a death in the family, and he's worried about how Katie will handle it." Dana reached over to flip back to today's page in the appointment book. "It's almost five—do you suppose we'll have any walk-ins?"

"Hard to say. We've got another half hour. If anything important comes in I could call your cell phone and get you back here."

"Could you stay till maybe six, then transfer incoming calls to the cell? That would give me a bit more time without interruption."

"Barring emergency."

"Thanks, Fran. I'll tell the kids where I'll be." Dana slipped off her lab coat and took it back to the office, then grabbed her truck keys off the desk and jogged the hundred yards up to the house.

Inside, the TV was blaring, and the raised voices indicated that yet another argument was in full swing.

"Just leave my stuff alone!"

"I never touched your stupid computer. Maybe there was a power surge or something." Molly's plaintive voice turned sharp. "Anyway, it's not like you never had problems with it on your own! It's so old it won't even take CDs!"

"If you go in my room again, I'll—"

"Alex!" Dana stepped into the living room and folded her arms across her chest. "Molly!"

"Mo-om, he says I messed up his computer. I never even went in there today."

"I didn't say *today*," Alex snapped. "You used it yesterday. Now it only goes into Safe Mode, and I can't even log on to the Internet."

Dana looked from Alex's angry scowl to the mutinous set of Molly's jaw. "Look, I can't deal with this right now. I have to run over to Zach's place for a while. When I get back, I'll help you, okay? Maybe we can try Scandisk, or something, and figure it out."

Alex glared at his sister. "I did that. I defragged it. I read the book and did everything else it said. *Nothing.* Do you know how far it is to Denver? How long it will take to get my computer back from a tech?"

"Just wait, okay? When I get back—"

"It's always like this!" He threw up his hands. "You're *never* here. I'm stuck here with Molly, you're gone all the time—it's so unfair!" He spun on his heel and headed down the hall to his bedroom. "I hope *you* have a great time." Seconds later his door slammed shut.

Molly stared after him. "I didn't hurt his stupid computer," she said in a small voice. "Honest. One minute he's nice, the next minute he's mad about everything."

"Being a teenager can be difficult. Not having a dad probably makes it even harder. Come here, sweetie." Dana opened her arms and enveloped Molly in a bear hug. "Zach needs my help for a few minutes. When I get back, I'll put some steaks on the grill, okay?"

"Maybe they could come over?"

"Well…"

"Please? Katie is really cute. And you could talk to her dad. Wouldn't that be fun?" Molly stepped back and flashed a grin. "I'll run downstairs and get another package of steaks from the freezer. I could make the salads too, and there's a cake mix in the cupboard."

"Wait, this really isn't the right time—"

But Molly's footsteps were already thundering down the basement steps.

SINCE LEARNING of Janet's death, a hollow feeling had settled in Zach's heart. Regrets and dim memories played over and over through his thoughts. Janet, barely walking yet, playing with her blocks on the living room floor. Bedtime stories, with the two of them curled up with their mother on the sofa.

Flashes of long-ago scenes that slipped away like mist through his fingertips—too fleeting to savor.

He'd been just five, and hadn't been very tolerant of the little one who toddled after him with pure adoration in her eyes.

She'd giggle and grab at the trucks he'd lined up so carefully in his garage under the coffee table. Grab crayons and scribble over the latest masterpiece in his coloring books. Or was he only remembering what his mother had told him?

What he'd give to have just a few of those moments back.

The crunch of tires on the driveway and the cacophony of geese honking in the backyard told him that Dana had arrived, but he stayed on the living room floor with Katie, his back braced against the sofa and elbows propped on his upraised knees.

She'd fallen asleep on a blanket, her doll firmly edged in the crook of one arm, her damp, pale curls clinging to her forehead and plump, rosy cheeks.

In her new purple sundress and little white sandals, she might have been any suburban toddler. She'd come a long way from the dirty and bedraggled waif who'd appeared on his door back in April. She was doing so much better.

And now she had to be told the most devastating news a child could ever hear.

"Hello!" Dana let herself in the back door. "Anyone here?"

He rose in one swift movement and met her in the kitchen. "Katie needed a bath after playing with Buffy outside, and she dozed off afterward." He shoved a hand through his hair. "I'll go—"

"No, please." He looked so drawn and gray that she laid a hand on his forearm and nodded toward the kitchen table. "We can visit for a while. Do you have any coffee?"

He gave her a blank look.

"Sit. I'll get it started. You've had a really bad day." She turned back to the sink and rinsed the coffee carafe, then started a new pot brewing. After finding coffee cups in one of the cupboards, she set them on the counter and settled into a chair opposite his. "So tell me. You've lost someone close to you?"

One corner of his mouth lifted, though the grim expression in his eyes never wavered. "Not nearly close enough."

"Who?"

"Katie's mother."

"Oh, my God. How? What happened?"

He sighed heavily. "It's…a long story."

"How awful for both of you. Losing her mom will be so hard on her." His hands were folded on the table, and she reached over to lay her hands on top of his. "And you—even if you were divorced, you had a child together. There's a bond that doesn't end."

He shook his head slowly. "I need to explain something, here. I should have done it earlier, but—"

Small footsteps shuffled across the vinyl flooring, and they both turned to see Katie approach, rubbing her eyes with one fist and dragging her doll along by one arm. When she lifted her arms in silent supplication, Zach shoved his chair back and swept her up onto his lap. "You still look tired, honey."

She leaned her head against his chest and closed

her sleep-glazed eyes, looking as content and secure in his arms as Dana had seen her. *They've bonded well, now. She's going to need that more than ever.*

He rubbed her back gently and met Dana's gaze, then closed his eyes and rested his cheek against her tousled hair. After a long moment, he began talking to the child in a low voice. "Remember the night you first came to see me? Your mom brought you to my house, and she brought a bag with your clothes. Remember?"

Katie gave an almost imperceptible nod.

"And she said, 'I need a place for my daughter. A safe place.' She brought you to me because she knew I would take care of you and love you, forever and ever, if she couldn't come back."

Katie straightened, pulled away from him. A radiant smile lit her face as she tried to scramble off his lap. "Mommy's here? Where is she?"

He held her in place, his arms looped gently around her back. "No, Katie. She isn't here. I promised her that I'd take care of you and love you. But she went far away, and she got very, very sick. She got so sick that her body stopped working, and now she's up in heaven."

Fat tears welled up in Katie's eyes as she twisted, back and forth, trying to check the windows and door. "I want my mommy back! I want to go *home*."

The ravaged expression in Zach's eyes made Dana's heart stumble. "She can't come back to us, Katie. She is with the angels now, where she can watch over us. But..." He took a shaky breath. "I know she will love you forever. Even from heaven."

"I want her back!" She slithered out of his grasp and ran to the door. With both hands on the doorknob, she tugged and twisted, her face wet with tears and her little feet slipping against the floor. Her voice rose to a shriek. "I want to go home!"

"I made a big damn mess of this, didn't I," Zach growled in a voice too low for Katie to hear. "I should have talked to you first and found out how to tell her."

"No. I couldn't have suggested anything better. She isn't really going to understand this for a long, long time, Zach. Young kids think Mom or brother or the family dog can come back someday." She rose and went to the door, then kneeled next to Katie. "Come here, sweetie. I need a hug, don't you?"

Her hands still clasped over the doorknob, Katie gave a sharp shake of her head. "*No!* I want my *mommy.*"

"I know you do. We all wish she could be here. But she can't." Dana shifted into an Indian-style sitting position and gently pulled Katie into her lap. "You've got your daddy, though. He won't go away. And you've got Buffy, and those silly geese. And Molly and Alex and me."

Deep, racking sobs shook through Katie. "I don't *got* a daddy."

"Sweetie, you have lots of people who love you, and your daddy, too." Dana rocked back and forth holding the child tight. She began singing all of the lullabies she could remember from when her own children were small, keeping her voice low and soothing, until Katie's sobs quieted and only an occasional hiccup shook her thin chest. "Why don't you two come over for supper tonight, Zach?"

"No..." Zach rose and moved to a window where he braced his arms on the window frame and stared out into the empty yard. "I don't think I'd be very good company."

"We're throwing some steaks on the grill. It might be good for both of you to get out of here for a while, don't you think? Molly and I can help with Katie."

After a long pause, he gave the child a somber smile, though his eyes were filled with infinite sadness. "I guess. Just let me check my e-mail before we leave. There could be some more news."

While he was gone, Dana crossed the room to the washer and dryer alcove, found a clean washcloth in a laundry basket on top of the dryer and washed Katie's hands and face with cool water.

"Doesn't that feel better, sweetie?" she murmured as she held the cloth at the child's flushed cheeks. "We're going to have a yummy supper, and you'll even get to see some brand-new kittens this time. Molly found a litter in the barn just last night."

"W-what color?"

Reaching for a hairbrush on the counter, Dana began gently working through Katie's sleep-tangled curls. "I need you to tell me. Can you do that? I haven't seen them yet. Maybe you and Molly can even think up some good names."

"Do they have *spots?*"

"Are those your favorites?" When Katie nodded, Dana gave her a quick hug. "Well then, let's cross our fingers, okay?"

Katie ran back to the kitchen table, where she picked up her dolly off the floor. "Ready!"

Zach reappeared at the kitchen door and regarded Katie with troubled eyes. "Maybe we should stay here," he said heavily. "Wouldn't you like that? We could put one of your tapes in the VCR, and—"

"No! I want to go." Katie's lower lip trembled. "They got *kitties.*"

"I'm sorry I mentioned it, Zach," Dana murmured. "I just thought being around people tonight might make everything a little easier for both of you."

He stood in the doorway as if the weight of the world rested on his broad shoulders. "You're right. This would be good for her. I'll just…go get Buffy and put her in while we're gone."

When Katie slipped out the door ahead of him, he stared after her. "Does she even understand all of this? It's like she…"

"Forgot already?" Dana crossed the room and looped her arm through his. "No. At her age, she just doesn't understand the finality. Maybe she's even trying to block out what you told her. Some young kids barely seem to react over bad news, then fall apart later."

"What if I mess this up—say the wrong thing?"

"You won't. Just love her, Zach. That's what she needs." At the pain in his eyes, she nearly reached up to lay a hand against his cheek but caught herself just in time. "My kids were older when they lost their dad, but I couldn't tell you if that's less or more difficult. We all just do the best we can."

"It's going to be even harder on her if she finds out how her mother died."

"An accident?"

"Janet had a problem with substance abuse from her teen years on." He sighed heavily. "I tried to help, but you can't help someone who refuses to even talk to you."

"So she died of an overdose?

He looked out the door to check on Katie, then lowered his voice. "I just got another e-mail. The autopsy showed that she died of a skull fracture. She also had a ruptured liver."

"My, God. How?"

"The Medical Examiner's report noted that someone tried to make it *look* like an overdose...smart move, given her history. Janet was murdered, and her body wasn't found for days. If Katie ever finds out the truth, what will it do to her?"

THE CHATTER of Dana's kids, the rich aroma of grilled steaks, the friendly warmth of her house all faded into the background as he mentally reviewed the facts.

It didn't take long to add up them up and reach a total that spelled danger. To Katie, and everyone else around him.

All along, Zach had figured Janet was on the run

after some back alley drug deal had gone wrong. It wouldn't have been her first.

But now, the relative timing of her murder and the e-mail from El Cazador were too close to ignore. Zach had learned to never discount anything as mere co-incidence.

Maybe El Cazador hadn't somehow traced Zach's e-mail address. Could he have gotten the address from Janet, and then killed her after he had all the information he needed?

Despair rushed through Zach, threatening to crush his heart. She'd been just thirty years old, the mother of a beautiful little girl who would mourn her loss for a lifetime. She'd been badly beaten and had suffered before dying, and then her body had been alone and undiscovered for days.

The sadness of it all was nearly unspeakable, the guilt almost unbearable. *After all the years I tried to help her, I might be the real reason she died.*

"Zach? Are you all right?" Dana set aside her napkin and studied him from across the table, her eyes filled with concern. "You look awfully pale."

Until he knew the truth, he wouldn't be all right. Not when his sister lay dead and her killer was on the loose. Not when all the pieces were beginning to fall into place.

The e-mail.

Janet's death.

A stranger in town, and that black Mustang.

There was a very real chance that El Cazador was already here in Fossil Hill. Which meant it was time for Zach to take Katie and disappear, unless he could figure out a way to identify and take the guy down. He'd start with that damned e-mail.

"I...think it must be something I ate earlier. A little indigestion."

She frowned. "Can I get you something? Some antacid, maybe?"

He set aside his napkin and rose. "Thanks, but I have a prescription." He looked down at Katie, who silently sat next to him. She'd made mountains and valleys in her mashed potatoes and built little stacks of her finely cut pieces of steak, but hadn't eaten a single bite. Her face was pale and drawn. "I just need to run home for a minute. Come on, Katie."

"I wanna ride the pony," she whispered.

"We'll come back, in just a little while."

"No!"

"Katie..." He reached out to tousle her hair. "I promise it'll only take a few minutes."

She twisted away from him and stood at the other side of her chair, her lower lip thrust out in a mutinous pout. Her voice rose to a wail. "No!"

He felt uneasy about leaving her behind even for ten minutes, but the sudden tears in her eyes showed just how overwrought she was.

"We'll keep her," Molly offered. "You'd like that, wouldn't you, Katie?"

The little girl gave an almost imperceptible nod.

"See? She'll be fine."

Zach scanned the expanse of lawn leading out to the driveway. A small band of mares industriously grazed the hill just beyond the barn, while a half-dozen farm cats lay like sphinxes on a stack of hay by the barn door. Old Gabe snoozed under an oak at the edge of the yard. Nothing unusual. Nothing out of place.

Not yet.

"Thanks," he murmured. "Give me fifteen minutes, and I'll be back for dessert."

BACK AT THE RENTAL HOUSE, Zach turned Buffy out into the front yard, then strode into his bedroom and lifted one of the gun safes from a high closet shelf. Laying his fingers in the shallow, handprint-shaped troughs of the keypad, he tapped in his secret code to unlock the safe, then withdrew his lightweight Glock 27.

From a second locked safe he retrieved two empty clips and loaded each with hollow-points. Slamming one into the butt of the gun, he chambered a round, dropped the clip to replace that cartridge, then slid the clip back into place.

After turning on his laptop and bringing up his Internet provider, he reread the old e-mail message from El Cazador, looking for some clue he might have missed before.

Nothing. Not even in the thirty-two lines of jumbled words and numbers in the header.

Knowing that an expert, given the right software, could probably trace the message back to the source, he'd immediately forwarded a copy to Jerry, Paul at the Dallas DEA office, and also to an old friend who'd just retired as a computer forensics specialist with the FBI.

None of the three had responded yet. *Contact me, dammit. Help me track this guy down.*

The dialogue box on the computer screen indicated one incoming message.

The message was chillingly brief.

Knowing you can be deadly, even in rural Colorado. I wonder how many other people you care about are going to die before you do?

El Cazador had definitely reached Fossil Hill.

Spinning away, Zach grabbed his wide elastic ankle holster from a bureau drawer and fastened the holster and small gun in place. He was now armed and ready...but for what?

He still didn't know who he was looking for. Any stranger on the street could be a tourist. Or a cold-blooded killer.

And Zach might not know the difference until it was too late to react.

CHAPTER ELEVEN

DUSK HAD FALLEN by the time Zach strode through the front door of Dana's house, his face grim. Molly and Katie were already out in the barn with the pony, and Dana had almost finished racking dishes in the dishwasher.

"Guess I missed dessert," he said as he entered. He scanned the room quickly, then focused on her. "Where are the kids?"

"We decided to save dessert until you got back and the girls were done riding Penelope. Alex, of course, is puttering with his computer." She tipped her head toward the counter, where an electric coffeemaker gurgled and spat. "Want some coffee? It's just about done."

The phone rang, and he moved to grab it before she did. "Rocking H." After listening for a moment, he held it out to her. "Guess it's for you. Horse with a leg injury."

"I think we could have guessed. It never fails—you come over, and I'm in demand."

Dana slid the last plate into the dishwasher, filled the detergent dispenser and slammed the door shut, then turned on the machine as she lifted the phone to her ear.

Zach watched her intently as she talked to the client on the phone and wrote down directions. The moment she hung up, he peered over her shoulder at what she'd written.

"I thought you knew everyone around here," he said.

"Not outside of Fossil Hill. There are some towns south of here that have been growing—city people who buy twenty or thirty acres so they can hobby-farm, maybe have a few horses."

"You've never met this caller before?"

"Nope." She flashed him a grin, hoping to lighten his mood. "Guess my fame is spreading far and wide."

"But it's practically dark."

"Yes, so…is that a problem?"

"I don't think you should go. You don't know this guy. How do you know you'll be safe? A lone woman out on isolated roads—it could be a setup."

"You must watch too much TV."

"Not at all. I read the newspapers." He lifted a dark brow. "Tell me what you know about self-defense."

"What?"

"What you would do if a man grabbed you from behind and tried to wrestle away your keys? Or maybe aimed a gun at your heart and offered to blow you to kingdom come if you weren't really, really coopera-tive about a little roll in the hay?"

She felt the blood drain from her face. "This sounds really creepy, Zach. What's gotten into you?"

"What would you do if your *kids* were threatened?" he insisted.

The fierce intensity in his gaze almost frightened her. "You know, I think it's maybe time you left." She planted her hands on her hips and glared at him. "You aren't my husband, my boss, or my boyfriend. I'm not sure where this is coming from, but my life really isn't your business."

"No."

"Well, then. I'm glad you agree."

"You misunderstood. I was saying 'no, I'm not leaving right now.'" His voice softened. "I'm worried about you, Dana. You're a beautiful woman. You're alone, with two kids, on an isolated ranch."

"We've got Ben."

"Whom I've seen for *maybe* a total of five minutes during the four weeks I've been out here. He'd be a *big* help if you had trouble. Where was he when that neighbor of yours came by and got angry when you turned him down?"

Dana shook her head in exasperation. "Why would Ben worry? He's known Tom since the guy was in diapers."

"Most attacks are made by people familiar to the victim," Zach said patiently. "But these calls by people you don't know—luring you into the night—are just plain dangerous. If you have to go, I'm coming along."

This was all because he was truly *worried* about her? Even as she resented the intrusion into her private life, the thought spread a feeling of warmth through her chest.

"I appreciate the concern. But I go out on ranch calls at all hours. It's my *job,* which will dwindle into nothing if I don't serve my clients when they need me the most." She glanced at her watch. "Right now, I need to load my portable X-ray unit and hit the trail."

He paced to the window, then turned back to face her. "The girls are on their way up to the house. Call Ben, tell him to keep a close eye on things, okay? The kids should lock the doors and windows. I'm coming with you."

"I really don't think—"

"Please. Janet was on the run, and now she's been murdered. She was afraid for Katie's safety. I've just received a e-mail from someone threatening harm to people around me."

"*Threats?* But she was in Dallas, right?" Dana stared at the face she'd dreamed about for years after Zach's unexpected departure, reading there a depth of concern that shook her to the core. She had no doubt that he would protect her and her children with his life.

She did doubt that there was any real danger.

"Why on earth would anyone come after you?"

"I...don't know for sure." He paced to the kitchen window, looked out toward the barn where Katie and Molly were petting the pony.

"Who sent the message? Do you know what he looks like?"

"Not yet."

"Maybe it's from some crackpot who heard about Janet's death and gets his kicks from harassing people."

"No. This guy is for real. He may be in Colorado already—maybe he even knows that I come over here. That could mean that you and your family are at risk."

"And how would this person ever find you in Fossil Hill? We're eight hundred miles from Dallas, in the middle of nowhere!"

"This is a very real threat, Dana."

"All right," she said, throwing her hands up in defeat. "You can tag along this time if it'll make you feel better. Tell Ben to keep an eye on the kids while I check the supplies in my truck. We need to leave in five minutes."

But instead of heading straight to the clinic, she watched him for just a moment as he headed outside to meet the girls on the lawn.

He didn't walk with the casual assurance of a successful computer salesman. His bearing was military, focused, radiating an element of control and power that spoke of an entirely different line of work. He seemed to have a very clear sense of danger on his heels.

What had Zach been doing all these years—and why was he *really* back?

THE INJURED HORSE, a pretty sorrel with three white stockings and a blaze, stood cross-tied in the aisle of the barn. Nervous and clearly in pain, its eyes were rimmed with white and its ears swiveled like radar antennae as Dana moved between its foreleg, the equipment she'd laid out nearby, and the vet truck she'd parked at the barn door.

After this second e-mailed threat, he'd been afraid to let her travel alone. Who knew whether or not someone could be waiting on a darkened curve of the road? In the depths of an isolated, darkened barn?

This vet call had been for real. The next one could be a set-up.

But given Dana's reaction to his concerns, she wouldn't be changing her response to night calls any-time soon.

Straightening, he rolled the stiffness out of his left shoulder. What he knew about horses came from a few visits to riding stables and the silver screen, but Dana clearly knew her stuff.

"I believe we're looking at a coffin bone fracture," she said finally, giving the gelding a rub behind the ears. "He won't bear weight, he has a bounding dig-ital pulse, and you saw his reaction to pressure with the hoof tester."

Amen, Zach thought. She'd used something that looked a lot like a big set of pliers to apply gentle pressure at different angles on the hoof, and the horse had nearly hit the ceiling.

"But because the fracture is inside the hoof wall, there's not obvious swelling or a fracture site that we'd be able to see if it were someplace else," Dana continued. "The X rays I took will tell us for sure, but I might need some different views. Can you bring him in tonight? Once we know for sure, I can get to work on him."

The owner, a bent and weathered cowboy with a steel-gray mustache, rested an arm on the sorrel gelding's withers and nodded. "Bad deal, going down like he did. Will he be okay?"

She took a quick look at the gelding's teeth. "With a young horse like this—what is he—three? There's a fairly good prognosis, but the healing is usually slow. If it's the coffin bone we'll cast him for a couple weeks. Then he'll need a heavy support shoe and thick leather sole pads for maybe five months. After that, a light bar shoe. Some horses do fine, some need to stay in a bar shoe for life."

The cowboy stroked the sorrel's neck. "So you don't think we'll need to put him down?"

"Until I see the X rays I can't give a final prognosis. But based on what I see so far, I think he's got a really good chance for recovery to full use." She picked up the portable X-ray machine and the wooden box containing a long-handled hook tester, hook knife and other paraphernalia. "You'll bring him in?"

"Right away."

"Good. This is a darn nice colt. I'll go get some bandaging material so we can get that leg stabilized for transfer."

She strode to her truck and began rummaging through the compartments of the vet box.

The cowboy gave the gelding's neck a final pat and then turned toward Zach with a lopsided grin and a hand extended in greeting. "Bob Creighton. Guess we didn't introduce ourselves. Something happens to one of my horses, and I can't think about much else. You're her husband?"

Zach had been in a few long-term relationships, but whenever that word started slipping into a woman's conversations he'd always started backing off, suddenly finding a dozen reasons to be anywhere else. Now the word *husband* had an almost...pleasant... sound to it. The cool night air and the scents of clean sawdust bedding and horse must have affected his brain.

"No. Just a neighbor."

The cowboy's grin widened. "That's one purty gal."

"And she's not looking for commitment any more than he is." Dana shook out a towel onto the floor next to the horse, then laid out an assortment of wrapping materials. "Some of us gain wisdom with age."

She went down on one knee next to the horse and began wrapping its lower leg in fluffy sheet cotton. "How about you, Bob?"

He chuckled. "A mite wiser than you two. My Betty is in the house, watching our grandkids. We've had forty-two years and the good Lord willin', we'll have forty-two more."

"That would be quite a record," Dana said dryly as she began wrapping over the sheet cotton with elastic bandaging. "You got some sort of youth potion in one of your wells out here?"

"Nothing but common sense to appreciate what we

have and a hope that it don't end.'' Bob watched her work for another minute, then jingled the keys in his pockets. ''I'll go tell her I have to leave, and then I'll hitch up the stock trailer.''

Dana wrapped white bandaging over the sheet cotton until it covered the gelding's leg from the hoof to just below the knee. She eyed it critically, then rose and began picking up leftover supplies. ''This ought to keep him more comfortable until we get him into the clinic.''

Zach moved to help her, but she brushed him aside. ''I've got it.''

''You don't need help at all, do you,'' he observed.

''Nope.'' At the truck, she sorted through the supplies and put everything away. ''Everywhere I look, there are responsibilities that would have kept me running even if Ken were still alive. Ultimately it's all up to me and no one else.''

''Ironic, isn't it? You and I ended up alike. Take charge, get the job done.'' He gave a short laugh. ''I figure when I'm in control, the world will keep turning, and I'll be happy. Then I meet someone like Bob and wonder if I've ever known what real happiness is.''

By MIDNIGHT the horse's leg had been x-rayed from three other angles and the diagnosis confirmed. Dana had applied a heavy cast. The patient was now settled in a deeply bedded stall in Dana's barn, and his owner had headed for home.

''Come take a look,'' Dana whispered to Zach.

He followed her through her kitchen, into the living room and up the open staircase. She held a finger to her lips as she slowly eased open one bedroom door after another to check on the kids.

In the room next to Molly's, Katie lay sound asleep on the double bed, her arm curved over Gabe's rangy body. The dog was snoring.

"Well, everyone is sound asleep. Isn't Gabe sweet? He's like a big pacifier—he seems to sense when someone needs a friend."

A sense of guilt washed through Zach. "I shouldn't have left her here, today of all days."

"But she did fine. Look at her, peaceful as a little angel. Why don't you leave her here overnight? If she wakes up on the way home…"

"I don't even want to think about it. She'd never go back to sleep, and we'd be up the rest of the night."

"Do you want to stay, too, in case she wakes up? It might be really upsetting for her if you aren't here."

The first thought that came to mind was one he quickly censored. *We're just friends. Only that.* But Dana's skin seem to take on a luminous glow in the dimly lit hallway, and her eyes were dark and mysterious.

Dangerous ground.

He scanned the darkened room. "I could doze in that chair in the corner until morning."

"You're kidding. How about that big sofa in the living room? It's just about long enough for you, I think. I'll grab a few blankets and a pillow, and you'll be a lot more comfortable.''

''I don't mind the chair.''

''But I do. What kind of hospitality would that be?''

The safe kind. Up here with Katie, I'd be reminded every moment about what matters most, instead of thinking about things we shouldn't even consider.

''I'll take your silence as assent.'' Dana spun on her heel and headed for the linen closet, where she retrieved a stack of sheets, blankets and an extra pillow that she piled into his arms. ''Come on downstairs, and we'll get you settled in no time.''

With swift, matter-of-fact motions, she switched on a single lamp in the corner, shook out a set of folded sheets and had the makeshift bed set up in a few seconds. ''There. Did you want anything to eat? Drink? Wait—before I go, we've got some new toothbrushes in the bathroom cupboard, and you're welcome to one of those—''

''Stop.'' He reached out to take her hand and felt as if he'd just corralled a tornado. ''This is crazy. Having me here is making you nervous, and I don't live that far away. I'll set my alarm early and come back before Katie is even likely to wake up. You can call me if she wakes up during the night, okay?''

It was a good plan. Touching her wasn't.

Because even as he said the words, he felt the warmth of soul-deep awareness speed into his veins like a caffeine rush, until the last thing he could possibly think of was sleep.

"You want to leave?" She eyed him uncertainly, and then he knew that she felt that same awareness and hunger and need that they'd both felt so long ago. Only now it was far stronger, fueled by the absence of a lifetime and the emptiness of other experiences that had never come close enough.

"What I want," he said finally, "and what we should do are two entirely different things."

"And what I want seems reckless, given what happened between us once before. Tell me," she said with a hint of wistfulness, "why you left town after the prom without saying a word."

Knowing this moment had to come didn't make it easier. She deserved the truth, yet he couldn't give it to her. Not all of it.

Not when he knew how much it would cost her.

"I waited for you at the park outside of town Sunday noon, after prom," she continued. "I waited and waited, but you never came." Her voice wavered. "I loved you, Zach. I would have followed you to the ends of the earth. It hurt to learn I didn't mean anything to you."

"That wasn't true at all." He closed his eyes, sorting through the memories that slammed back into his thoughts. Painful memories he'd tried to forget ever since that last night in Fossil Hill. "You meant everything to me."

"Then why? You left without a word. You never wrote, or called. For all I knew, you could have been dead all these years." Her voice hitched a little and she pulled her hand from his.

"It...seemed better just to disappear. I couldn't come back. And later, I figured there wouldn't have been any hope that you'd even see me again."

"Better? To just *disappear?*"

"After I moved here, it didn't take long for the sheriff and his deputies to brand me as trouble," Zach said slowly. "I was a loner, a teenager with a chip on my shoulder. They probably figured I was a threat from the start."

Dana gave a short laugh. "I remember. We were pulled over a half-dozen times when you took me out. The deputies always seemed disappointed when they didn't find open bottles, or worse. And my mother was always warning me about you."

I'll bet she was. "There were other encounters with the law when you weren't along. Ordinary stuff, I suppose, for a rural community trying to corral its wild teens. But then..." Even now, his anger rose at the injustice. "I got stopped on prom night, after taking you home. The deputy made my options damned clear. He said he had enough evidence to put my mom and me in jail for embezzlement from the bar where she worked."

"What? That's ridiculous!"

"He claimed to have witnesses, documents, everything. We could get out of town immediately, or Mom and I would be arrested."

"Why—who?" She stared at him. "In all these years, there's never been a word about this around here. We could have stood together and proved it wasn't true. Who accused you?"

"The person behind it all had some real connections. When I tried to get the deputy to tell me, I earned a concussion and a laceration worth eight stitches. Any last convincing I needed was done when I stared down the barrel of his gun."

Dana drew in a sharp breath. "I never knew."

"He gave Mom and me a few hours to disappear, and said the accusations would be waiting if we ever came back."

"That's ridiculous!"

"Was it?" Zach lifted a shoulder. "He sounded plenty serious to me. I knew there wasn't much hope for a barmaid from the wrong side of the tracks and her kid. If we'd been tried in a backwoods courthouse with a public defender, we wouldn't have had a chance."

"But—"

"We had nothing. No connections, no money. My mom had…legal problems over several bad checks the year before. Not intentional, just a lack of money and sheer desperation, I think. Any additional charges against her could have spelled real trouble. I knew we couldn't risk staying."

Dana fell silent for a long moment. "Did you ever find out who wanted you out of town?"

"Nope. I have some suspicions, but I'll never know for sure unless someone feels guilty enough and volunteers to incriminate themselves. Since my mom and I weren't guilty, there wouldn't be a paper trail to follow."

"You should have told me. I could have helped you."

All of the fear and anger came back. The absolute certainty that there'd been no choice. But because he'd agreed to leave town that night, he'd been free to go on to school and ended up with a good career. His mother had been free to eventually marry a good man in another town and had finally made a good life for herself.

"It was the right choice at the time, Dana."

"I wasn't worth fighting for," she murmured. A sad smile curved her lips. "It's okay."

"God, no. That isn't true. But it was *hopeless*." She looked so lost that he slowly, with deliberate sensuality, slid his thumb along the high curve of her cheekbone. Then across the fullness of her lower lip. "No one has ever affected me the way you did. *Nobody*."

"You don't have to say that. I'm a big girl, now." Stepping back, she waved a hand toward the sofa. "You're welcome to stay, or you can go home. I'm heading upstairs."

Catching her arm as she turned to leave, he gently pulled her into an embrace with his hands locked at her lower back. "You can't run away from this. Not just yet."

She stilled in his embrace. Stared into his eyes. Then slowly relaxed. "You asked what I would do with an intruder?" Her eyes gleamed. "I could show you, right now."

He winced at that. "Maybe another time. When your old friend Tom shows up again?"

Her answering smile faded as a heavy silence lengthened between them. "I don't think there's anything else to say," she said finally. "We had a high school affair. We feel some of the same old magic. But that doesn't change who or what we are now, so it doesn't matter."

"Liar." Since coming to Fossil Hill, he'd tried to deny the chemistry he felt whenever she was near. It hadn't helped. "Making love to you in the moonlight after prom was the single most magical moment in my life. And if I don't kiss you, right now, I think I'm going to die."

Her eyes widened. "Really?"

Reaching up, he framed her face between his hands and brushed a kiss against her lips, then threaded his fingers through her hair and cupped the back of her head. "Absolutely."

"And if I say—"

He didn't give her a chance to say anything else.

CHAPTER TWELVE

SHE COULDN'T HAVE SAID another word if her life depended on it.

The hunger in his beautiful dark eyes nearly took her breath away. His dazzling, confident grin after that first kiss sent her heart into a lazy somersault that made her knees go weak.

"You are," he said with grave certainty, "the most desirable woman I've ever met."

He brushed another kiss across her temple, then bent lower to trail an electrifying series of light kisses across the exquisitely tender flesh below her ear. Dazed, she arched her neck and savored the liquid rush of anticipation that seemed to set every nerve ending on fire.

"Another minute of this and I'm going to collapse," she whispered.

She looked up just in time to catch the wicked gleam of satisfaction in his eyes. "That, my dear, is the idea. You'll be in my clutches, helpless and confused, in no time flat."

Laughter bubbled inside her as she reached up and pulled him down into another kiss—deeper, longer than the last, willing him to feel the emotions raging through her.

It wasn't enough. She wrapped a leg around one of his, trying to get closer, frustrated by the fabric between them. Needing to feel the heat of his skin against her own.

Unbuttoning shirts was way, way too complex. Fastening her teeth around a button at eye level, she pulled back.

"Um…Dana?"

The words didn't register at first.

Disoriented, she tipped her head back to look into his eyes, the button still clenched between her teeth. "What?"

"This isn't a good idea."

She felt the heat of embarrassment slide into her cheeks. After practically forcing him to stay, she'd attacked him on the spot. And now he was planning to gently decline.

"Because," he growled, "there's no lock on your living room door."

He bent and swept her up into his arms, and the room spun in a dizzying rush. "Your room?"

Confused, she stared up at him.

"*Where* is your room?" he amended with a laugh.

She flung a hand and pointed down the hallway. "At the end. All the way down."

By the time he had kicked the door shut and locked it, he'd also somehow unfastened most of the buttons on her shirt. By the time they fell onto the bed, she'd nibbled open at least four of his.

With Ken, God rest his soul, loving had been earnest and kind, with mutual concern. But this—this was like a torrent raging through the high country, taking everything in its path. And the humor—how had she forgotten that?

He pulled her beneath him, then rolled above her, his muscular forearms braced at either side of her. "I have thought about this since I first saw you again. I won't deny it. But this is as far as it goes if you have any hesitation at all. Tell me."

There was no mistaking the heavy weight of his desire, the tension in his corded muscles. But above all else she felt swept away with the intensity of his resolute gaze that spoke of absolute, uncompromising honor. He was a guardian, a protector, who would stand by his word no matter what the cost.

She lifted a hand and rested it against his stubble-shadowed cheek. "I want you," she said simply.

"You're sure? No regrets later?"

"How could there be?"

With a deep sound of satisfaction, he gazed straight into her eyes.

Then he lowered his mouth to hers, and suddenly everything changed. Where there had been flirtation and humor, the testing and sampling of new beginnings, now his kisses were fierce, possessive; so consuming that she was swept away to a place where the world narrowed to the heat of his mouth, the strength of his hands, the broad, muscular expanse of his chest.

"I think," she whispered against his ear, "that you've forgotten something?" She slipped her hands beneath the hem of his shirt, then slid them slowly up the indentation of his spine, savoring the feel of his muscles flexing and tensing beneath her fingertips. "Like this shirt." She skimmed her hands downward, slid them beneath the waistband of his Levi's. "And these?"

His answering laugh rippled across her sensitized skin, sending shivers dancing clear to her toes. "Not forgotten, sweetheart. Just delayed."

Pulling back, he stood by the edge of the bed, reached up to jerk the shirt over his head, then skimmed his jeans and briefs down his narrow hips and long legs. He leaned over and fumbled briefly with something—the laces of his running shoes?— then shoved his clothes under the foot of the bed.

When he straightened, the moonlight filtering through the curtains sent highlights and shadows across the muscular planes and hollows of his chest. And lower, to the evidence of his arousal.

Dana sighed with pure satisfaction. "Not bad, Forrester. Not bad at all."

His eyes glinted. "Fair is fair, sugar." He bent over her and whisked away her clothing. When she twisted in sudden embarrassment, reaching for the edge of the blanket, he caught her wrist in a gentle grasp. "Please, no. You are so incredibly beautiful."

He lifted her hand to his chest, where she felt the pounding of his heart beneath his heated flesh.

"We've got until dawn, so we can do this right," he said, flashing a wicked grin. "And after all these years apart I think it's going to take a long, long time."

"Swear?"

"You, sweetheart, are *mine*."

As a teenager, his aura of wild recklessness, of danger, had intrigued and entranced her, luring her on a primitive level that she couldn't understand. Now she recognized that appeal in the testosterone-laden baritone of his voice that bore powerful sexual promise.

But desire could be a raging force that took one's breath away, or it could be soft and immeasurably sweet.

What completely stole her heart was the trembling of his hand as he cupped her face and settled his mouth against hers.

Tears burned beneath her eyelids as a rush of emotions too powerful to name swept through her.

Only you, Zach. Always and forever, only you.

HE'D FIGURED that leaving would be awkward. He hadn't realized it would be so difficult.

Every instinct told him to get up and move to neutral territory before any of the kids awoke and knocked on Dana's door. But the sweet warmth of nestling close to her, with her back to his chest and skin-to-skin contact from shoulders to toes, was intoxicating. The silken feel of her skin and soft fragrance of her hair were textures and scents he couldn't give up. Not just yet.

At three in the morning he finally slipped away from her bedroom, leaving her asleep in a tangle of sheets, pulled on his jeans and went out to the couch, where he sat with his forearms resting on his thighs and head bowed from sheer exhaustion. Had she seen the holster on his leg? He'd fumbled with it in the darkness, trying to take it off without alarming her over the gun he carried.

Knowing Dana, she would definitely have spoken up.

"Asking forgiveness for sleeping with my mom?"

Startled, Zach straightened and scanned the darkened room until he found Alex sitting in an easy chair in the far corner, his face twisted in a scowl. "I didn't see you over there, son. Isn't this a bit early?"

"I'm not your son," he bit out. "And you could also say it was just a bit *late*."

"I suppose you could, at that," Zach said mildly. The kid was all righteous indignation, his hands clenched and voice a half octave higher than usual. Zach recognized it for what it was, the challenge of a young male as head of the house, and settled back against the sofa. "Are you always awake at four?"

The boy's gaze slid away.

"Just making sure your mom is okay? That's a good thing, caring about someone. We didn't get back from the clinic until after midnight. Thanks for watching over Katie, by the way. I'll pay you in the morning for the two times you've done that."

"I don't want your money."

"Not for some new CDs? Seems like a kid your age has a lot of places he could spend his money."

"Why are you still here?"

Ignoring the belligerent tone, Zach searched for the right words. "It was too late to take Katie home. We figured it would be best just to let her sleep. I stayed so she wouldn't be upset if she awakened in a strange place and didn't have me close by.''

He awaited the next inevitable questions about where he'd slept, but Alex just stood and crossed the room, his hostility evident with every stride. At the foot of the stairs, he turned back. ''We don't need you here, you know. I don't want another guy hanging around, thinking he can be our dad, and neither does Molly. My mom does just fine on her own without anyone else.''

''I'm sure she does.''

''Especially if that guy is a liar.''

''What?''

''It's creepy, you know? If a guy would lie about one thing, he'd lie about something else. My mom says a guy's honor means everything, and it's something he can't ever get back once he screws up.''

''I...guess she's right.''

His lips curled in distaste, Alex leveled a look of pure disdain at Zach. ''Then maybe you shouldn't come around here anymore.''

''*Alexander Hathaway!*''

Zach and Alex turned in unison to look toward the hallway leading to the downstairs bedrooms, where Dana stood at the doorway, a thin robe wrapped around her and a look of horror on her face.

''You need to apologize to Mr. Forrester at once, do you hear me? You know better than to talk to any adult that way!''

''Then maybe you'd better talk to your *boyfriend*, and find out what he's doing with that little girl,''

Alex sneered. "Because Katie says he wasn't married to her mom and she sure as heck doesn't think he's her father."

COMMUTING WAS HELL in Colorado ranch country.

In Dallas, everything was convenient…and anonymous, if need be. With over a million people in the city, it was damn easy to blend in.

Here, he'd had to stay in a run-down motel off Interstate 25 to be less obvious, registered as someone called Alberto Marquez, then drive well over an hour just to observe his target. Not that it wasn't worth his time. Now he knew where Zach shopped, when he usually came and went. How often he visited that pretty little neighbor.

It had almost become a game, drifting through town, then cruising out on that highway past Zach's place, hoping to catch a glimpse of his quarry. Forrester usually looked edgy, hyperalert. As if he *knew* he was being watched. Maybe he was even starting to feel some real fear.

But now the e-mailed threats and surveillance weren't enough. With Janet dead, it was time for the next step. With every passing day his impatience grew.

Safe behind his keyboard, he'd once managed the finances of a cocaine trafficking operation that brought millions of dollars into the family's coffers. He'd once been a wealthy man.

The traitor who ended all of that deserved to die.

Smiling to himself, he turned off the headlights of

his car. He drove slowly down the long lane to the little blue house, his right-side tires on the grassy edge to limit the noise, then eased the car around so it faced the highway again.

From a nearby hill he'd watched the Blazer leave earlier in the evening. By three o'clock in the morning he knew the guy wasn't coming back anytime soon.

Perfect planning. He opened his car door and stepped out into the cool night air.

But he hadn't planned on *geese.*

Squawking, flapping their huge wings, their long necks and beaks extended like vicious snakes, they burst out of the shadows behind the house with enough noise and confusion to wake the dead. Held back by the fence around the backyard, they beat their wings against the barrier, frustrated at their inability to attack.

From somewhere behind them came the bloodcurdling scream of...a woman? Some other creature straight from hell?

His heart jerked straight up and lodged in his throat, quivering like a beached jellyfish, as he waited, frozen.

Surely every last person in Fossil Hill had heard those damned geese. Maybe Forrester had doubled back. Maybe he'd launch out of the little house with his guns blazing.

Seconds ticked by. Minutes.

Nothing happened.

As he scanned the area, a ragged white form, illuminated by a shaft of moonlight, seemed to rise out of the darkness down by the barn.

Horror rushed through him as he focused on the mutilated target of a male figure. Hundreds of holes had pierced the paper—almost all dead center.

Until now it had almost seemed like a game. The chase provided an exhilarating sense of power, an almost sexual pleasure. But this was no game. It would be a duel for life and death, and Zach would be the one who went down.

It was time to deliver the final threat.

The house would make a pretty bonfire, out here on this endless damned prairie. Too bad nobody would see it go up in flames.

He slipped into the barn and found a can of gasoline sitting next to a lawn mower just inside the door, then started for the house. The geese went crazy again at his approach. *Cooked geese,* he thought, smiling at his own wit. With any luck they were penned close enough to the house to roast.

But just as he poised to begin dousing the clapboard siding of the house, he heard a sound from inside. The cries of a puppy. God, he couldn't burn an innocent little puppy. He stopped in frustration, then tried the windows and doors. Every one of them was locked, dammit.

Blindly kicking through the grass at his feet, he searched for a rock or a stray board, something to break through the windows. His anxiety rising, he checked his watch.

If Forrester returned, he'd be trapped. There was

only one way to drive out of this place, and it could be blocked with a single vehicle.

With an oath, he pivoted away from the house and hurried to the barn. He splashed gasoline along the outside wall. Then he lit a makeshift wick and ran for his car.

Sparing one glance at the beautiful ball of flames exploding into the night sky, he smiled to himself, then stomped on the accelerator and headed toward the highway.

This was his final message. The next trip to Fossil Hill would be his last. He'd wait, until the moment his quarry's guard was down.

And then justice would be served.

"Go to bed, young man. *Now.*"

"A real popular place to be, around here." Alex gave Dana a look of disgust, and then she knew that there was far more behind his outburst than the information about Katie. "Aren't you gonna—"

"This is not your business. I'll take care of it."

"Right." He headed up the stairs, his back rigid. "Great example, Mom."

When his bedroom door slammed shut, Zach cleared his throat. "I'm sorry," he said quietly. "I never should have stayed the night."

"I knew it would be hard for him if I ever…started seeing someone."

"You were seeing Tom, though."

"Never overnight. I'm not sure if we ever had more

than a brief kiss in all that time, but Alex didn't like him either.''

"It's a primitive guy thing.''

"I know.'' She listened for sounds coming from upstairs, then beckoned for him to follow. "Let's go out in the kitchen, where we can close the door.''

When they reached the kitchen, she shut the door behind them and started a pot of coffee. "Want anything to eat?''

Zach stood at the window and looked out into the yard. "It's a little early for me.''

He did look tired. They'd gotten to bed late...and they sure hadn't slept once they got there. "Me, too. I could have used another hour or two. Look, I'm sorry about my son. These teen years aren't easy for him, and he says—''

"He was right.''

"He...was?''

Zach turned to face her, his expression grim. "I never said the words, but I did let you all assume Katie is my daughter. She isn't.''

A sick feeling pooled in her stomach as Dana remembered all the promises Zach had made as a teenager, all the promises that had been broken when he disappeared.

Ironic, how she'd seen such integrity in him when they'd made love last night...and sad, because she clearly wasn't any better at judging character now than when she'd been a girl of seventeen. "Maybe you'd better explain.''

He seemed to choose his words with care. "My

sister said she needed a *safe* place for her daughter. I figured it would be better if people didn't know too much about Katie, even out here.''

"Why would anyone harm a little girl?''

"I don't know, but Janet's death is evidence enough of how serious her enemies were. There's been good reason to keep Katie's background under wraps...but I'm truly sorry for not telling you sooner.''

The ease with which he'd misled her was a warning signal that might as well have flashed in neon lights. What else could he tell her that wasn't true? How would she ever know? "You should have known any secrets were safe with me.''

His jaw hardened. "I trust you. But what about your kids? Ben? Your friend Francie? What about John Doe on the streets of Fossil Hill? If someone casually stopped by and asked a few questions, could there be a chance that one of them might inadvertently reveal Katie's location? *'Yeah, there's a guy outside of town. Has his sister's little girl. Is that the one you mean?'*'' Zach shook his head slowly. "Blind trust and common sense are two different things.''

Dana tried to mask her hurt. "Of course.''

Crossing the kitchen, he gently lifted her chin with a forefinger and looked down into her eyes. "Tell me you understand.''

"I...do. It's just unsettling to see how easily I can be fooled.''

"Since coming here there have been so many times when I wanted to explain. But—''

At the sound of Gabe barreling down the steps, they both turned. A second later the dog was clawing furiously at the door, barking frantically.

"Whatever it is out there, I'm going after it," Dana said. She reached for her Ruger 30-06 bolt action rifle on the top shelf of the closet by the door. "Darn coyotes, probably."

"Wait!" Zach grabbed her wrist and hauled her back. "Don't be a fool. Someone might be out there."

Molly came running into the kitchen, her face pale. "Look out the windows!" She jerked open the window shades to the west.

On the horizon an immense orange glow rose into the night sky, pulsing as if it were a living thing.

"I think that's your place, Zach!" Dana spun around, her face pale. "Molly, call 911, then go wake up Ben. He needs to stay in the house with you kids. I'm grabbing my clothes."

Without waiting for her, Zach grabbed the keys from his pocket and raced out to his Blazer, thankful for the concealed weapon at his ankle.

Gut instinct told him that the fire was no accident.

A sick feeling rose in his throat at what might have happened if he and Katie had been at home.

If this was the work of El Cazador, it might not be too late to catch him.

The bastard who'd dared threaten Katie was going to pay.

CHAPTER THIRTEEN

THE ENTIRE BARN WAS ABLAZE when Zach slammed on the brakes a hundred yards north of the buildings.

There'd been no sign of another vehicle as he drove in. He turned off his headlights, drew his weapon and scanned the area before opening his door.

In the eerie glow of the fire he could only see shadows dancing in the darkness and choking billows of smoke.

He quickly searched the backyard of the house, tested the door locks. The house was still secure, the peacock and geese huddled at the far end of the fenced yard, well away from danger. From inside the house he could hear Katie's puppy frantically yelping.

Moving on, every sense alert, he circled the barn with his gun drawn, watching for any suspicious movement. Even at fifty feet away, the intense fire heated his skin and his eyes watered from the acrid smoke. With every step closer to the barn, the sharp smell of gasoline grew stronger.

Arson.

If the guy had tossed the can into the inferno, there'd be little chance of fingerprints. If he fell under the thank-God-criminals-are-stupid classification, that gas can would be somewhere along the driveway, or out along on the highway.

Embers rained down like falling stars, flaring into a thousand miniature grass fires that were already coalescing into a low wall of flame advancing across the dry grass toward the house.

Discordant sirens wailed in the distance, echoing across the vast grassland.

Turning on his heel, Zach ran to the house and unlocked the front door. He grabbed the puppy's cage, his laptop, sensitive case files and the gun safes. Then he filled a box with Katie's toys and clothes. In two trips he had most everything of importance in the Blazer.

"Sorry, buddy," he murmured to the terrified pup cowering at the back of its cage. "You're a whole lot safer in here."

He slammed and locked the car door, then retrieved the garden hose from the backyard. After attaching it to a freestanding hydrant out by the overgrown garden, he began soaking the roof of the house.

Steam sizzled skyward where embers glowed ominously against the shingles. The stench of hot asphalt burned his lungs. Fitful breezes carried clouds of heavy, choking smoke toward the house.

Dana's truck pulled up behind his Blazer, the sound of its motor masked by the roar of the fire. After climbing out of the cab, she hoisted a heavy coil of hose from the back.

At the edge of the yard she dropped all but one end of the hose, then ran toward the house to hook it up to an outside faucet along the foundation. "I'll start on this grass fire," she yelled. "How are you doing?"

"The barn's a loss—I'm just trying to save the house." He rubbed a forearm across his face to wipe away the sweat and soot trailing into his eyes. "Sounds like the fire trucks are almost here."

Minutes later, the Fossil Hill volunteer fire trucks— an ancient tanker and a 1950s ladder truck—pulled in with six volunteers.

Within seconds the yard was a scramble of dark-coated firefighters. Hoses snaked in every direction, and hoarse voices shouted orders above the roaring flames.

Billows of smoke rolled skyward as the firefighters struggled to contain the grass fires now spreading in every direction.

When one of the firefighters gave a thumbs-up and a nod toward the house, Zach stepped back to let the man take over with his much more powerful hose.

Two hours later, the dying blaze hissed and crackled, and the heavy, choking smell of wet cinders and damp, smoldering hay clogged the air. The barn was a loss, just as Zach had thought, but the house had been saved and the firefighters had stopped the spread of fire across the pasture.

The firefighters began coiling hoses, their adrenaline rush over and their steps weary and slow.

"Can you come over here for a minute, sir?" One of the younger men pointed to a patrol car parked next to the ladder truck, where a heavyset, balding deputy stood scowling at the clipboard in his hands.

Even through the low-laying haze and predawn darkness, anyone could see the alligator pattern of charring across the entire lower front foundation of the barn that was strongly suggestive of arson.

The officer gave Zach a tight nod of acknowledgment. There was something vaguely familiar about him, and if related to law enforcement in this area, it probably wasn't good.

"Your name, sir?"

"Zach Forrester."

"Have any identification?"

Zach hesitated, then withdrew his wallet and slid out his driver's license, thankful that he'd left his badge and DEA credentials in one of the gun safes.

His career, and reasons for being here, were topics he had no wish to discuss while standing in a curious, milling crowd. With luck, perhaps he'd never need to reveal them while in Fossil Hill.

"How long have you been at this residence?"

"May twenty-ninth. Martha Benson gave me a four-month lease on the place. I'm on a medical leave for three, but I wanted a little leeway, just in case. I hope to be back to work soon as I can."

The deputy peered at him over his half glasses. "Where do you work?"

"Allied Computer Systems in Dallas." The company belonged to an old friend, and he'd used it as a cover several times before. Unless a new employee answered the phone, his cover would hold.

The deputy gave him a keen look of appraisal. "Do you remember me, son?"

Zach gave him an easy smile. "I've been trying to place you, but I've come up dry."

The deputy didn't smile back. "You and me had a run-in a time or two. I didn't ever expect to see you in these parts again."

Studying him, Zach mentally subtracted fifteen years and twenty pounds and added a full head of hair. On his last night in Fossil Hill, it had been dark as pitch on that country road. Everything had happened too fast, and in that adrenaline rush of fear, most of that night was a blur. Had this guy been the one who'd stopped him? Threatened him?

"I haven't been here for years," Zach said slowly. "I'm sure not looking for trouble."

"Right." The deputy's doubtful gaze shifted briefly to the house, where the geese still squawked and flapped their wings whenever anyone drew too close to the backyard fence. "See or hear anything suspicious this evening? The sound of a car?"

"Not at all. I'm sure those geese would have let me know."

"Any idea how this blaze started?"

"Looks like arson, to me. The barn's electricity was turned off, and there sure wasn't any lightning."

Rocking back on his heels, the deputy frowned. "Some folks come to an isolated area, figure it's a safe place to do a little business outside of the law. Sometimes," he added, "we bring in the drug dog from over in Blackburn just to check things out."

Did the guy think he'd been cooking meth? The irony nearly made Zach laugh. "Be my guest. Search the barn and bring out the dogs. If someone was doing anything illegal out there, I'd be the *first* who'd want to know.''

''So you were here all night, and saw *nothing?*''

The venom in the man's voice stopped Zach short. He had an idea of who started the blaze, but had no real name, no physical description. A moment ago, he'd been on the verge of quietly revealing information about the e-mailed threats and asking for help from the local authorities. Now he knew that such a revelation would only cast greater suspicion upon himself.

And unless he dared unleash a cascade of inquiries looking into his own past—which might bring agents into the area and end his chance of apprehending El Cazador—he wasn't yet ready to discuss being part of the DEA.

The deputy straightened, hitched up his gun belt. ''Got nothing to say?''

Hell. Zach stared back at him, knowing he couldn't admit spending the night with the pretty town vet. Small-town gossip being what it was, both her reputation and her practice might suffer. ''Guess I'm a heavy sleeper—I didn't hear a thing.''

''He was with us at the ranch,'' Dana called out. She sauntered up and threaded an arm through Zach's. To an onlooker she might have appeared fully at ease, unless one noticed the tense set of her jaw. ''He went with me on a late farm call, and when we got back his…Katie…was sound asleep. Zach stayed on my sofa.''

The deputy gave her a dismissive glance. "You don't live far away."

Dana snorted. "You think he somehow slipped over here, set this barn on fire and went back to my place? Gabe would have barked like crazy at anyone sneaking through our yard at night. Easy answers aren't always the right ones, Robinson."

"I'm not looking for *easy*. I'm looking for facts. And this guy and I go *way* back."

"The kids and I can account for every minute with him since yesterday evening. Maybe you need to look a little further—like those troublemakers over in Gresham, or Culver. Didn't they burn the Graysons' calf shed just south of here?"

Ignoring her, the deputy met Zach's eye. "Don't worry. I'll find out how this happened, and I'll make damned sure the right person is charged."

DAWN SHADED the rolling hills to the softest hues of rose and violet as the fire trucks slowly headed down the lane to the highway. Dana stood on the porch of the little house with her hands on her hips.

"It's good you're moving out for a few days," she called. "The smell of wet, charred hay is overwhelming."

Zach emptied the last of Katie's clothes into a suitcase and snapped the lid shut, then carried it out onto the porch. "I've got everything packed."

"With all the smoke, I'll bet there isn't one thing in the house you and Katie could even wear."

Ashes smudged her brow and her eyes were bloodshot, but she was still the prettiest woman he'd ever seen. Resisting the need to pull her into his arms, he hooked his thumbs in the front pockets of his jeans and leaned against the wall. "There's a Laundromat in town, right?"

"A small one, a block north of Main and Third."

Finding it wouldn't be a problem. Main Street wasn't more than ten blocks long. The business district was just half of that, and the entire town was only three or four blocks wide. "Know of any motels? I don't remember seeing one."

"There aren't, but Flossie and Leo Cooper have a string of cabins called the Shady Oaks. It's behind their house on Fourth. They don't have much of a sign in front, so you really have to look for it." Her voice sounded hoarse and strained with fatigue. "Last I heard the going rate was forty bucks for a room and as much of Flossie's gossip as a person could bear."

"Thanks." He still felt damned uneasy about the whole situation. There'd been no specific threat against Dana, but this fire had been set and El Cazador's last e-mail had read, *How many will die before you do?*

Perhaps the bastard wouldn't associate Dana and her kids with Zach. In the eyes of a stranger, they might simply be neighbors, nothing more. But perhaps that wasn't good enough. "You're going to be really careful, right? Keep your windows and doors locked. Take me along if you're called out to a stranger's place at night."

"There's never been any trouble before."

"Dana, this fire tonight was no accident. Someone *set* it."

"Gabe barks at intruders. Ben has a rifle and lives a hundred feet away. I've got my Ruger 30-06," she said patiently. "I can also call 911."

"There *is* someone out here—someone who could harm people close to me."

She stubbornly lifted her chin. "I can take care of myself and my kids, Forrester."

"I know it'll sound like I'm angling for a place to stay, and I'm not. But maybe Katie and I should come out to your ranch. I can help keep an eye on things."

"If Flossy doesn't have a vacancy, okay," Dana said slowly. "Otherwise, I think it's a bad idea. I...just don't think I could handle it very well."

"We're talking *security,* here. I swear I won't even touch you again, if that's what you want."

She bit her lower lip. "No—yes. I just need distance, Zach."

"You'll call the sheriff if you see or hear anything suspicious at all? *Promise* me. And you can call me anytime, day or night. Okay?"

"I don't believe anything else is going to happen. How do you know this fire wasn't caused by local vandals? But yes, I'll call."

Zach pushed away from the wall with a sigh, then went back inside for the last suitcase and set it on the top step of the porch.

She didn't believe there was a risk. All he had to do was look at the charred hulk of the barn to know there was.

On the north side, blackened timbers jutted skyward like rotting teeth. The rest of the building had collapsed in a tangle of rubble. He'd wondered what the firefighters—and deputy—would think of the bullet-riddled target next to the barn, but it had been completely destroyed by the inferno.

"Could you board the puppy for a few days?"

Raking her hands through her hair, Dana gave him a weary smile. "Of course, but Katie will sure miss that pup. I…suppose she could stay in Molly's room, and you could have the guest room."

The offer was straightforward western hospitality, but her hesitation was just as clear. He reached out and rested both hands on Dana's shoulders. Waited until she lifted her gaze to meet his. "I won't force this. But if you have any trouble, I'll be at your place in a split second."

"Thanks. I'll give Flossie a call and tell her you're coming," she said with a hint of wistfulness. "That really would be for the best."

"Dana—" Zach gave a deep sigh, then moved behind her and wrapped his arms around her waist, gently guiding her back until she leaned against his chest. "I'm sorry about misleading you regarding Katie."

"It's…only right that you'd want to protect her."

"If things were different, nothing could stand in my way. There's no one I could ever want more than I want you," he murmured against her ear. "I think about you during the day. I find myself dreaming about you at night. Making love to you was the most incredible experience of my life.''

When she shivered, he drew her even closer, until her head lay against his shoulder. "With every day, it's harder to remember that there isn't a future for me here.''

Her breath hitched. "At least we're being honest, this time around.''

Honest. If only she knew.

He wanted to kiss the delicate skin of her nape. Trace the fine shell of her ear with his tongue, and then turn her within his arms and kiss her with all of the heat and desire that had been escalating within him from the moment he touched her. God, he wanted her so much.

Instead, he forced himself to step away.

Several boxes were already loaded in the Blazer. "Guess we're done here,'' he said, lifting the two suitcases. "I'll come back out to take care of the peacock and the geese every day until the house airs out enough to live in again.''

"Are you going straight to town?''

The distance in her voice echoed in the empty spaces of his heart. "Not yet. I'd better be around when Katie wakes up.''

The drive back to the Rocking H felt like the longest trip of Zach's life.

THE SHADY OAKS CABINS might have been shady, if there'd been any trees. They certainly weren't conducive to rest. When the good women of Fossil Hill heard about the fire they began coming in droves and the steady traffic hadn't decreased yet. If Zach had accepted half of their dinner invitations, he and Katie could have been occupied for the next six weeks.

He'd spent endless hours over the past three days combing through the charred remains of the barn and searching the ditches on either side of the driveway and highway for evidence.

It appeared that the fire had been set using the gas can that had been stored inside the barn. The can, now buckled by the intense heat with its paint blistered away, had been tossed inside. No latent prints could be lifted from its damaged surface, and there wasn't another shred of evidence to be found.

On Monday afternoon, Martha Benson knocked at his cabin door. "Coffee at the Pink Petticoat Inn in a half hour? We need to talk about the fire at my place. I would have been here sooner, but I was out of town."

He almost smiled at the elderly woman's patrician manner and complete confidence in being obeyed. This was one invitation he couldn't turn down. "Of course." Glancing toward the corner desk, where Katie was somberly coloring, he added, "We're getting close to nap time, so I can't guarantee how long we can stay."

"Understandable. Though I hear," she said in a voice loud enough to catch Katie's attention, "there's a new dollhouse back in the corner, and good little children can play with it while their parents enjoy a moment of peace." She turned to leave, then offered her first smile. "That child seems to be doing so much better than when you first came to town. People said she seemed so…frightened. You're a good father, Mr. Forrester."

A good father. Could he be?

But Katie had been quietly despondent since the death of her mother and had already faced so much uncertainty and change in her young life. She deserved better than a single guy with erratic work hours and little experience with kids. Yet what would it do to her if she was uprooted once again? Would she be better off staying with him?

That was selfish thinking, Zach knew. He would do what was right for Katie, even though he couldn't imagine life without her. He just wondered how he could ever let her go.

AT THE PINK PETTICOAT, Martha had settled at a prime table by the front window when Zach and Katie walked in. She gave Katie's yellow sundress and be-ribboned ponytail an approving nod, then smiled and waved a hand toward the empty chairs.

Zach hesitated, uncomfortable with the exposed location, then reached up and twisted the wand on the miniblinds so no one on the sidewalk could look in. Catching Martha's frown, he gave her a smile in return. "Terribly bright sun, don't you think?" he said as he took the chair facing the front entrance.

Martha harrumphed and peered at him over her half glasses. "Same as always at this time of day."

"Look!" Katie breathed when she caught sight of the dollhouse in the far corner.

As tall as her shoulders, the white wooden house featured windows draped with frothy pink curtains, and each room boasted a full collection of furniture. For the first time in days, her somber expression lifted.

Cindy appeared instantly, her order pad in hand. "After you eat, you can play over there, okay?"

Giving the dollhouse a last, longing look, Katie dutifully scrambled up into her chair.

"Let's get to the point, shall we?" Martha said after the waitress delivered coffee, plus cookies and lemonade for Katie. "The sheriff called in a fire investigator from the Colorado Bureau of Investigation. He concurred with what you told me on the phone that day. Arson."

"Not a professional job, but it couldn't have been anything else."

"There's never been any question in my mind about you being responsible, you understand." Martha sipped at her coffee, then cradled the cup in her hands. "Though I hear the deputy was a tad disappointed when he heard you had an alibi."

"Dana and I went on a late vet call."

"Right." She gave him a knowing look. "Be that as it may, I just wonder if you've any idea about who might have been involved."

"Even if I'd seen someone, I probably wouldn't know who they were. I've been gone over fifteen years."

"It just seems strange…the place has been empty

for so long without the least bit of vandalism. You've been here for what...a month? And an arsonist burns down the barn.''

"Maybe activity around the place attracted the attention of a passerby?"

She snorted. "I'd guess activity would *discourage* someone from driving up that long lane. Unless, that is, they had a bone to pick with you." After another long sip of coffee, she folded her gnarled hands on the table. "I hired several women to work on your house yesterday and today. They've washed the curtains and rugs, and aired out the place. It should be okay if you want to return. If not, I'll understand and will cancel your lease."

From the corner of his eye, Zach caught several young women at other tables watching him with interest. One of them artfully crossed her slim legs and ran a hand through her long, curly brown hair the moment she caught his eye.

"We'll be moving back there as soon as possible," he muttered.

Martha glanced at the other table, and her mouth quirked into a wry smile.

Katie held up her empty lemonade glass to show Zach. "Can I go see the dollhouse?"

"Go ahead, honey. Just don't wander any further, okay?"

With a nod Katie slid out of her seat and darted to the back of the café, then dropped to her knees next to the dollhouse. Zach hoped she might squeal with delight, but she just stared at it for several minutes.

Then she reached inside the living room, tipped a female figure on its side and rocked back on her heels, her eyes infinitely sad.

They both watched the child for a moment, then Martha abruptly turned back to Zach. "You probably don't remember me from when you lived here last. Young bucks like yourself usually see old folks around town as just so much wallpaper, and I know you weren't in town for very long."

At a lift of his brow, she shrugged. "Being post-mistress meant I always knew about what went on in Fossil Hill. And I've known Vivian—Dana's mom—since we were both in diapers. So naturally I'd be even more aware of her family than most."

Zach nodded.

"When Dana started going out with you during your senior year, I remember worrying about her. You weren't a local boy. You had an air of…danger. Of trouble looking for a place to happen."

"I was just eighteen."

"But you were a boy who'd seen a lot during those eighteen years. I knew you and your mom moved around a lot, and that she worked at a bar." Martha cleared her throat delicately. "Well, I'm sure you know what I mean."

A flicker of anger burned in Zach's gut as he remembered the endless new towns, the many schools. The small-minded people who had expected the worst from a kid who'd given up on the thought of ever having roots and friends and the white-picket-fence life he'd only seen on TV.

His mother had never been able to find the right job, the right man, during his youth, but her inability to settle down hadn't been his fault.

"I'm not sure where this is headed."

Flags of color appeared in Martha's parchment-pale cheeks. "I still worry about Dana, young man. She's a sweet girl, and she's like a niece to me. I remember how destroyed she was years ago when you left."

"You never…heard rumors about why my mother and I left town so suddenly?"

She gave him a blank look. "Rumors? We all knew you up and left, if that's what you mean. Ed, down at the bar, said your mother didn't even give any notice."

So the details of that last night hadn't become common knowledge. Interesting.

Martha waited a beat, then continued. "And now, with you and Dana seeing each other again…" She flapped a hand in consternation. "I just worry about what sort of business you might really be in, and if trouble might have followed you here. I don't want her to be hurt."

"Trouble?"

Martha had the grace to look uncomfortable. "It's just that something doesn't seem quite right. Your references proved valid—I checked before I rented you the house. Yet I can't see you working as a software salesman."

"I'll hope my boss doesn't agree with you. I could find myself job hunting."

She ignored him. "And lately, a stranger in town has been asking questions about you."

Though his thoughts started racing, Zach tried for an easy grin. "I've no idea who that could be."

Martha's mouth thinned. "Are you running from someone?"

"Whatever you think of me, I've never been on the wrong side of the law. Not once. Maybe this guy is on vacation, and my boss told him to look me up. What did he look like?"

She studied him for a long moment, her eyes filled with doubt. "Not very tall—maybe five foot six or seven. Hispanic. Wiry build. Ball cap. Sunglasses...I wouldn't know if they were prescription or not."

"Did he give his name?"

"Not that I heard."

"Any idea of what sort of car I should watch for? Did he say where he was going?"

"I just saw him from a distance for the second time this morning," she murmured. "Odd though, I think he was driving a rusty, beat-up Ford pickup. Why would a tourist drive long distances in something like that?"

To blend in better with the locals. "Maybe it's a loaner while his own car is in the shop."

For almost two months Zach had tried to recall the events of that last evening in his condo. A face...or anything out of the ordinary, beyond the black Mustang. Now and then pieces of that day returned, like brief flashbacks, but never enough to go on.

Could this be the guy? "Any idea where that truck was headed?"

"I was outside the drugstore, talking to Fern Jones…" Martha thought for a minute. "West. No, east. I think he was headed east."

East. Toward the little blue house, and Dana's ranch. A coincidence, or something more?

"Thanks for the information." Zach glanced at his watch, then stood and dropped a five and several ones on the table. "I completely forgot about promising Katie we'd go out to Dana's clinic to visit her puppy before supper. Will you excuse us?"

"Of course."

Even with the prospect of seeing Buffy again, Katie thrust out her lower lip as he scooped her up and strode for the door, but at least she didn't start a scene.

If this guy was lurking around Dana's place, Zach wanted to get there, fast. El Cazador had been on the loose long enough.

CHAPTER FOURTEEN

"I CAN'T WAIT to get away from here," Alex grumbled as he hauled the last of the trash to the back door of the clinic. "It's not like this ranch has been in the family for generations or anything."

Francie looked up from the cocker puppy nestled in her arms. Too weak to nurse and rejected by his mother, he'd been on formula at the clinic for a week now, and was doing much better. "So what's your latest plan?"

"College. A regular job someplace cool, in a big city where there's lots to do."

"In three years you'll finish high school and can do anything you want."

"Yeah, right." Keeping the clinic and the ranch running took endless hours, with Dad gone. If Alex left home, what would Mom do?

"Why not? You're a bright kid. You'll earn lots of scholarships, I'll bet."

"Maybe." *But none of them would replace having me help out around here.* The sympathetic look in Francie's eyes made him squirm. Sometimes he wondered if she could read his mind. "Guess I'd better go work the colts for a while."

"You've done a great job with them this year." Francie bent to put the pup back into its warm nest of blankets in a cardboard box at her feet. "If the Rocking H colts do well at the futurities this year, it'll mean a lot for the reputation of the ranch."

He shrugged away the compliment, even as a warm sense of satisfaction slid through him. There was so much more in the world, outside the narrow confines of Fossil Hill. He could imagine it. Feel it. Almost taste the excitement and wonder of traveling far away. But working with the horses gave him another kind of satisfaction that almost made up for everything else he was missing.

"Maybe someday you can start taking some of these horses out on the show circuit," Francie ventured. "Wouldn't that be fun?"

"We couldn't afford it, and Mom would never have the time."

"Well, how about the chance to work with a new horse—one of mine?" Her cheeks turned pink. "I asked Tom if he'd go with me to a sale in Denver next weekend, and help me pick out a good show prospect. He said he would. If I find a nice mare maybe I could hire you to help me work with her. That way you could earn some extra money."

"Maybe...if Mom says okay. She's seemed sorta weird lately. Like her mind is a million miles away."

Francie gave him a pensive look. "Do you think she's happy out here—really, truly happy?"

Was she? The thought had never occurred to him. "I dunno. I suppose."

"If she had a dream," Francie persisted, "Of going anywhere, of being anything, what would it be?"

He raised his palms. "I don't know."

"You men," Francie retorted with a twinkle in her eye, "are all such observant creatures." The silver bell above the front door tinkled.

She turned and started up the hallway muttering something about fairy godmothers being highly underrated, but Alex couldn't catch all the words. Weird.

Anyone—especially adults—ought to know that dreams and wishes were a big waste of time.

THREE DAYS LATER, Jerry called Zach. "I've got some information you might want," he said. "I'm not sure how much it will help, though."

Bracing the phone between his ear and shoulder, Zach grabbed a pen and pad of paper from the kitchen counter of his rental house. He glanced at Katie, who was happily playing on the living room floor with the puppy, and lowered his voice. "Ready."

Before moving their things back into the house, he'd stopped by Dana's place, and had even driven another half hour east, but hadn't seen any sign of the old pickup Martha mentioned. Since then, he'd patrolled the streets of Fossil Hill every day, and the highway on either side. He'd seen nothing suspicious. With luck, maybe Jerry had found out something worthwhile.

"I did a tracer on the e-mails you forwarded to me and came up blank. But your retired FBI friend did better. He finally tracked them both to a run-down motel in West Dallas.''

"A guest room?"

Jerry snorted. "Not a place I'd want to be a guest, believe me. I drove out there yesterday. Big old two-story motel, the kind with rooms opening onto an outside balcony. One wing was boarded up. The clerk's desk was behind bullet-proof glass.''

"Did she give you any information?"

"Only after I slipped her twenty bucks. Most of the clients hanging around there looked like ex-cons, low-end dealers and other losers. She remembered the guy who rented that room because he was better dressed than most and came back a coupla times.''

"Did you get a name?"

"That's another reason she remembered him. He paid cash and signed in as Jeff Anderson, but he was Hispanic and had an accent to boot. What are the odds of that? Oh, and he wrote down a phony Texas license plate number that doesn't match anything in the registration system.''

"Damn."

"On the upside, I got a description. She's got one of those height markers on the entry door to her office. Guess they have a lot of trouble with their clients, because she always writes down extra information about anyone who walks in.'' Jerry gave a short laugh. "Probably makes things easier when she has to call in the cops.''

Zach paced impatiently at the end of the telephone cord. "Well?"

"The guy's maybe five foot eight. Slender. Hair probably cut pretty short, though he wore a ball cap so there could have been a ponytail hidden underneath. She thought he was in his late thirties."

Bingo. "Tattoos? Scars?"

"Not that she noticed. The lighting isn't good in that office, though." Papers rustled. "She did say it looked like he'd once had a major case of acne."

"What about his voice? His clothes?"

"Most of the guys hanging around that joint were bare chested, with unbuttoned jeans hanging at half-mast. I saw lots of leather vests and a hell of a lot of tattoos. Our guy wore a package-wrinkled oxford shirt, new jeans and loafers. She said it was almost like he'd bought clothes for the occasion."

"Or maybe was decking himself out after a long time in prison orange."

"She also remembered his voice. Real high for a guy, sort of soft. She wondered at the time if he was some pretty boy looking for a little rough action." Jerry cleared his throat. "I did ask around, but none of the guys staying there remembered anything significant. Or so they said."

"Not even for a ten or twenty?"

"Strange, isn't it? Most of those motel room doors were open, and the guys were aimlessly wandering in and out of the rooms as if they were stoned. You'd think they'd sell their granny for another hit."

"Maybe our guy has more connections than we think." As soon as Jerry hung up, Zach glanced at the clock. Four o'clock here, five o'clock in Dallas.

With luck, Paul was still at his desk, or maybe Sara Hanrahan was in. He'd worked with Paul on a number of cases over the years. Sara was newer, but both were efficient, effective agents.

After ten minutes of transfers and far too much canned music while on hold, he finally reached Sara.

"Hey, boss. How's the vacation?" Sara's feminine lilt and pretty blond features belied a bulldog tenacity that matched that of any male agent, something that had stunned more than one suspect into confusion and an easier arrest.

"It's hardly that." He quickly filled her in on the details of the e-mails and Jerry's report. "I need you to take another look at some of the older cases I was on in the Dallas area. The department has been checking, but I'd like you to zero in on anyone who has served time and was released since this past March. I think the actual arrest may go back much farther than we thought. And look for cases where there might have been brothers involved, or other close relatives. I have a feeling this involves revenge."

"Revenge for what?"

"Maybe this is someone I caught and sent to jail, who's been angry about it ever since. Or someone avenging family honor or restoring a gang's reputation after we raided the headquarters. Why else would anyone spend so much time sending threatening notes and e-mails? This guy is hoping to scare me before he finally strikes. He wants someone else to suffer like he has, I think."

"Why didn't you call me sooner?" Sara said quietly. "We haven't heard from you since the end of May."

"Back in Dallas, this guy tracked me every time I moved. I figured it was safer to just stay out of sight."

She fell silent. "You can trust me, Zach."

"I know. But I've got a three-year-old girl who's a target. If there was a tap, or someone on the inside who overheard...I just needed to cover every possibility."

"You think this guy is close by?"

"I believe he is."

"Have you talked to the sheriff out there?"

Zach moved to the left and watched Katie playing sock tug-of-war with Buffy. She released her grip on the sock, then giggled as the pup rolled over and pedaled at its prey with all four feet in the air.

"Zach?"

"No...not yet. Just get me that information as soon as you can, okay? If you come across any suspects matching the description of this guy, send some photos via e-mail attachment."

"You be careful. Say the word, and I'll be up there on the first flight. Better yet, maybe you should come back to Dallas."

"In Dallas he'd be one of a million faces. Out here, it's much harder for a stranger to hide. I need to figure out who this guy is, and what he looks like, before I risk being in large crowds of strangers with Katie."

Zach cradled the receiver and stepped out onto the front porch. The Glock 27 at his ankle was a reassuring presence; the boisterous peacock and territorial

geese a measure of insurance against unseen trespass-
ers. With the gradual healing of his shoulder, wrist
and ribs, he'd regained most of his accuracy and a
good share of his strength.

But with every passing hour, he felt as though the
walls of this house and the surrounding hills were
closing in on him. As if he could nearly explode with
the stress of being here, away from the action, the
adrenaline and split-second decisions that had made
his life exciting for the past ten years.

But that wasn't it. Not really.

It was the certified letter from Janet's father that
arrived today.

My wife and I appreciate your care of Katie during this difficult time. We have, however, con-
sulted legal advisors, and plan to remove Katie
to the care and custody of her Aunt Diane, our
youngest daughter. She's happily married, and
can provide the kind of family environment Katie
has lacked.

Though we were estranged from our daughter
Janet over the last few years, we feel it's our duty
to secure a stable future for her child.

Despite his earlier resolutions, Zach's first reaction
to such finality was a fierce desire to fight for custody.
His second was the hardest he'd ever had to face.
Whatever he wanted, no matter how painful it was,
he knew he had to think of Katie first.

Tonight he would contact Jerry about a background

check on Diane, and ask some of his other friends to start checking into her life as well. If she was warm and loving, with a stable family home, maybe Katie would be better off with her.

Even if Zach's heart lay shredded and bleeding on the ground.

ZACH PACED the narrow confines of the little house. He'd made supper and cleared the dishes away. Then he left a message on Jerry's answering machine about investigating Katie's Aunt Diane.

Katie, scrubbed and fresh from her bath, now sat in the midst of her toys and looked up at him with hopeful eyes. These moments with her were precious, but right now he couldn't dispel an unaccountable sense of foreboding.

"Stories?" she begged.

He glanced at the clock on the kitchen wall. Seven o'clock. The Hathaways should be inside by now, shouldn't they? He'd called fifteen minutes ago. Five minutes ago. No one answered.

There were a lot of strangers who passed through Fossil Hill, because National Forest lands and the incredibly beautiful Rockies were less than forty miles to the west. Still Molly's offhand comment about a stranger stopping by for directions had bothered Zach ever since. What were the chances, given the fact that someone had been hanging around town asking questions, that the guy at the ranch had been El Cazador?

He smiled down at Katie. "First, let's take a little

drive and wish Molly and Alex good-night, okay?"
And while you're with them, Dana and I need to talk.

Katie had already gathered an impossibly heavy load of picture books for her bedtime stories, and now stood in the middle of the living room with most of them slithering out of her grasp. "Can Buffy come?"

Buffy, her rounded puppy tummy full, lay upside down and fast asleep in a pile of shoes that she'd fetched from the closets. "She looks pretty tired, honey."

"Please? She likes the car." Katie appeared pretty tired herself, and now her lower lip trembled. The books all hit the floor. "She's scared by herself."

"I'll get the carrier, then. Can you find your shoes?"

"Wif my *jammas?*"

At her abrupt, wide-eyed look of delight at something so silly, he spun back on his heel and scooped her up into his arms.

Her damp blond curls smelled of daisies, her dewy skin felt silky—like a fresh, ripe peach. The softness of her, her fragile weight, made him feel as if he could take on the world just to keep her safe and happy and secure.

A wrenching loneliness swept through him as he remembered that he wouldn't be there every day.

What would she look like in six months, a year? Would he be able to see her as often as he liked? Would she even remember him a year from now? What would she dream of? Talk about?

Already she'd begun to talk more. Whether it had

been emotional trauma or a lack of enough stimulation, she'd had so little to say at first. And now she strung maybe six or seven words together in a sentence, her eyes alight with curiosity and excitement over the toys and animals around her.

And she'd started returning his bedtime hugs and kisses with shy efforts of her own. That first wet little kiss, planted haphazardly on his cheek, had nearly made his heart burst.

When she started wiggling, he shook off his thoughts and gave her nose a playful tweak. "You want down, huh?" he growled. "I...don't *think* so!"

Giggling, she wiggled her chubby fingers along his neck and he laughed, pretending that her tickles were unbearable.

"Now!"

"Nope! I think I'll just hold you forever and ever."

"Even when I sleep?" She pulled back and studied his face.

He'd carried her into the house a few times when she'd been fast asleep, the totally relaxed weight of her like a sack of flour at his shoulder, her cheek warm and soft against his neck. That complete child-like trust had taken hold of his heart and never let go. "Even then," he whispered.

"Always?"

It would end all too soon. He gently put her down and turned away, suddenly needing distance. "In my heart, Katie. Always in my heart."

CHAPTER FIFTEEN

THE ENGINE OF Dana's truck was running when Zach pulled his Blazer to a stop next to her clinic. Before he'd even gotten Katie out of her car seat, the door of the clinic banged shut and he looked up to see Dana fly to the back of her truck, a box of supplies in her arms.

"What's the rush?" he called out as he unbuckled Katie and lifted her to the ground.

Busy stowing away the supplies, she didn't turn around. "A mare with lacerations, over in Bixby."

Zach strolled over to her side, trying to curb his impatience. "That must be almost an hour from here. There isn't a vet closer?"

"There is, but he's on vacation, and there aren't that many of us out in ranch country." Slamming the lid of the compartment shut, she opened the neighboring compartment and peered inside, then closed it as well and started toward the driver's side door. "All set."

"Is it even cost-effective for you to go?"

She paused, one hand on the door handle to give him a look of disbelief. "These people have a horse bleeding heavily. I can't just say, 'Oh, dear, it's a long drive.' And at any rate, the farm-call rates do vary by mileage. The expense is covered.''

''Have you been there before?''

''Not this again. Really, Forrester, you need to find a new hobby. Worrying about my career is going to get you nowhere.''

''Weren't you supposed to let me know about late farm calls for unfamiliar clients?''

''And why is that? Has anything happened around this place? Have I been threatened? I've been on my own for three years now. I can take care of myself.''

''But what about the kids?'' he persisted. ''Is Ben here?''

''Of course he is.'' She opened the door of the truck and slid behind the wheel. ''And my mother is on her way, because Ben is going to Denver later this evening to stay with his youngest daughter for a few days. I'm not stupid.''

Zach moved ahead a step and held the door open. In her rush to treat an injured horse she probably wouldn't register half of what he said, but after this farm call he would lay everything out in detail.

''Do you mind?'' she said, running a hand through her bangs in exasperation. ''I appreciate your concern, but I need to hit the road.''

''Let me go with you.''

''That really isn't necessary.''

''Swing up by your house so I can drop off Katie with your kids. Ben needs to stay in the house with them, and they need to lock the doors while you're gone.''

"But..." She eyed him closely, then sighed. "Okay, but let's make this fast, all right?"

At the house, Zach brought Katie inside and talked to Alex and Molly, then he jogged to Ben's cabin and rapped sharply on the door.

The old man appeared after several seconds, one loop of suspender hanging down to his knees and a disgruntled expression on his face. He seemed unimpressed by Zach's warning.

"That's what we got ol' Gabe for. Somebody comes, he barks."

"Unless someone shoots him."

"Now who would go and shoot an old dog? This ain't some big city with crazy people in the news every day."

Zach stifled a curse. "Then think about the problem if one of *those* people came out here wanting to make trouble. Do you have a rifle handy?"

The old man looked affronted. "Does a horse have teeth? Course I do."

"Then load it, and go up to the house and stay with the kids. I don't think there'll be any problem, but I want to be sure. And don't let anyone except Vivian through that front door."

Muttering to himself, Ben wheeled away. He reappeared in a moment with an old Winchester rifle and a box of ammunition.

From over in the driveway came the impatient sound of a truck's horn.

"Don't hesitate to call 911 if you see anything." Zach started for the truck. "Got it?"

"Won't nothing happen here." Ben strode toward the house, his rifle cradled in his arms. "But when you get back, there'd better be some explaining."

"Explaining about what?" Dana asked as Zach climbed into the truck. "I'm sort of curious myself."

Zach waited until they were out on the highway headed east, where the narrow, two-lane road rose and fell through gently rolling grassland that stretched as far as the eye could see.

"Remember why I let you and everyone else think Katie was my daughter?"

Dana shot a quick glance at him, her eyes filled with alarm. "You said that your sister was afraid of someone, and wanted you to keep Katie safe. Have you heard something else?"

Once and for all, he wished he could tell her everything, so someday there might be a chance she'd understand, and forgive the fact that he hadn't revealed the truth earlier. But he couldn't explain his connection to the DEA. Not yet. After years of undercover work, he knew that the less he revealed, the more effective he could be. "The man she feared is now after Katie and me. He calls himself El Cazador. I don't know his real name."

Stepping on the brakes, she pulled over to the side of the road and faced him. "Then why on earth is he after *you?*"

"A past business deal, maybe. Or maybe he figures I know something that could hurt him."

Dana drew in a sharp breath. "Have you told the sheriff?"

She looked so earnest, so filled with trust that the system would provide complete protection, that he wanted to pull her into his arms and protect that innocence. "No. El Cazador said if he saw the law being called in, he would target Katie, and I didn't want to take that risk. Now…maybe it's better if she and I leave the area."

Dana stilled. "What?"

"Maybe the guy will try to follow me, and then I can figure out who he is."

"But—"

"I can't put you all at risk any longer."

He reached for her then, cupping the back of her head and leaning toward her until he could lower his mouth to hers for a swift, hard kiss, perhaps the last one he'd ever have. He felt his heart clench, then slowly rip in two even as he strove for the right note of nonchalance. "We both knew this was just a temporary stay, right? It's been fun, but life goes on."

At her sharply indrawn breath and the shock in her eyes, he knew his breezy dismissal recalled the last time he'd left Fossil Hill, and that this was the last chance he'd ever have with her.

"You're right, of course," she said coolly, drawing back. "It's always best to just run."

He winced at the look of naked pain in her eyes, but he'd done the right thing. It was best to make a clean break. To leave, and keep her safe. Even after he caught El Cazador, who knew if someone else from the past might appear someday, as intent as El Cazador for revenge? Would she be in danger then?

She would never know how much this moment hurt him.

Without another word, she shifted the truck into drive, then eased back onto the highway.

The miles sped past in a blur of barren grassland. At the top of a low hill she slowed, bit her lower lip and then pulled to the side. When she rolled down her window, the pungent, peppery scent of sagebrush rushed in on the cool evening air.

"This doesn't look right," she muttered, picking up the directions she'd written in a spiral notebook. "We've gone thirty-eight miles east of Banner Creek Road. This says we should have hit a gravel intersection three miles ago. Allowing for reasonable error, we should have seen it long before now."

"Do you have the phone number?"

She gave a short laugh. "Wouldn't do much good. The cellular reception way out here is poor, and I haven't seen a ranch for the past half hour. There's no way to call."

Opening her door, she stepped out of the truck and moved to the front bumper to scan the terrain farther east. Zach grabbed the notebook and joined her. "Your notes say that the place was to be another twenty miles north of that turn."

"And I don't see a sign of any roads up ahead." She shook her head slowly. "I don't come this way very often, and I just don't remember."

Uneasiness hummed through Zach's veins. "Was it a man or woman who called?"

"I didn't take the call. Francie did."

"Let's head back."

"We should go another few miles, to be sure," Dana said, glancing at her watch. "What if that road is just over the next hill?"

"Then those people will call again. In the meantime, we can't call your place from out here, and I think we need to get back. Now."

Her eyes widened. *"My God."*

"Is Ben pretty good with that rifle?"

"Only if he's got his glasses on."

Damn. "We're leaving right now."

Dana pivoted toward the driver's side of the truck, but Zach caught her arm. "I'll drive."

"Hey! I'm perfectly capable—"

He propelled her toward the passenger side. "Shut up, and get in."

The second their seat belts were fastened, he threw the truck into gear for a three-point reverse of direction, then he gunned the motor. By the next rise the speedometer had hit eighty-five and Dana had braced a hand against the dashboard.

Her stomach lurched as he took a curve in a squealing, controlled skid. "Are you *crazy?*"

"No, I'm in a hurry." He shot a glance up at the rearview mirror, then riveted his gaze on the road ahead. "I had an uneasy feeling about this. Figured I'd better go with you just in case. But maybe you weren't the target after all."

"Target?" An image of Molly, Alex and little Katie flashed through her thoughts. They were at home, in her kitchen. Eating ice cream and probably driving

poor Ben to distraction with their chatter. *Dear God, let them be doing exactly that.* ''W-why would anyone harm them, Zach?'' Her voice rose in panic that she couldn't control.

A muscle jerked along the lean plane of his jaw. ''I could be wrong, but I can't take that chance.''

''Who are you, really? What's going on here? *Tell me!*''

As they rounded a curve, the truck rocked deeply to one side. From the vet box in back came the sound of breaking glass. Zach didn't spare her a glance. ''Later.''

Twelve miles east of the Rocking H, on a long stretch of straight highway, the speedometer crept up to ninety. Dana closed her eyes and leaned over, willing away the nausea rising in her throat as she thought about old Ben and the children. *Please let everything be okay. Please, please, please let everything be okay.*

At the sound of an approaching siren, she sat bolt upright. Maybe a quarter mile ahead, the light bar of an oncoming squad car flashed dizzying streaks of crimson across the darkened landscape. The car slowed, pulled to a stop, its lights still flashing.

Maybe he's coming to find me. Please don't let it be bad news!

Zach eased off the accelerator and struck the steering wheel with the palm of one hand, then slowed to a stop on the shoulder of the highway next to the patrol car. ''I don't need this now,'' he muttered. ''Not here and now!''

The deputy—Carl Robinson again—stepped out of

his car and slammed the door shut. His face was a dark, angry mask.

"What the hell are you doing with a man like this, Dana?" he growled.

Dana unbuckled her seat belt and leaned over to see him better. "We've got to get back to the ranch."

"Not with this guy, you won't." Carl drew his semiautomatic and motioned for Zach to step out of the car. "Now I can haul your ass in for more than just arson, Forrester," he growled. "Get out of that truck, and keep your hands where I can see them."

Zach stilled, his hands on the steering wheel.

"She's right, Deputy. We've got to get back. There's someone who—"

"Now." Carl stepped forward and reached for the door handle.

"Sorry, Officer. It has to be later." Zach threw the truck into gear and floored the accelerator.

"Zach!" Dana gripped the door handle and the edge of the seat as he rapidly shifted gears and sped away. *As if he were no stranger to escaping the law.*

Behind them, a nightmare of flashing lights and the earsplitting wail of the siren rushed closer. Came within yards of the truck's bumper.

The patrol car swung wide, as if planning to pass or force them to the shoulder.

Zach jerked the steering wheel to the left. From behind them came the squeal of brakes as the cruiser fishtailed, caught the edge of the asphalt, spun around and ended up skidding into the ditch.

"My God, Zach, what are you doing?"

"He wasn't talking about a speeding ticket back there. What he *thinks* he knows could have come from only one source—someone who wanted me out of the way. I just hope we can get back to your place in time."

CHAPTER SIXTEEN

INTENTLY SEARCHING the shadows, Zach drove around the clinic, then past the barns and house. Apparently satisfied, he swung the truck back to the front of the house, slammed on the brakes and hit the ground running.

Dana followed, her heart in her throat. There were no unexpected vehicles here. Her mother's car was under the old ash tree, where she always parked. Which surely meant everything was okay—*didn't it?*

The sound of hysterical crying burst into the night air as Zach yanked the front door. Molly brushed past him and flew into Dana's arms, nearly knocking her off her feet.

"Mom! They're gone," she cried, burying her face against Dana's shoulder. "And Ben—he's bad, really bad." Sobs shook through Molly as she held on tight, her cheeks wet with tears. "What if he dies, Mom? And what if that guy k-kills Alex and Katie?"

Horror avalanched through Dana. She pulled away and grabbed Molly's shoulders. "What are you talking about? What guy? Who is gone?"

"Y-you weren't here, Mom. Why weren't you here?" The heartbroken accusation came on great, gulping sobs. "He came right through the window. There was glass everywhere, and h-he went after Ben, and Katie was screaming, and he said aw-awful things. Alex and Katie are gone!"

Her heart lodged in her throat, Dana grabbed Molly's hand and started to run, dragging her along. "Come on, Molly. Hurry!"

At the porch steps, Molly balked. "Th-there's blood. It's everywhere. Oh, Mom! I got so scared—I heard arguing through the floor vent in my room. A-and gunshots—"

Dana kept moving, pulling Molly along despite her resistance. "Where's Grandma?"

"She's with Ben, an' she's scared, too. She got here just before you."

Wrapping an arm tightly around her daughter's shoulders, Dana strode up the steps. "I don't want you out here alone, sweetheart. "

"But—"

A siren wailed in the distance.

"Did you call 911?"

"The ph-phone wouldn't work. I've been hoping and hoping you'd come back."

So that siren would only be the deputy. Her mind racing, Dana grabbed the cell phone from her shirt pocket and rapidly dialed for an ambulance as she crossed the porch and hurried inside the kitchen.

Molly hadn't been far wrong.

Zach had dropped to one knee by Ben's head to take his pulse. The old man lay in a pool of blood, one arm outstretched and his face ashen. Smears of blood covered the counter, the front of the cabinets.

Her hands bathed in his blood and her face streaked with tears, Vivian knelt next to him holding a crimson-stained kitchen towel at his wounded side.

Zach rose. "His pulse is weak but fairly steady. All of you stay here. I'm going to search the house."

"Thank God you're here," Vivian whispered as Zach disappeared into the living room. "Is help on the way?"

Nodding, Dana dropped to her knees, waves of cold fear turning her blood to ice water as images of Alex and Katie rushed through her. "Has he talked to you? Do you know what happened? What about the kids?"

Vivian's lower lip trembled, and fresh tears welled in her eyes. "I—I don't know. I got here a couple minutes ago. I—I should have been here sooner, but the library meeting ran longer than I thought, and I had to get gasoline, and—"

"Mom, that doesn't *matter*. What about Alex and Katie?"

Zach strode into the room, his face grim. "The kids aren't here, anywhere. There are signs of struggle in the living room, and some blood on the floor."

Blood? Could Alex have struggled with the intruder? Was he *hurt?* A thousand images crashed through Dana's thoughts—of her son's terror, of the pain he could be in right now. Or worse.

"Don't touch anything in here," Zach ordered. "The investigators need to search for latent prints."

A vehicle skidded to a halt on the gravel outside. A car door slammed.

Zach went to Molly and took her face gently in his hands. "You've been a brave girl, honey. Now you need to tell us everything—everything you saw or heard. The other kids are depending on you, sweetheart."

"I—I heard men shouting. Ben, and someone else. I couldn't hear all they said, except the other guy said h-he—"

The front door burst open, and Carl Robinson strode inside, his face mottled with fury and his gun drawn. "Step away from that girl, Forrester. Make one wrong move and you're a dead man. And that's a promise."

Molly screamed in terror and threw her arms around Zach's waist.

Dana, stunned speechless, stared at the deputy, then Zach.

"You don't know what's going on here, Officer," Zach growled.

"And you sure as hell aren't the guy I'd ask," Robinson snapped. "Molly, be a good girl and go to your grandma. *Now.*"

She hesitated.

"Go on, Molly, it's okay," Zach said. "No one here is going to get hurt."

She wavered, then stepped away, her gaze darting between the raised gun and Zach.

"We need assistance, Carl," Dana said sharply, "not a gun held on the one man trying to help. Someone broke in here. He's got Alex and Katie, and Ben is badly hurt.''

The deputy ignored her. "Against the wall, Forrester—arms and legs spread." When Zach didn't move, he cocked the hammer. "Now."

"Didn't you hear her?" Vivian snapped. "There isn't time for this nonsense. The kids are in trouble!"

Carl quickly patted down Zach's sides and the pockets of his jeans, then handcuffed his hands behind his back. "The promise stands. One mistake and you won't be here to stand trial, got it?"

"My ID is back at the—"

"Yeah, right. I know what you are. *Trouble.* Now *shut up.*" Carl backed away, keeping one eye on Zach. "I called for backup before I came in. We'll have this bastard out of here in a few minutes. How's Ben doing?"

"He's been shot. Lost a lot of blood." Hot tears welled up in her eyes as Dana looked up from unbuttoning Ben's shirt. "I've been trying to talk to him, but he hasn't answered."

Vivian glared at Carl. "I don't know why you cuffed Zach—he wasn't even here when this happened. You're wasting time while two children are in danger!"

The sounds of distant sirens came through the open front door as Carl snorted. "Both of you have been led down the primrose path by this jerk a second time. Don't you wonder why this guy is here? What kind of man he really is?"

Dana stared at Zach in numb disbelief, Carl's words

coming at her through a great vacuum. Why this, why now? What mattered was seeing Alex and Katie walk through the door right now and fall into her arms. Fear rolled through her in waves, until her knees felt ready to buckle. *Please God, keep them safe.*

"Dana, Ben is moving!" Vivian cried. She cradled the old man's head with one hand. "Ben, can you hear me?"

His eyes fluttered, then opened partway as he gave a wheezy gasp. His voice was nearly too weak to hear.

"K-Katie knew that guy," he whispered. "When she saw him she screamed, then he slammed her against the wall. Told her to shut up." He coughed, and his body spasmed as if in deep pain. Cold sweat beaded his forehead. "I tried…to stop him…"

The deputy hunkered down nearby. "What did he look like? Did you see his car? Any idea of where he was headed?"

"Wiry guy. Dark…" Ben's eyes fluttered shut. After a long pause, he coughed again. "Alex…went after him." His head lolled to one side.

Cold fear gripped Dana's heart. "Oh, Ben." She leaned over him to feel for a carotid pulse. Thready, but still beating. "Why doesn't that ambulance get here? We've got to go after Alex!"

"Not you. *Me*," Zach said. "I—"

The deputy rose, pivoted and, in one swift motion, swung his elbow into Zach's midsection. He smiled with satisfaction as Zach doubled over, gasping for breath. "This *friend* of yours hasn't changed over the years, Dana. He's been a busy guy, from what I hear.''

"What are you talking about? He sells computer software, for heaven's sake."

"Really? The young gal I talked to at the company had never heard of him. And I also found out that he goes by more than one name."

"You're crazy!" she retorted.

"Am I? Ask him who Tony DiMarco is."

Zach drew in a sharp breath.

"Ask him about his business, Dana. Then ask him where those kids are. Maybe he even set this whole damn thing up, planning to demand money for their return."

"Zach?" Dana stared at him, frozen.

Indecision crossed his face, then he set his jaw. "It's…not what he thinks."

The deputy slashed the air with the side of his hand. "He's lying. Your buddy here has a rap sheet a mile long—for possession, for dealing…even attempted murder. If someone is coming after him, then your son and that little girl are in the hands of another drug dealer or some addict crazy enough to track him clear out here."

VIVIAN FOLLOWED the ambulance to the hospital to stay with Ben. Her mind numb, her heart racing, Dana paced as two deputies, the sheriff and some sort of investigator milled around the house, looking for evidence, taking blood samples from a number of sites.

She wanted to race out the door and search for

Alex, but where would she go? Which direction? Was he still in the area? Still in Colorado? *Was he still alive?*

She'd tried to hold back her tears for Molly's sake, tried to be brave. Now she was strung so tight that she felt as if she could break at any moment. Her hand trembling, she held back the kitchen window curtain and peered out into the darkness for the thousandth time, imagining that every flicker in the shadows was someone bringing Alex and Katie home.

Some of the men had fanned out into the yard with flashlights an hour earlier, and now all she could see were beams of light swinging wide through the darkness.

One deputy had hustled Zach out the door and taken him back to town as soon as they all arrived. Had he—or his enemies—anything to do with this?

"Do you think Alex is all right?" Molly whispered. Her arms wrapped tightly around her waist and her face white as snow, she hadn't stirred from her kitchen chair. "If I'd only come downstairs, maybe I could have done something. Stopped that guy, or helped Alex and Katie, or…" Her voice trailed away.

Dana pulled a chair next to hers and sat down, then embraced her…even as she ached to be holding Alex, and Katie as well. "There's nothing you could have done. *Nothing.* No child is a match for a man, much less one who has a gun. Understand? You did the right thing to stay where you were. Just think how you saved Ben, right? If you hadn't stopped that bleeding before Grandma came, he might have died."

Molly sniffled. "I close my eyes and all I see is blood, and I hear Katie screaming...and Alex yelling."

Me, too, honey. With every heartbeat. "I know, sweetheart."

"A-and I don't understand about Zach. How could he be like that? He loves Katie so much, and is so nice to the puppy. How could he be so bad?"

"We don't know the truth yet," Dana said slowly, choosing her words with care. The deputy had seemed so certain.

Whatever the truth, one fact remained. Alex was missing, and if Zach Forrester hadn't come to town, none of this would have happened. For that, she could never forgive him.

The phone rang.

Molly gave a startled cry. "Maybe they found Alex!" She raced for the phone and listened, the sudden joy on her face fading. She held the receiver out to Dana. "It's Grandma."

"We're at the community hospital," Vivian said as soon as Dana picked up the phone. "They were afraid to risk transferring him, so they took Ben into surgery right away. He's still in recovery and so far he's stable." Vivian's voice was weary, anxious. "No one will tell me anything, and I've called the sheriff's office three times. Have you heard anything?"

"Nothing." The sick feeling in the pit of Dana's stomach grew. "Nothing at all."

"And Zach?"

"No word, but Carl sure seemed certain of his facts."

Vivian fell silent.

Dana knew she was thinking back over the years to when she'd railed endlessly about his background, his family and his dim future for months after Zach had disappeared. The entire topic became such an obsession that Dana had ultimately changed plans and decided on a college farther away than she'd planned. She steeled herself against her mother's inevitable diatribe.

"Maybe..." Vivian hesitated. "There's more to this than we know."

Astonished, Dana paced to the windows and back again before finding her voice. "What do you mean?"

A heavy sigh came through the receiver. "Just that sometimes we look for all the wrong things. Hold on—" After a moment, she came back on the line. "The nurses say I can go in to see Ben now. I'll call you again in a few minutes."

"What is it, Mom? Is Ben okay?" Molly's voice trembled.

"He's in recovery now. Grandma will call after she sees him."

One of the deputies walked in the door just as Dana hung up. "We've just received a call on the radio. I'm supposed to take you and your daughter to the local sheriff's office, ma'am. Right away."

Fear sliced right through Dana's heart. "Alex? Is it—is it bad news? You've got to tell me right now. Don't make me wait."

. "I'm sorry, Doc. I tried to get more information, but the dispatcher refused to say anything more on the radio. All I know is that they want you there immediately."

FOR MOLLY'S SAKE, Dana held back her tears on the endless trip into town.

From inside the cruiser, the screaming siren and flashing lights faded into nothing as she held Molly close. A single litany of prayers filled the cotton batting of her thoughts. *Please, God, let this be good news. Please, God…*

When they pulled up at the sheriff's office she sat numbly in the back seat, barely aware of the deputy's extended hand. "Come with me, Doc. We need to go inside."

If I go inside, this might all be real.

"Come on, Mom," Molly sat up straighter and gripped Dana's hand. "We've got to go."

Feeling like an automaton, as if every slow, hydraulic movement came from an outside force, Dana finally climbed out of the car and followed the deputy inside the small building barely the size of a two-stall garage. She'd been there once before to dispute a parking ticket, and remembered the small reception area, with an office and a single holding cell in the back.

From the entryway she could see that the barred door of the cell was open. "What? Where is—"

"In here, ma'am," the deputy said as he opened

the door to the office and ushered Molly and her mother inside. "The deputy will explain."

Dazed, fear clogging her lungs, she held Molly close and stepped through the door.

Robinson sat behind his desk and averted his eyes as she walked in. A tall, imposing blond man she'd never seen before, dressed city-casual in knife-pleated khakis and a black oxford shirt, stood next to him, with his arms folded across his chest.

Zach, his handcuffs gone, stood at the other side of the desk loading cartridges into a gun clip with calm precision.

He seemed like a complete stranger when he glanced up at her with a grim smile and an expression of steely determination in his eyes. He radiated the absolute confidence of a man in charge who would let nothing stand in his way.

"What's going on here?" She demanded. "What have you heard about my son?"

"This is DEA Special Agent Mike Haley," Zach said, nodding toward the stranger. "He came in to assist. There are a number of other agents on the way."

"What about my *son?*" she demanded, her voice rising.

Haley cleared his throat. "When Robinson went out to Zach's place to collect Zach's identification, there was a message on the answering machine. This El Cazador guy says he has both children."

"Where are they? *Tell me.*"

"Apparently Alex tried to save Katie, and the guy

nabbed him, too. Both of them were put on the
phone—just for a few words. He wants to deal.''

Relief flooded through her. ''Money? How much
does he want? I'll get whatever it takes.''

''It's a little more complex than that.'' The agent
shifted his attention to Zach. ''Do you still want a few
minutes alone?''

Zach gave a single nod, then waited as Robinson
and Haley left. ''Do you mind if I talk to your mom
alone for a minute, Molly? We won't be long.''

Molly shot a fearful look at Dana. ''I want to know
about Alex, Mom. Please!''

''He's okay, honey. They heard him talk on the
phone, remember?''

''But—''

''I'll come and get you in a minute. It's okay.'' She
waited until Molly closed the door, then turned to
Zach. ''What's going on here?''

He'd seemed to be in complete control, but now his
face took on a ravaged expression. ''I'm sorry for all
of this, Dana. You've got to believe that, if nothing
else.''

''Who *are* you? What is this?''

He reached into his back pocket and flipped open
a wallet-size case. Inside were a gleaming gold badge
and official-looking cards on both sides. ''After I left
here I drifted awhile, then finished a degree in criminal justice and became a Special Agent for the
DEA.''

She stared back at the man she thought she knew.

The man who worked as a sales rep for a computer company. A man she'd slept with. Loved. And all of it had been based on lies. "So…"

"I do a lot of undercover work, Dana. Over the years I've been involved in too many cases to count. High profile, often dangerous…dealing with people you'd never want to meet."

"And you led one to Fossil Hill?" she asked in disbelief. "To my *children?*"

"Not intentionally. I needed a safe place for Katie while I was on medical leave. I never thought this guy would be able to follow us."

She could see his pain. Understood that he'd never meant to bring harm to anyone by coming here. But it didn't matter. "You lied to me, Zach. I don't care if you're a Special Agent or the man in the moon, I can't ever forgive you for this. Because of you, my son is terrified, maybe injured." Her voice caught. "Or worse, I could lose him."

"I regret this more than I could ever say." He picked up a shoulder holster from the desk and slipped it into place. "I'll get him back for you. I promise."

"Forgive me if I feel some doubt, Forrester. Your credibility rating is pretty low in my book."

The other two men looked at her, then at Zach.

"Time to go," Zach said. "I don't want to be late."

"Got the wire?" Haley asked.

Zach nodded. "Pull into the pasture west of the house and hide your vehicle. Don't move any closer than you need to for reception. I don't want any mistakes out there.''

"You're sending him alone? Without any help?" Dana looked frantically between the two other men. "What if something goes wrong?"

"He has to go out to his house to wait for the next phone call," Haley said. "If that guy sees either of us, there's no telling what he might do."

"But what happens after the call? Won't Zach need a ransom, or something?" Uneasiness washed through her at the abrupt silence. When she saw Zach pick up a Kevlar vest, her heart fell. "What happens then?"

"The message said El Cazador will call my house at midnight to set up a meeting. Just with me. I'll put a bug on my phone when I get out there, and these guys will hear all the details about the location. I'm also wearing a wire. The only important thing is getting the kids back safely, Dana. No matter what it takes, I'll make sure that happens."

As he walked through to the front door of the building, her panic rose. "Let me go with you."

He stopped but didn't turn around. "No."

"It wouldn't look strange if I went along, at least that far. The guy already knows you and I are—were close. If something goes wrong, if anyone is hurt, I can help."

"And have you killed in the process? No."

"*Please.*"

He turned around, then, and gave Haley a pointed look. The agent stepped forward and took her arm.

"Let him go, ma'am. He's real experienced at this. If anyone can get those kids back, it's Zach."

She watched him stride out the door, then jerked her arm away from Haley's grip and went to the front window. Moments later the taillights of the Blazer disappeared down the street.

A premonition of danger swamped her—images of blood and death and the crying of children. Maybe Zach thought he could handle this alone, but he was wrong.

Her own vehicle was back at the ranch, so now she just needed to find a way to join him.

CHAPTER SEVENTEEN

"MOLLY AND I NEED to be at the hospital," Dana said after Zach left. "My mother is with Ben, but we should be there, too. Can one of you give us a ride?"

When Haley and Robinson exchanged uneasy glances, she added irritably, "You can't tell me that we're under arrest here, or anything. It's only a mile— I suppose we can walk."

"You understand that this whole situation could explode if anything goes wrong, don't you?" Haley said. "There was a clear message regarding outside interference of any kind."

"And we're supposed to sit here when you two leave? I'd like to be with Ben, if you don't mind." Dana nodded to Molly. "Let's go."

"Wait. Robinson, we've got a good two hours until we can take position. Run them out to the hospital, and see that they get inside safely."

The deputy gave a grudging nod and lumbered toward the front door. "I'll be back in ten minutes."

Outside, he waved Dana and Molly toward the back seat of his squad car without a word. When they were all inside and heading down Main Street, Dana leaned forward. "Just out of curiosity, what made you think Zach was a drug dealer?"

A dull red flush, visible even in the dim light of the instrument panel, crept up the back of his neck. "A tip."

"From whom?"

"Uh…that's confidential."

"From the guy who has Katie and Alex?" She didn't try to mask her incredulity. "And you *believed* him?"

"I never saw him. There was a note shoved under my door one morning that gave all those details. When I researched that DiMarco name, I came up with the background, just like the note said."

"But he's with the DEA. That would have been a *cover.*"

Robinson sighed. "On the good side, that alias gave the agents the tip they needed. Now they've figured out which undercover operation this El Cazador guy was involved in. They're even pretty sure about the guy's name—Vincent Alvarez. A rap sheet and photos of him just arrived by fax. No matter what happens here, he won't be on the streets long."

A chill slithered down Dana's spine. "Nothing will go wrong, Molly," she soothed, patting her daughter's hand. "We'll have Alex and Katie back in no time."

Robinson's gaze jerked up to the rearview mirror, and she knew he'd just caught his blunder.

"Of course you will," he said quickly. "There are more agents coming from Denver right now, plus all of us here. Those kids will be okay."

They pulled up at the hospital emergency entrance. An orderly lounging by the door stood up abruptly and started for the cruiser, but Robinson waved him off.

"I hope Ben is okay," the deputy called out as he watched Dana and Molly walk into the hospital.

Dana nodded and raised a hand in farewell without turning around. "Come on, Molly, we need to move along."

The hospital, with just twenty beds, wasn't much larger than a roadside motel. Dana headed for the first nurse she saw. "Where's Ben?"

The nurse, hurrying down the hall with an armload of linens, stopped and smiled. "Hi, Doc. He's in Room Fourteen. He's doing well, all things considered. Grumpy as ever."

At the door of Room Fourteen, Molly hung back. "Maybe I shouldn't go in," she murmured.

"He's okay, honey. They've cleaned him all up, and he's in a nice comfy bed."

Molly hesitantly followed, gave the bed a wary glance, then edged over to her grandmother's side.

Vivian gave her a big hug. "I'm so glad to see you two. Any news?"

"Nothing yet." Dana quickly summarized what had happened at the sheriff's office. "So now we just have to wait. This is so darn hard, Mom."

"Zach is a *Special Agent?*"

"Big surprise there, right? As if he wouldn't still be just as much of a liar as when he was a teenager." Dana stalked to the small window of the room, then back again. "The one positive thing is that they say he's good at what he does. If anyone can get the kids back in one piece, it's him.''

''But?''

''The bad thing is that none of this would have happened if he'd been more honest. Better yet, if he'd never even showed up in town.''

Vivian pursed her lips. ''So he had no good reason to keep his secrets, then.''

''Yes...no...it doesn't matter, Mom. Since when has he been truthful about anything?'' At Molly's wide-eyed expression, Dana took a deep breath. ''I'm sorry. I'm just too upset to even think straight. This waiting is driving me crazy.''

Vivian laid a gentle hand on Ben's brow, then reached for her purse on the bedside table. ''Should we go to the lounge? They've got some coffee down there. You can have a bite to eat.''

Molly brightened. ''I'm starved.''

Metal glinted from the pocket of the sweater Vivian had tossed over the back of her chair. *Car keys?* ''Um...you two go along. I don't think I could eat a bite.''

''I think you should. You look awful.'' Vivian gave Dana a worried head-to-toe glance. ''And you're a nervous wreck.''

''Everyone looks sick under these bright lights. I'll just stay here. With Ben.''

''But, Mom,'' Molly started. ''Don't you—''

''Go along,'' Dana said firmly. ''While you're gone, I'll call and leave a message on Francie's answering machine. She's out of town, and I don't want her to hear about all of this from someone on the street.''

EL CAZADOR—now Alvarez, apparently—had warned against any law enforcement officers in the area. With darkness as his cover and the perfect bait, he could take aim and kill Zach, then turn his gun on the children now able to identify him. Only a fool would risk a life sentence for kidnapping if he could easily eliminate the witnesses.

Dana wouldn't let that happen.

A mile before the lane to Zach's house, she cut the headlights and drove past by the light of the moon, uncertain about whether or not Mike Haley and the deputy were already hidden somewhere in the low hills surrounding Zach's house. She saw no sign of a car, but that could have been hidden, too.

She didn't turn the lights on until she hit the approach to her own driveway. The place seemed dark, eerie with everyone gone.

Driving past the clinic, she quickly searched the shadows. Watched for unexpected motion in the darkness.

At the house, her heart skipped a beat when something moved to the side of the car and rose up against the window.

Gabe. With a weak shudder of relief she opened the door and gave him a hug. ''I'm so glad you're here, old guy.''

Snapping her fingers at her side, she brought him

to heel and headed for the house, where she let him bound in ahead of her.

Frantic pawing and squealing from the cage in the corner greeted her as she turned on the lights. "Hey, little pup. Need to go outside? Maybe you two should stay locked in the yard while I'm gone."

She quickly retrieved her rifle and a box of cartridges from high in the back closet, then scooped up the puppy and took both dogs outside. At the edge of the yard, she closed the gate and locked it after she put the puppy down. "Sorry, Gabe. But you've got to baby-sit tonight, okay?"

The old dog's whines followed her to the barn, where she laid the rifle and cartridges on the top rail of the corral fence.

In the barn she flipped on the lights, grabbed a bridle and strode down the aisle to Blaze's stall. As she slid open the door, the gentle gelding lifted his head from the hay to give her a curious look.

"I know it's late, buddy, but this won't take long. I'm even going to let you head home on your own. How about that?"

After bridling him, she led him out the front door of the barn to the corral. She loaded the rifle and slid the box of remaining cartridges down the front of her shirt, where they were held securely by the belt at her waist. Then she climbed up several fence rails and stepped over onto his broad back.

He tossed his head and pivoted away, anxious at the change in routine, but she rested a hand against his neck until he calmed down. Then she retrieved the rifle and reined him toward the western pasture fence.

There was no livestock in this field—not until next month, when the cattle would be rotated to fresh pasture. At the gate she leaned down and unchained it, letting it swing wide-open. Then she urged Blaze into a lope.

Crickets chirped a never-ending symphony in the moonlight. Above, shadowy forms swooped through the night air after insects. Moonlight lit the way in tones of pewter and charcoal.

Anxious thoughts spun through her even as the rhythmic three-beat movement of the horse surged beneath her, his warm hide comforting as a favorite easy chair. The long grasses muffled the sound of his hooves against the earth until it seemed as if they were sailing over a soft and silver sea.

But somewhere out in the darkness Alex was afraid, maybe hurt. Katie was terrified. She urged Blaze on as her anxiety grew. *Please, God—help me do the right thing. And please keep Zach and the children safe.*

ZACH PACED through the nearly suffocating confines of the small house, willing the phone to ring. The tap was in place. He'd tested the hidden wire, then discarded his earpiece once Haley confirmed good reception from his position a half mile away.

Now they could only wait.

Had Alvarez spooked? Had he seen Haley pull up

at the sheriff's office, and guessed at the guy's reason for coming to town?

With luck, he hadn't. The lives of two children depended on it.

At a soft sound outside he drew his gun, then released the safety as he moved to the window of his darkened bedroom and pulled back the curtain a few inches.

Nothing moved out in the yard. His Blazer was parked at the end of the sidewalk, ready to roll.

All he needed was a destination, and the operation could begin.

Five minutes to midnight.

Four.

Reaching down, he checked for the tenth time the ankle holster and the Glock it held. The deputy had missed it in his excitement at finally having the chance to arrest him after all these years.

Zach hadn't had the heart to point it out back at the sheriff's office in front of the others.

Before he headed back to Dallas, though, he would need to have a talk with Robinson. The guy's strong-arm tactics were going to get him in deep trouble someday. And failure to find a hidden weapon could get him killed.

Two minutes after midnight.

Five minutes.

Six.

Zach swore, trying not to think about what had gone wrong. *He's got a slow watch. Forgot to check the clock.* "Call me, dammit," Zach muttered. "I'm here and ready. Pick up the damn phone and call."

When the phone did ring, he pounced on it like prey and gripped the receiver for another ring. Then he took a deep breath and lifted it. "Zach here."

The voice was soft, faintly accented. "Drive nine miles east. There's a dirt road leading up into the hills. Stop at three point five miles and get out of your car, nice and slow. One fast move and one of these kids dies, got it? Anyone else shows up, and they are both dead, and so are you." *Click.*

He'd been on a countless number of cases. Life and death could become a way of life, and over the years he'd become hardened to what he had to do.

But never had the lives of two young kids been on the line. Never his little niece Katie, with her trusting eyes and delighted laughter, and the way she smelled so sweet and innocent after her nightly bath.

Zach opened his eyes and realized he still held the receiver in his hand. He put it down, then spoke loud enough for the wire.

"Got it? Any sign of trouble, and the kids die. See if you can find another approach. Stay way, way out of sight. I don't want anyone on the scene unless there's gunfire, and then get there fast. Forget about me—just call for an ambulance and get to those kids." He repeated the directions, grabbed his car keys from the counter.

Then he stepped out into the night.

CHAPTER EIGHTEEN

ALVAREZ CHECKED HIS WATCH, then continued to scan the horizon below for any sign of approaching headlights.

He'd picked the perfect location. No one could approach from any direction without being seen, and he had a good view of the highway leading into Fossil Hill—at least three miles of it. If anyone followed Zach as a backup, they'd never think to cut their lights so far away.

The sound of renewed whimpering from the back seat of the car set his teeth on edge. He'd bound the kids and left them there as insurance in case things went wrong.

But the little girl's endless crying had been driving him crazy. Even with duct tape over her mouth, he could still hear her whine. The boy's coldly defiant expression made him nervous.

He was stuck with them until this was over. Once Forrester was dead, the brats could be disposed of and he could go home in peace with the honor he'd craved every last minute he'd spent in prison, thanks to Tony DiMarco. Maybe he'd changed his name to Forrester, but that hadn't kept him safe. Not with El Cazador on his trail.

With a short laugh over the nickname he'd given himself, Alvarez paced back and forth behind the car. He fingered the trigger of the semiautomatic in his hand, resenting the cold sweat that made the metal feel slippery. The sweat didn't mean he couldn't do this, dammit. His entire future depended on pulling the trigger with perfect aim.

And no one, especially not some two-bit traitor from Dallas, was going to rob him of all that awaited him when he returned.

He had all the account numbers. He had the right contacts. With his skills at management, the family operation would soon—

Tiny headlights appeared over the horizon. Coming slow. This would be Forrester, watching for his turn-off. Maybe, Alvarez thought with a smile, he was wondering if these moments would be his last. With luck, maybe he would even plead for his life.

The headlights crept onward, then turned onto the dirt road. Alvarez lost sight of the vehicle several times, as it traveled slowly over the gradually rising hills.

He released the safety on the gun in his hand and stepped behind the hood of his car.

The Blazer's lights blinded him for a moment as they crested the hill, then they swung away, and the vehicle came to a halt with the passenger side facing Alvarez. Zach turned off the lights.

Smart move, but it wouldn't save him.

The car door swung open and Zach stepped out,

leaving the door slightly ajar, just enough to cut the interior lights. Did he think he would be escaping?

"Come out where I can see you," Alvarez shouted.

Zach moved forward just far enough to be seen in front of the windshield, a gun extended in a two-fisted grip. "I want to see the kids. Prove to me that they're okay."

"I've got them here, in my car."

"Show me."

"You'll have to come here, Forrester."

Zach waited. And waited.

With a curse, Alvarez reached in the open back window of the car and ripped away the duct tape over the boy's mouth. The boy yelped in pain. "You tell him you two are okay, for now. You tell him any more, and you're gonna die right now."

"We're both here," the boy called out in a shaky voice. "But he's got a gun."

"You hear that? Come out here so we can talk. Let me see your hands in the air."

"Tell me what you want. Money? Weapons? A passport? I can help you. In two days you can be out of the country, free as a bird."

Alvarez took careful aim and squeezed the trigger. A sense of power sped through him as the front tire of the Blazer hissed.

Zach ducked back behind the Blazer. "Dammit!" He turned and looked over the countryside. "Let's talk, *now*. Meet me halfway."

Had there been a prearranged signal? Were there others hiding nearby? Alvarez swallowed. He pulled open the rear car door and reached inside, grabbed the girl and hauled her into his arms. "I've got her with me. Right here. Put your gun down and step out where I can see you, or she dies."

"You leave so much as a scratch on those kids, and you'll be dead before you can blink. Believe that even if you've never believed one blessed thing in your life."

"The gun, man. If you want this kid alive, put down your gun!"

Zach slowly put his gun on the hood of his SUV. Stepped cautiously away from the protection of his vehicle. "Let's talk about this, Alvarez."

"Help me? I watched you day and night, back in Dallas. You never made a move I didn't see." His voice rose, rising with the anger that boiled through his midsection. "Your sister ran from me twice. Hid her daughter. But now she's dead and the kid's gonna die, too. Who has the power, here? Not you."

"But *why?*"

The raw pain in Forrester's voice filled Alvarez with a rush of satisfaction. "Your sister thought she could keep me from finding you, and that was a stupid move. The kid? I'm not serving life because some brat can ID me in a lineup."

"Why did you want me in the first place? Hell, I don't even *know* you."

Alvarez gave a harsh laugh. "I had over ten years in the pen. Every last minute I spent figuring out how to pay you back. Remember that operation in West

Dallas? Everything was perfect until someone called in the Feds. And I think that traitor was *you*."

Zach edged forward. "Right now you're in a lot of trouble, but maybe I can help you," he wheedled. "We can both get out of here. Cross the border and live like kings."

"Because of you, I lost ten years of my life and my father and brother are dead. The only place you're going now is straight to hell."

Did Zach's arm *move?* Alvarez took fast aim, squeezed the trigger. The explosion ricocheted through the hills, echoing on and on. Kicking wildly, the brat in his arms struggled to escape his grasp despite the tape that bound her wrists and ankles. He thrust her aside and lifted the gun again with both hands.

Forrester staggered. Rolled forward. Reached for something at his ankle.

Panic surged through Alvarez. His hands shook as he took aim again.

But something else moved at the periphery of his vision. In that endless heartbeat of time, he wavered between Zach and the new intruder.

"You're dead, Alvarez," Zach growled.

A split second later, the sharp crack of a rifle rang out.

Followed instantly by another explosion.

Alvarez stared at Zach as something heavy, so very heavy burned with molten heat through his chest.

Odd, how time seemed to stand still. He needed to

fire. Needed to finish Zach and those damned kids, and get in the car before it was too late.

The stars and the night sky swirled around him at dizzying, blinding speed.

And then the blackness fell.

IN MINUTES the hilltop swarmed with cars and men shouting orders. An ambulance arrived seconds later, though there would be no need for lights and sirens on the way back to down.

Despite the heavy bleeding from his upper arm, Zach shoved away medical help in his rush to get to Katie. He knelt next to her and held her tight, her face buried against his chest and his head bowed low over hers.

Ignoring his pain and the paramedic who hovered close, examining and then wrapping a tight bandage around his arm, he whispered, "I love you, Katie. You're safe now and forever, I promise."

Dana hugged Alex and asked him questions until he finally squirmed out of her arms, his face bright red.

"Mo-om," he said in a pained voice. "Those men are *watching*."

"I don't care. I love you so much that I don't ever want to let you go."

He almost looked relieved when an officer beckoned and started questioning Katie and him.

Still in a daze, Dana wandered back to the ambulance and watched from several yards away as they zipped up the body bag and lifted Alvarez onto the gurney. Zach broke away from hovering near Katie and joined her.

"I killed him," she whispered. "I—I took a man's life."

Zach hesitated, then curved an arm around her shoulder. "No. He did this himself—and if he hadn't died, he might have killed Katie and Alex."

"Time to go, sir," one of the paramedics urged. "We need you in the ER to take care of that wound. It looks as if the bone is involved, and that isn't good."

"In a minute." The bandaging on his arm and shoulder shone ghostly white in the moonlight. His face was ashen, but his voice was as firm and in control as ever. "I just want to know what the hell you were doing out here, Dana. Haley told you to stay in town. You could have been killed."

"My son was out here. And Katie. And…you. I knew what would happen, and I couldn't let you all die."

"I had the vest on. I was armed. The other men were on the way from the first sound of gunshot. You shouldn't have been here."

"But that bullet missed the vest," she retorted. "Maybe his next shot could have killed you, if I hadn't fired."

Zach gave a growl of frustration. "I *did* fire, Dana. One of us hit him, and it was probably me. How on earth did you get here?"

"I rode Blaze through the pasture between my place and yours. Then I crawled from the barn to your

SUV, climbed into the back seat and hid on the floor under a blanket." She gave him a half smile. "Luckily, your geese didn't see me."

The paramedic reappeared. "Come on, sir. Time to go."

"I'm not ready yet." Zach waved the man off and reached out to rest his hand against her cheek. "I'm sorry, Dana, for all of this."

She stilled, searching his face. The deep regret in his eyes told her there was more.

"I think this guy used my sister to find me, then killed her." The grief in his voice was palpable. "After he bombed my condo—"

"What?"

"He abducted Katie afterward. That's probably why he wanted her back, so she couldn't identify him to the police."

"Did you ever ask her?"

"Stone silence. It's as if she blocked out the entire experience." He gave a harsh laugh. "The poor kid went through all of this, yet she didn't remember a thing."

"Except maybe the night someone stopped at the ranch for directions? Molly said Katie cried at the sound of that guy's voice."

"I remember," Zach said heavily. "At the time, I thought she was just fearful of all strangers. Hell, she was even frightened when that perky waitress at the Pink Petticoat Inn got a little too close."

"Couldn't you have told the sheriff when this all started?"

"The guy warned me that if he saw any evidence of the authorities being called in, he'd escalate his efforts against Katie. Until I could identify him, how could I protect her?"

The urge to comfort him came from nowhere, catching her unaware. "You were willing to give your life for the children," she answered softly. "I—I know you didn't want any of this to happen. I can't ever thank you enough for saving my son."

"Sir?" The paramedic was back, and this time he'd brought another one with him. "You need to come with us. That arm needs attention."

Zach gave Dana a resigned shake of his head. "I'm not sure how long I'll be. Can you take Katie?"

"Of course. They'll probably airlift you to Denver for surgery. I'll change that tire while the officers finish talking to the kids, then I'll take Katie and your Blazer to my place. Whenever you're ready to come back, just call." She managed what she hoped would pass for a smile. "I suppose you'll be wanting to get back to Dallas now."

He studied her face, his eyes filled with sadness. "Yes. I guess so."

She watched him leave with the paramedics, then she headed back to where the sheriff and one of his female deputies were gently questioning the children.

Katie gave a cry when she saw Dana and rushed forward into her arms. "Oh, sweetie, it's all okay. You'll be home with Zach in no time, I promise."

But even as she comforted the weeping child, her heart weighed heavy as lead inside her chest.

After seeing the kind of danger Zach faced in his job, she knew how hard it would be to love a man like him and never know, when she kissed him good-bye in the morning, if he would come back to her alive at night.

How did the wives of agents and law enforcement officers handle the endless stress?

She'd already lost a husband and had shared the children's grief over the loss of their father. To bring them all into a relationship with high potential for another loss was unthinkable.

But he'll be leaving now, and he won't be back. It's for the best.

Exactly what she'd known since the day he arrived.

"I'LL BE GONE just a minute," Dana said in a low voice. "I'm locking the doors, and I don't want any-one getting out of this car, okay?"

In the back seat, Katie was fast asleep. Alex rolled his eyes. "We're under the brightest lights in town, Mom. Right outside the hospital."

"I don't care. I hate leaving you two out of my sight." Dana slipped out of the Blazer and tapped the door locker device on the key ring twice, to set the alarm, then she spoke to the security officer taking a smoke break by the rear entrance. "Keep an eye on my car, would you?"

Striding quietly down the hallway to Ben's room, she eased the door open and peered inside. Molly, sound asleep, had curled up in a chair over in the corner. Vivian gave a start and sat up straighter, blinking as she blearily patted the bedside table for her glasses.

"Sorry I'm so late, Mom," Dana whispered. "How is Ben doing?"

"Better. Where on earth have you been? What about the children?"

"It's a long story. Katie and Alex are outside."

"Oh, thank God," she cried, stumbling to her feet. Her eyes filled with tears. "Are they okay? What happened?"

Dana wrapped her arms around her mother for a long hug, then gave her an abbreviated explanation. "The children are shaken but fine. It could have turned out so differently."

"Molly was afraid you'd gone to help Zach, and she was terrified that you might be hurt."

"I did go. The only one who got hurt was Zach, but he'll be fine. Given his medical track record, I think the man needs to find a new line of work." Dana moved to Molly's chair. "Hey, sleepyhead. We need to get you home, okay? Time for bed."

Mumbling incoherently, Molly stumbled to her feet, her eyes half-open.

"I think I'd better hang on to you, or you're going to hit the floor."

Vivian rested her hand on Ben's arm, then rose stiffly to her feet. "I suppose it's okay to go. The nurses said he'd sleep for hours, yet."

"You need a good night's sleep too, Mom."

They both helped ease Molly into the back seat of the SUV next to Alex, where she almost immediately closed her eyes again. Suddenly her eyes flew open. "Alex? Katie?"

"Shh," Dana warned. "Katie's asleep. We can talk later."

Molly awkwardly gave Alex a hug. "I'm so glad you're back! What *happened?* Did that guy get you, too? Did you ambush him?"

Ducking his head to hide his reddened cheeks, Alex pulled away. "Later," he mumbled, gesturing toward Katie.

Vivian sat up in front. "You didn't tell me—is that awful man in custody?" she whispered as Dana eased the car out of its parking space.

"His real name was Alvarez, and he's dead." A knot of guilt coiled in Dana's stomach at the thought.

Once again, she saw herself lifting her rifle and taking rapid aim. She'd been so terrified for Zach and the kids. Would another split second have made the difference in her aim? Could she have stopped Alvarez with just a bullet wound, instead of sending him to the morgue?

Waves of guilt and regret washed through her over what she'd done. No matter how evil the man had been, she'd *killed* him. With sudden, horrible clarity, she knew she'd never be able to forget that moment, or forgive herself for what she had done.

Frowning, Vivian reached over and laid a hand on Dana's arm. "It must have been awful, dear. Did the kids see what happened?"

"I don't think so. It was dark. Katie was on the ground and Alex was tied up in the car."

"Those poor children. Poor, poor children."

"But it's over. Alvarez will never be able to threaten them again."

And now I'll have to live with the fact that I took someone's life.

"We owe Zach a lot, Dana." Vivian fluttered her hand in dismissal. "Oh, I know you figure none of this would have happened if he hadn't come back, but he still really came through for us."

Another surprise. "This is quite a switch, Mom. You had nothing good to say about him for years."

"People change." Vivian fell silent, pensively staring out the window as they drove the last few blocks to her duplex on Third Avenue. After Dana pulled to a stop, Vivian started to open the door, then paused. "If you could have anything in the world, what would it be?"

"After tonight, that would be my kids. Having them safe forever."

"For yourself, Dana. If you could do anything, be anything you chose."

Dana frowned. "There's no question. I've got the clinic to run, a ranch to keep afloat. Kids to raise."

"Think about it." Vivian gave her a sad smile. "Sometimes we aren't as trapped by our choices as we think we are."

"Trapped? I see it as taking responsibility. Following through. Being accountable. It's what adults do."

"And was my legacy to you, when I chose to stay here after your father died. It was a hard life when he was alive, and afterward?" Vivian looked down at her gnarled hands. "If I'd opted for joy, I might have taken a job I loved in a much larger town and given you a better childhood, instead of resenting my life every blessed day. Sometimes...that bitterness made me do things I regret even now."

Dana released her seat belt and slid over a few inches from behind the wheel to give her a hug. "I couldn't ask for anything to have changed. You were a great mom, honest."

"I'm not asking for thanks," Vivian insisted. "I see you working yourself to the bone, day after day after day. Pulled in a dozen different directions. Worrying about money. Dreams are a powerful thing, honey, but if we don't figure them out soon enough, it's too late."

Dreams? Who had time for that? Maybe when the kids were grown. When the clinic debt was clear. When the mortgage on the ranch was paid off. Maybe.

Dana waited at the curb for her mother to go safely inside. But suddenly Vivian turned on her heel and marched back to the car.

With a nod toward the children in the back seat, she motioned Dana out on the sidewalk. "Years ago, Zach never called or wrote you about why he left town so fast. I don't know why he didn't—God knows he must have been angry. And I—I've been afraid. Afraid he knew who was behind it. Afraid you'd never forgive me if you found out." She reached out and gripped Dana's hands. "I was *terrified* when he showed up in town again."

"What are you talking about?" Even as Dana said the words, a cold feeling spread through her.

Vivian's eyes welled up with tears. "Your dad and I married way too young, and we had a hard life. Not much money—scrimping to save every nickel. I wanted so much more for you, Dana—such a bright little thing you were, with so much promise. I—I was afraid you'd end up like me. And then that handsome, no-account boy came into town and you fell head over heels for him. I knew that..."

Realization hit Dana like a heavy blow to her heart. "It was *you*."

"His mother was just a barmaid...they drifted all over. What kind of life could he have given you? I just wanted him to leave town, before..."

Pulling her hands away, Dana jammed them in her pockets. *"What did you do?"*

Vivian lowered her head. "One of the deputies was a good friend of mine back in high school. I told him everything, and he said Zach was a born trouble-maker. He said he'd take care of it and no one would ever know. Zach and his mom were gone the next day."

Closing her eyes, Dana tried to imagine what she might have done if her own daughter were at risk, and hoped she would never have been so cruel.

"Honey?"

She felt her mother lay a tentative hand on her sleeve, then opened her eyes. "Zach recently told me that deputy got really rough with him, Mom. He was just a kid, and the guy said he and his mom would face trumped-up charges and jail time if they stayed. Zach figured no one would ever believe his side of the story."

"I never meant it to go that far." Vivian's voice broke. "God forgive me, I never wanted to hurt anyone."

"Until now, I thought maybe Zach's story was a fabrication. At least now I know the truth."

"If you think Zach isn't an honest man, you aren't as smart as I thought," Vivian said softly. "I thought I was protecting you, and now I see all the ways that I hurt you instead. If I could do it over again, I'd never interfere. Believe me, I'm so sorry."

WHEN THEY ARRIVED back at the ranch, Alex woke up Molly enough to take her up to her room, while Dana carried Katie into the guest room. The exhausted child barely stirred when Dana slipped off her shoes, socks and dirty coveralls.

"We'll give you a big bubble bath in the morning, sweetheart," Dana murmured after kissing Katie's forehead. "Right now, it's better that you just sleep."

In the kitchen, Dana glanced at the clock above the stove, then drew water for a pot of herbal tea. Nearly four o'clock in the morning, but her nerves still buzzed and her thoughts were still racing through the events of the night.

Alex appeared at the door. "I don't think I can sleep, either," he said, though there were dark shadows under his eyes.

Even in the subdued lighting of the single light

above the kitchen sink, the angry red marks over his mouth and on his wrists made Dana want to weep. "Want some hot cocoa? I've got the teakettle on, and there are some packets in the cupboard."

"Yeah. I'll make it." He brought out spoons and stoneware mugs for both of them, his motions tense and restless, then he wandered over to the window where he braced his hands on the sill and rested his forehead against the glass.

When the teakettle whistled and he didn't move, Dana smiled to herself and made the cocoa and the tea, then brought them to the table. "I think you're more tired than you thought, honey. Do you just want to go on up to bed?"

He stayed where he was. "I heard what Grandma said in the car, Mom. I just want you to know that I agree with you."

Startled, Dana looked up from the tea bag she'd unwrapped. "About what?"

"I've been giving you a lot of grief about wanting to leave this ranch, but I'm not going to do that anymore. There's way too much work here for just you and Ben, and I know Dad would have wanted us to keep the place. He always said he bought it hoping the Hathaways would stay here for generations."

His voice was flat and filled with determination that surprised her, and when he finally came to the table he no longer had that glint of teenage defiance in his eyes. Instead, there was just weary acceptance.

"But that's not want you want."

He bowed his head over his mug, stirring the cocoa

as if it took every bit of his concentration. "It's the right thing, Mom. I've screwed up everything so much. If I hadn't—" His voice caught, and his head bowed even lower.

"Honey, I can't think of one big mistake you've ever made. We…ah…won't count that solo trip to town in the pickup when you were thirteen."

She'd hoped for an answering grin, but he just stirred the cocoa, on and on and on. "Tell me what it is that you ever did that was so wrong."

Silence lengthened in the room until she was sure he'd never answer. But then he squared his shoulders and lifted his chin. "Tonight I screwed up again, big time. I tried to stop that—that Alvarez guy. I couldn't. I was gonna take his car keys so he couldn't leave, but he caught me. Zach and Katie could have been killed tonight because I failed."

"Oh, Alex." Dana reached across the table and rested her hand over his. "He was a vicious man. An *adult* who'd been in prison for terrible things. No one could ever expect a boy to best someone like that."

"I should have done something different. Something better." Alex pulled his hand away. "Just…like when Dad died."

"But you weren't even in the car with him."

"He wouldn't have left that night if I hadn't forgotten to give him Ben's message about the baling twine. We had to bale hay the next day, and because of me, he had to hurry into town before the store closed."

"It was an *accident.*"

"And he never would have been in it, if not for me," Alex said stubbornly. "You can't say it isn't true. And now, look at how hard it is here without him…and how much we m-miss him." Alex bowed his head.

When Dana saw the first tear hit the tabletop, she felt her own eyes burning for all her son had silently borne. *Maybe now you'll be able to heal, sweetheart.* She went to him and wrapped him in an embrace. "Your dad took a lot of last-minute trips to town. He was always forgetting one thing or another. Don't you remember? I think maybe he sometimes just liked an excuse to grab a cup of coffee with his buddies down at the feed mill."

Feeling Alex pull away, she held him a little tighter as she continued. "He took that trip a thousand times. He knew the road, and was a good driver. That accident was the fault of the truck driver who crossed the center line, not you. It could have happened on any other trip of his. No one has ever blamed you, and you can't blame yourself. He wouldn't want that, honey. You and Molly were the light of his life."

Alex hugged her back. "I'm s-sorry, mom."

"Even now you miss him terribly. *I know.* But promise you'll come and talk to me about this anytime you're feeling down, okay? You'll feel a lot better, and so will I."

Long after he'd gone up to bed, Dana sat holding her cup of tea and thought about the past. She wondered if she, too, had held on to it far too long. When her mother had spoken of dreams and making choices, she hadn't really understood. Until now.

But was it already too late?

CHAPTER NINETEEN

THE FOLLOWING MORNING, Deputy Robinson brought Vivian out to the ranch just as Francie and Tom returned from their trip to the horse sale in Denver. Dana met them all at the clinic door with a wiggling chocolate lab puppy in her arms.

With Tom in tow, Francie sailed in and thrust a sheaf of papers forward with a flourish. "We had a *wonderful* time," she gushed. "Tom was a fantastic help. Just look at the bloodlines on the mare I bought!"

Looking between Francie's flushed cheeks and the affectionate smile Tom gave her, Dana guessed the trip had been a success in other ways as well. "This must be one fantastic horse." She grinned up at Tom. "I hope you both had a good time at the sale."

The new light in his eyes spoke volumes. "You were right, Dana," he murmured too low for anyone else to hear. "I didn't understand until now. Thank you."

"Congratulations on the mare," Vivian murmured. She'd been subdued since her arrival, almost wary, but now she managed a wan smile. "We'll all look forward to seeing her."

Dana took the pup back to the kennel room. When she returned, Francie and Vivian were in deep conversation.

"My, God. I'm so sorry I wasn't here during the past couple days," Francie exclaimed, her face pale. "It must have been absolutely *awful*. How are Ben and Zach?"

"Ben will be discharged later this morning," Vivian murmured. "I'll take my car into town and bring him out here for you, Dana. I'm not sure you'll even want him back, though. He's testy as a bear."

Dana laughed. "That wouldn't be anything new."

"And Zach?" Francie asked.

"I called the hospital all night. They wouldn't say anything at first, then the desk said they couldn't find him. How could they lose a man that size? His arm didn't look good. Maybe he's in surgery and they wouldn't say?"

At the sound of the front door of the clinic, she looked up and found Zach standing in the entryway.

He still looked haggard, and his arm was heavily bandaged and suspended in a sling. But he never took his eyes from Dana's face as he started across the waiting room.

"We need to talk," he said.

Francie looked between them, grinned, then grabbed Tom by the arm and started for the door. "I think this is our cue to leave," she called out over her shoulder. "I'll call you tomorrow."

Vivian watched the door shut behind them, then turned back to Zach. "I need to go pick up Ben. But before I leave, I want to thank you, Zach. And I need to apologize. I—''

"No," he said gently. "There's no need. Not anymore."

"You know—about *everything?*''

"I remembered how nervous you were when you first saw me back in town. As a kid, I could only see the deputy taking his distrust of me a step further. Later, though, it didn't take long to put the facts together."

"I don't expect forgiveness," she persisted, "because I can't even give it to myself. In blindly trying to protect my daughter, I hurt both of you. I was wrong to ask that deputy to warn you away."

"I'd protect Katie with my life," he said slowly. "I understand what you did. If I ever thought she was running with the wrong crowd, who knows what I'd do to protect her?" A wry grin lifted a corner of his mouth. He extended his good arm. "Bygones?"

She searched his face, then reached out and took his hand, but didn't release it. Tears welled in her eyes. "Thank you, Zach. Now I'll just pray that you can undo some of the wrongs I've done to you in the past."

"I'm sure going to try." Zach waited until Vivian had left, before he turned to Dana. "I thought you'd want to know that the preliminary autopsy report is in. You hit Alvarez in the thigh, but it wasn't the wound that killed him."

Relief flooded through her. "I wanted to stop him any way I could. But later..."

"I know. As an agent I've only had to fire my gun a few times, but we *never* draw without intending lethal force. Disabling a bad guy just gives him more time to kill you or someone else. Afterward, though, I wonder about the guy's family and friends, and wonder if I could have found another way to stop him. You never forget, and that makes it hard to sleep at night."

"I'm sorry." She wouldn't have expected that from a seasoned agent, but she admired him all the more for it. "Are you supposed to be out of the hospital already?"

A rueful smile tilted the corners of his mouth. "I think they've got an APB out on me. The nurse said something about me going AMA—against medical advice—and had some pretty dire predictions about my future."

"Then you need to go back!"

"No, I need to be *here.*" He stepped closer and looked down into her face. "Over the past twenty-four hours I've done a lot of thinking. About what matters most in my life and where I want to be."

Dana's heartbeat faltered, wobbled on a precipice of hope. "You have?"

"I'm going back East to talk to Katie's grandfather, because he wants her to live with her Aunt Diane. My P.I.'s investigation found nothing but good about the woman, but in my heart I know Katie belongs with me."

Her heart slowly settled back into place. "That's... good, Zach. I think you're right."

"I've got my lawyer working on the possibility of adoption. And with Katie counting on me, I'm not going to take so many risks anymore."

"But what would you do?"

"If I go back to Dallas, maybe I'll get involved in a drug awareness program for kids, where I can make a difference in another way."

"Anything else?" Dana whispered, almost afraid to ask.

"All I can come up with is that I want you and Katie in my life forever."

Her heart stumbled hard this time. "Oh?"

"I have no idea what kind of work I could ever do out here—or even if you'd have me. I know that what happened years ago has been a real problem, because you figure I just took off and never cared enough to look back. But that's not true."

Even as he spoke, all of the advice Francie and her mother had been giving her came tumbling back. And suddenly she knew exactly what her answer had to be.

"My mother told me about what she did to you. How she kept it a secret all these years." Dana took another step closer to him, until she could feel the heat of his body next to hers, and breathe in his faint masculine scent of soap and aftershave. "But I want you to know that what she said made no difference at all."

The light in his eyes faded. He studied her face for a long, silent moment. "That's your answer? That's *all?*" He seemed to withdraw from her even before he moved, his remote expression becoming that of a stranger.

Before she could react, he'd started for the door.

"Whoa!"

He stopped at the doorway, turned partway back. *"Whoa?"*

"Sorry, it's a reflex." She gave him an embarrassed smile as she caught up to him. "I think I've even told my kids to heel a time or two, but that sure never worked."

"I don't know if there's anything left to say."

"No. There isn't. Except that my mother's confession didn't make any difference, because I'd already listened to my heart. I already knew that nothing in the past mattered anymore. I love you, Zach."

Cautious of his sling and injured arm, she reached up and clasped her hands behind his head, then pulled him gently down until their lips met.

He definitely didn't seem very disabled when he slipped his good arm around the back of her neck and crushed her mouth against his—hot and seeking, as if he wanted to devour her whole.

Shivers of sensation shot through her, settling in her lower belly and making her toes curl. The clinic, bright Colorado sunshine and the entire world faded away as she lost herself in the exquisite sensation of his mouth and the powerful curve of his arm behind her.

He lifted his head and smiled. "There is one last thing to say…and this time, there'd better be no misunderstandings or I might just go into heart failure."

"Will you marry me?"

He gave a shout of laughter. "You got it. And the answer is definitely yes."

Then he pulled her close again and showed her just how much he meant it.

EPILOGUE

"I CAN'T BELIEVE you pulled this all together in four weeks, Fran." Dana lifted a hand to her brow and shaded her eyes from the sun as she scanned the meadow.

The people of Fossil Hill had been drifting in for the past half hour, chatting with each other and admiring the beribboned white chairs that had been arranged in a semicircle in front of a rocky outcropping that would soon serve as an altar.

To the west rose the magnificent Rockies, still frosted with snow, the jagged peaks a sharp contrast to the crystalline blue sky.

Francie snipped a last stray thread from the hem of Dana's gown. "Simple, classic, perfect," she said. "You look absolutely elegant. And the kids—it almost makes me cry just looking at them."

A few yards away, Alex stood straight and tall in his midnight-blue tux, talking to Zach. Molly, her pretty pink skirts bunched in her hands, raced past, with little Katie hot on her heels.

Both girls collapsed in the soft grass, giggling and flushed and looking as if they might have always been sisters…except for the contrast of Katie's pale-blond hair to Molly's long, flaming tresses.

How things had changed in a short time.

With Dana's heartfelt prayers for his success, Zach had flown to New York with Katie to meet with her grandfather. Once assured of Katie's attachment to Zach, his secure career plans and his impending marriage to Dana, her grandfather dropped his plans to bring Katie back East.

Knowing that they wouldn't face a heated custody battle made this wedding day an even more joyous occasion.

"I wasn't sure about the pink dress," Francie observed. "But Katie and Molly both wanted pink. And you know what? Molly looks stunning. Before long the boys will be tying up your phone line from dawn to dusk."

"I sincerely hope not," Dana retorted fervently. "For those years I can definitely wait."

Francie reached over and patted at the back of Dana's hair. "Are you ready for all of this? Are you going to be really and truly happy away from here?"

"Alex is thrilled. The girls are excited—at least now that Molly knows she can bring her horse and other pets to Dallas. And me? I took the Boards for several states when I graduated from vet school, and Texas was one of them. I can go work for someone else, or maybe even start another solo practice."

"Tom appreciates the chance to lease your ranch. He's been wanting to expand for a long time."

They both looked over the crowd to where Vivian stood with Ben, holding his arm. "I didn't want to sell, but that lease will cover the mortgage payments and more. Maybe someday we'll come back. Ben wants to stay, so he can keep up the buildings. And who knows? I never would have guessed, but maybe someday he and my mom…''

"You once told me about your dreams from long ago. What you'd really and truly like to do…''

Mystified, Dana tore her gaze from the crowd and turned to her old friend. "I don't even remember.''

"Sure you do. Think, Dana. For once, think about what you alone hoped to do one day. You ended up out here with Ken, living out his dreams. But what about yours?''

"I'd wanted to teach, but it was never possible, living out here. Maybe someday I still can.''

Francie reached into the canvas tote at her feet. All morning, she'd been pulling makeup, safety pins, needles and thread from that tote. Now she withdrew an envelope.

"When Zach came back to town I had this sudden inspiration. Maybe it was wrong of me…but I saw the advertisement in the back of *The Veterinary Journal* and figured it wouldn't hurt. You could always say no, right?'' She gave Dana a nervous smile. "I don't know what it says, so maybe it didn't even work, which would make this a truly *awful* surprise instead of a good one, but—''

"Francie! It's okay. Whatever it is, I could only be thankful that you thought of me.''

Francie held out the envelope with shaking fingers. "Open it quick—I can't stand this any longer.''

From the other side of the meadow came the soft,

haunting notes of a harp. The guests were seated now, the minister in place.

She took the envelope and slid a fingernail under the flap. She withdrew the letter inside and stared at the words without comprehension, at first, because tears seemed to be blurring her vision.

The letter had come from Texas A&M University, requesting an interview as soon as possible. Given her résumé—

"My *résumé,* Francie?"

Francie shrugged. "You had a file with your old transcripts in a drawer, and I already knew where you've been working."

"They want an interview for a teaching and research position at a livestock research facility just south of Dallas!"

"Uh…are you upset?"

"How could I be? If they hire me, I'll have the kind of job I'd always hoped for!"

The music swelled, sending a shiver of anticipation down Dana's back. That shiver developed into something much deeper when Zach gently took her arm.

"Are you ready for this?" he asked, his gaze fixed on hers. "No second thoughts?"

"I could never want for anything more."

Katie came running toward them, her cheeks rosy, the flower garland in her hair askew. "It's time, Daddy, we gots to go now. Molly says!"

She'd just called him Daddy.

He reached down and scooped her up into his arms,

only slightly favoring his damaged shoulder. "There couldn't be a happier guy on the face of this earth."

And then they walked together into the waiting crowd.

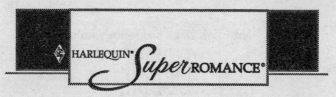

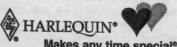